Cline Investigates

A Cut Throat Business

by

D South

Bloomington, IN Milton Keynes, UK

AuthorHouse™
1663 Liberty Drive, Suite 200
Bloomington, IN 47403
www.authorhouse.com
Phone: 1-800-839-8640

AuthorHouse™ UK Ltd.
500 Avebury Boulevard
Central Milton Keynes, MK9 2BE
www.authorhouse.co.uk
Phone: 08001974150

First published by AuthorHouse 12/11/2007

ISBN: 978-1-4259-4790-3 (sc)
ISBN: 1-4259-4790-5 (sc)

*Printed in the United States of America
Bloomington, Indiana*

This book is printed on acid-free paper.

In loving memory of Dorothy, and with thanks to Elsie, Christine, and Marilyn, without whose encouragement and support this book may never have been written.

Chapter 1

Jan. 1970

The swirling mist made concentration on the subject in hand almost impossible.

Jimmy would normally take a clean handkerchief, carefully and lovingly laundered by his fastidious mother and wipe his eyes clear of any moisture. His handkerchief would be of little use this time. Although it was a typical cold and dank January day, this was not the reason that he had blurred vision; it was the result of the fear that had been taking over his whole being, in anticipation of what would await him at the end of the school day.

His time at Bolderdale Comprehensive had only been for a short period, six weeks to be precise. He had started there when he and his family moved to Bolderdale when his father was transferred to the area by his company he worked for. From day one, Jimmy had drawn the attention of the school bully who had a sideline of selling drugs, mainly cannabis, to the other school lads. If you didn't buy, then you had to pay with your skin.

Today was payment day. Jimmy had already received several previous warnings from the bully everyone knew by the nick name "Biff"

There was just no way Jimmy could obtain the money to buy the drugs even if he wished, so today he had to take his chances.

The second hand on the wall clock above and behind the maths teacher's head seemed to be moving at twice the normal rate, he was sure he could even see the minute hand moving. Outside darkness had begun to fall, darkness that at any other time Jimmy would have hated because it kept him indoors at night. Tonight however things were much different, he hoped the darkness would grant him the invisibility to hide him from the clutches of "Biff" and his gang.

Earlier in the day, the school central heating had broken down and everyone in Jimmy's class was wearing their coats in an attempt to keep warm. Not Jimmy, he had been in a hot sweat all afternoon brought about by the fearful thought of what lay ahead at the hands of "Biff" and his gang.

Jimmy's attention towards Mr. Wilson the maths teacher had fast been waning, as the hands on the classroom clock approached four o'clock. The sudden sound of the school bell shocked Jimmy back into the real world, the adrenaline was now pumping through his body so fast, it wouldn't be a case of how fast he could run but how on earth would he be able to stop. He dashed out of the classroom as fast as his legs would take him, the fact that it was strictly forbidden to run on school premises was of no consequence. The only thing of importance at this time, was to reach home before "Biff" and his gang apprehended him and metered out whatever punishment was planned for him.

He ran down the long straight corridor through the double swing doors and out into the playground area. His mind was now racing ahead of himself trying to work out what next he should do to avoid capture. "If I take a short cut across the playing fields and past the sports pavilion I can save five minutes by jumping over the boundary fence. I'll be home safe and sound in another ten minutes. "Biff" and his mates will be waiting for me at the school gates and with a bit of luck, I'll be home before they miss me."

All Jimmy could see in the failing light of the cold damp winter's afternoon as he ran at helter-skelter speed across the playing fields, was the boundary fence still quite some distance in front of him and seemingly not getting any closer. At this point, it had never crossed Jimmy's mind that if he escaped the gang today, there was always tomorrow.

As he raced past the sports pavilion he never saw "Biff's" leg shoot out from behind the pavilion wall. Poor Jimmy had no chance to stop himself crashing onto the concrete footpath that ran around the pavilion, his own momentum adding to the force that resulted when flesh and bone hit solid concrete. The seething pain was nothing in comparison to the pain that was about to be inflicted on him from the effect of "Biff's" boots, boots that would crash into almost every inch of Jimmy's frail body.

Before Jimmy plunged into a state of unconsciousness, brought about by the excruciating pain, the last thing he remembered was seeing "Biff's" cocky grin. "Biff" knew he'd taken his pound of flesh but Jimmy also knew, that one day he would have his revenge, sooner or later it would make no difference.

If only "Biff" and Jimmy had been able to see into the future, perhaps that January afternoon may have turned out differently. It was however, probably for the good, that they didn't know that sometime in the future, one of them would be murdered and the other one behind prison bars.

Chapter 2

Saturday 7th July 1996

Peter Armstrong took the path that passed through the outskirts of the wood, just behind the upper class private housing estate where he lived with his wife Ruth. He was delighted with the day he'd had at work. He was the owner of a motor showroom in the centre of Bolderdale, selling luxury cars. Selling one car in one day was good by anyone's standard but selling four cars of the quality he dealt with in one day was excellent business. One of the sales was with a cash customer, handy with regards to cash flow but it presented some amount of security concern. Even though the showroom office had its own safe one never knew who might come barging in brandishing a sawn off shotgun.

It was always with a great amount of suspicion and no small amount of uncertainty when he had to deal in large amounts of cash. The last thing he wanted was to get involved with the law for handling stolen money, even though he usually relied on his perfect judge of character he could never really be one hundred percent sure of his clients integrity.

Although he was quite happy and content with the days takings, he still couldn't prevent the feeling of anger that would rage inside his stomach every time he thought of that bitch of a wife, who of late, was hardly ever at home. Sometimes she would stay out all night, always staying at her friend's house, at least that's what she told him when he eventually caught up with her. Of late, she seemed to spend more time with her friend Mary Duncan, than she spent at home. Most nights he would walk this way to the pub, which was at the end of the footpath, at least this way he didn't have to start cooking a meal for himself after a long day at the showroom.

Tonight however, he had to make a small detour before going to the pub. It was overcast making it dark along the woodland footpath. He thought it looked like the weather may turn to rain before the night was out, so he quickened his stride. If he didn't hurry, he would soon have some difficulty seeing where he was walking.

About one hundred and fifty metres from the public house he came upon a side shoot to the left of the main footpath. He turned and continued until he arrived at a fallen tree at the side of the path. One end of the tree was hollow where it had rotted away with time. Armstrong reached into his inside jacket pocket and removed a brown parcel and shoved it into the hollow end of the tree. Only after he had grabbed a number of twigs and pine needles off a nearby fir tree and rammed them hard home into the hollow to conceal the small parcel did he feel it was safe to return to the main woodland path and proceed on his way to the pub for the long awaited repast.

Having unburdened himself of the task of delivering the parcel into the hollow tree, his mind was free to ponder and concentrate on the forthcoming meal. He could already taste the hot mushroom soup along with the bread roll ladened with the homemade butter the pub was noted for. Next would come steak entrecote with grilled mushrooms to be washed down with copious amounts of a fine quality Beaujolais. The thought of the forthcoming meal must have deadened all his senses, especially his sense of hearing, so

6

much so, he never heard the sound of the vegetation as the assailant approached him from behind. The first he knew he was not alone, was when he felt the long thin blade of the stiletto knife penetrate his body below his left shoulder blade. He tried to turn and look over his shoulder to catch a sight of his attacker but he was not quick enough. As his head swung around, he felt an arm over his right shoulder. By now, it was too late to be thinking about entrecote steak and Beaujolais. As the knife blade sliced Peter Armstrong's throat, he didn't even have time to reflect on part of his life, not that it mattered any more.

Whether by luck or design, the stiletto blade had already punctured his heart, he was dead before he hit the ground. The only sound that could be heard was the sound of heavy rain hitting the footpath and the trees. It was as if the death of Armstrong was a sign for the heavens to open.

Under normal circumstances, you wouldn't have expected Armstrong's body to have been discovered until at least Sunday morning when the locals took their pet dogs out for their morning constitution. Earlier on Saturday night Graham Dawson had set out on his nightly ten mile run in preparation for his forthcoming half marathon run for a local charity. He was almost home when the heavens opened up. It was at that point he decided to take a short cut home through the woods. He had already run nine and a half miles half a mile less would be neither here nor there.

"God damn it, I should have brought a torch I can't see a blasted thing in front of me"

He never saw the body lying on the footpath right in his path. As he fell heavily, his head struck the trunk of a tree and he was knocked unconscious.

When Dawson eventually managed to raise himself to his feet, he had no idea where he was, or how long he had been unconscious. The only thing that he was aware of was the blinding headache, the result of having an argument with a tree trunk. He was still bleeding from a wound on his forehead although by now the bleeding had reduced to just a trickle. As part of his senses returned, he could just vaguely remember jogging through the woods. "What the hell happened?" I must have fallen over something on the path. He began to feel nauseous just before he lost his balance and fell to the ground again.

Although he could vaguely remember jogging, he couldn't understand what he was doing in the woods, it would have been obvious to anybody watching him, that he was suffering severe concussion. He eventually managed to stand on his feet again and begin to edge his way forward. He had no idea that he was walking back the same way that he had entered the woods, not that it really mattered, he was still in a state of shock. Graham could only walk very slowly, in fact, it was more like a stagger than a walk. After only a couple of paces, his foot touched an object in front of him. "What the hell is that?"

He bent down swaying from side to side, at the same time, moving his outstretched hand in front of him, until he felt a sodden heap on the ground. His hand had come into contact with Armstrong's tweed jacket, although to Graham, it felt like the end of an old sack. Immediately, he thought someone may have disposed of some dead animal in a sack and dumped it in the woods. "God how cruel and callous some people can be" He moved his hand further along what he thought was a sack, until his hand touched Armstrong's head. His hand withdrew from contact with Armstrong's head, as if it had been given an electric shock. " This was no dead animal that had died, or been killed, and then dumped in a sack in the woods, this was a bloody body" Now Graham began to panic, even though he was still not in command of all his senses and faculties, his instinct told him he could be in danger. "How did the body get here? How did it die? Was it male or female?" All of these questions were rushing through his confused mind. "I've got to get out of here as quick as I can and get help.If this body was murdered, the murderer may still be in the woods and I could be in danger." He struggled back up to his feet and slowly made his way out of the woods.

Unbeknown to him, the first sign of life that confronted him was the pub which Armstrong was making his way towards when he was so suddenly and brutally struck down. The pub was now in total darkness since it was well past closing time, but this didn't stop Graham hammering on the doors as hard as he could. What Graham failed to realise, was the effect the knock on the head was having on his senses; what he thought was loud hammering was in effect only a faint knock on the door. Even if the landlord of the pub had been leaning on the inside of the door, Graham's hammering would still have gone unnoticed. After what appeared to Graham to be an eternity, he left the pub yard and made his way into the housing estate. If he had been in possession of all his faculties and was able to think in a rational manner, he would have knocked on the first door that he came across. The only thing foremost on Graham's mind was to get to a phone. It took him another thirty minutes before he saw what he was looking for. At first, it appeared as a solitary light on the corner of two roads, but as he approached the light he could make out the outlines of a telephone box, standing invitingly on the footpath ahead of him.

He struggled to pull open the kiosk door, even a fit person had to be built like Mr.Universe to enter the phone box. In Graham's physical state of health, it took all of his reserve of strength just to get the door to move. By the time he'd made his way into the kiosk his whole body was shaking and all his energy spent. It was all he could do to remain conscious. With the utmost of difficulty, he managed to pick up the handset and press 999. He could barely keep on his feet as he heard a faint female voice calling "Emergency Services, which service do you require?" The female voice continued to repeat the message but by now Graham was too weak to reply. He fell into a heap on the floor of the kiosk striking his head on the way down. It took the Emergency services another twenty minutes before they could locate him .He was still unconscious when he was admitted to 'ST.ANDREW'S HOSPITAL' in Bolderdale town centre in the early hours of Sunday morning.

Chapter 3

Detective Sergeant Peter Jones looked at his watch. "Three twenty on a Sunday morning and we've still another four and a half hours to go." His companion Detective Constable Gary Moore was having great difficulty keeping his eyes open. "Gary I hope you are not falling asleep."

"No Sergeant, it's just that hard trying to see through these blasted windows with all the rain on the outside and the mist on the inside, it's straining my eyes. If I open the window I get pissing wet through. Just how much longer do we have to stay out here for anyway Sergeant? If you ask me, I think we're just wasting our bloody time."

"I wish you would give over moaning and be thankful of the overtime, you are starting to give me a headache. Your guess is as good as mine. According to that old fart of a Chief Constable, he's been getting it in the neck from his drinking mates, down at the Lodge."

"What's all this got to do with them?"

"Well Gary, apparently since all these muggings started on the prostitutes a few months back, the toms are steadily moving away from their usual haunt, here on the Turpin Road Estate and moving over to the more prosperous area of the Boulevard and you know who lives up there, quite a few of the Chief's Lodge and golf buddies."

"I suppose it's a case of not in my back yard, hey Sergeant?"

"You've got it in one Gary. The general idea is for us to sit here, until we catch the mugger and get him off the streets. Then it is hoped the toms will all come back down to this neck of the woods."

"Well Sergeant, as I said before I still think we're wasting our time, I'm surprised even the toms are out on a night like this."

"You might be right Gar......." Sergeant Jones was interrupted in mid sentence by the radiophone.

"Fox-trot one are you there?"

Jones gathered the handset. "Foxtrot one here."

"Break off your surveillance and proceed to the 'OLD MASTERS INN' a body's been discovered in the nearby woods."

"Ok we're on our way, we should be there in about five minutes. Are any of our lads on the scene?"

"Yes uniform are there waiting for you."

"Looks like your wish has come true Gary. Did you catch all that?"

"Yes Sergeant."

"Then why the hell are we still here. Let's get away from here before someone changes their minds and we finish up here for the rest of the shift."

As Moore and Jones drove onto the public house car park, they could see two Panda cars already parked up. A young looking PC stood in front of the car nearest the entrance. Moore and Jones got out their car as the PC approached them." Hope you've both got raincoats and boots Sir? You'll need them down there." The young PC was pointing over his shoulder into the woods, as he was speaking.

"Gary, get the gear out of the car boot."

"So what have we got down here then, constable?"

"From what we can make out so far, a jogger was running through the woods, sometime last night, when he fell over the body laid out in the middle of the footpath."

"What time was the body discovered?"

"We think about eleven thirty Sir"

"What do you mean, you think? That's over four hours ago. Why the delay in calling C.I.D. in?"

" We're not rightly sure about that Sir, It would seem from what we can make out, when the jogger fell, he hit his head and was knocked unconscious for a good length of time. When he managed to raise the alarm, he was so in and out of consciousness it took the Emergency Services, ages to locate the body. We arrived here at three fifteen, we've called S.O.C.O and the M.O. they shouldn't be too long getting here."

"So where's the jogger now constable?"

"He's over in St. Andrews Hospital. He won't be going anywhere, he's in no fit state. He keeps falling into states of unconsciousness, due to his head injury he sustained when he fell.

Just in case he comes to and starts talking some sense, there's a uniformed P.C. by his bedside. He's been ordered to stay there, until C.I.D. can get someone over there to relieve him of duty."

"The only sensible information, the hospital staff have been able to gather from the jogger, is his name, Graham Dawson."

"Ok constable lead the way, we'll follow."

Jones gave the PC and Moore instructions not to walk down the middle of the footpath, just in case they may destroy any vital evidence that may have been left by the unknown assailant. As they approached the murder scene, they could make out the lights of two P.Cs standing over the body. Sergeant Jones sent the PC, who had led them to the body, back to the public house car park, so he would be there when the S.O.C.O. team and the M.O. arrived.

One look down at the body and the surrounding area, was sufficient enough for Jones to see the imprints of size twelve boots within a foot of the body.

"You bloody incompetent pair of idiots, it will be difficult enough, finding reliable evidence from the crime scene with the damage caused by the rain, without your great clodhoppers all over the place. Get back over to the side of the footpath and don't move until I tell you to."

By now, Sergeant Jones was in a foul mood, cold, wet, hungry and miserable. It was bad enough being on surveillance all night but at least it was nice, warm, and dry in the car. Now here he was wet through to his skin, freezing and to cap it all, surrounded by idiots.

"How long have you two been here?"

"About fifteen minutes Sir."

"Then why on earth haven't you cordoned off the area? Get off and seal off both ends of the footpath and watch where you put your bloody feet."

"Don't you think you were a bit hard on them Sergeant?"

"It may or may not have escaped your memory Garry but at least two people have been down this footpath tonight. One is dead and for all we know, the other may be the murderer. If any of the evidence is destroyed tonight, I don't wish the blame to be at my back door."

Another ten minutes passed by, before Jones caught sight of the torches at the far end of the footpath. At least S.O.C.O. and the M.O. aren't walking down the middle of the path. Jones wondered if the young P.C had said anything to them. At least the rain had eased off.

As soon as the team arrived, they began taking photographs of the body and the surrounding area. A white plastic tent was then erected over the murder scene, in order to help preserve the site from any further contamination of evidence. Inside the tent, six tall, large powerful floodlights were installed.

Sergeant Jones instructed S.O.C.O. that he wanted photographs taken of the footpath from both sides of the body to where it entered and left the woods.

"That's going to take ages Sergeant. Can't someone else do that in the morning when it's light?"

"No I want it done now. I don't know how much damage has been done already to the area, with people trampling about with size twelve boots. Besides, I expect the killer would at some time, have decided to walk in the middle of the path, when they may have thought they were far enough away from the body. I know I am clutching at straws but this weather is not going to help matters."

On entering the tent, Sergeant Jones realized that this was the first time he'd really had a good look at the body. The M.O. was bent over towards the body, carefully making notes on a note pad, as he carried out his preliminary examination.

"Well Doc, What have you got to tell me?"

"As you can see for yourself, you don't need to know how he died. He's been stabbed in the back and if that wasn't sufficient to kill him, he's had his throat slashed as well. Who ever killed him, they wanted to make sure, that they made no mistakes."

"Any idea about the time of death?"

The M.O. turned the body over. "Do you see that Sergeant?"

"Do I see what?"

"That dry spot on the ground underneath where the body had been laying."

"What does that tell us?"

"Well it tells me, he was probably murdered just before or just after it started to rain last night. You can see that very small damp patch, and then we have a dry patch which was protected from the rain by his body. It must just have been starting to rain, that would explain the small damp spot

15

under his legs. His warm body at the time of death would have dried out any slight dampness on the ground. It started to rain somewhere between eight thirty and ten thirty last night. Hope that helps."

"Have you checked his pockets yet Doc.

"Yes, but I'm afraid there's no means of identification on him at all, even his wrist watch is missing."

"How do you know he was wearing a watch?"

"Well I can't say for sure that he was wearing one when he was murdered but from the white patch on his wrist I would say he normally had one on. Otherwise his entire wrist would have been tanned." "So Doc, it looks very much like we have a mugging that's gone wrong?"

"I doubt it, who ever killed this guy wanted him dead. You don't accidentally stab someone in the back and then slash his throat. I think the killer took the victims wallet and watch etc, to stop your lads finding out whom the victim is. Maybe they were just trying to gain some time before you come up with a name. One thing the killer missed, the victim's wedding ring. I've tried to get it off his finger but it won't budge. Perhaps the jogger disturbed the killer before they could cut the ring off. You will have to wait till we get the body back to the lab, with a bit of luck there might be an inscription on the inside."

"Ok Doc, I guess we can't do much more here tonight, I suppose D.I.Cline will be out here in the morning, to join the search team and no doubt he will be paying you a visit later in the day."

Chapter 4

Cline looked out of his bedroom window. "Thank God the rain has eased off." He'd been looking forward to a Sunday off for the past nine weeks. It was to be the first opportunity for many a week, for him to visit his sister and brother-in-law Ben and the kids. In fact, he couldn't remember the last time they had all spent time together. A forty minutes drive to Doncaster, then a short drive to the Peak District and he could forget all about work for the day. He had just finished having his morning shower and had one leg into his trousers, when the phone rang and broke his train of thoughts.

"No, not today of all days, leave it John, they'll think you've gone out."

Whoever was trying to contact him was a persistent so and so, the phone just would not stop ringing.

"Perhaps it's nothing. It's Sunday morning, nothing ever happens here on a Sunday morning, certainly not important enough to call out a D.I."

Hopping on one leg, his trousers trailing behind him he struggled over to the phone and reluctantly picked up the hand set thinking at the same time how he must look, standing there with one leg in his trousers and his under pants slowly slipping down to his knees as the elastic waist band decided, that enough was enough and now would be a good time to succumb to old age.

"Cline here."

As soon as he heard the voice of Superintendent Knowels, he knew his long awaited trip to the Peak District wasn't to be.

"I want you back here at the station straight away. There's been a murder and I want you in charge of the investigation right away."

"Surely there must be someone else who could take the case?" He knew before the answer came back, that it would be of no avail trying to plead with Knowels. For too long, they had been at loggerheads with each other, for either one of them to expect any favours.

"NO BUTS OR ARGUMENTS GET BACK HERE NOW."

By the time Cline reached the station it was gone nine thirty and Knowels was pacing backwards and forwards in his office.

"What took you so long? I told you to get here right away."

Cline ignored the question thinking why should he explain to the pompous sod, that he had to let his sister know he would not be going with them to the Peak District.

"I've picked your team for you. They are waiting for you in the incident room. D.S. Jones will brief you, now get on with it, you've wasted enough time already"

Cline was well respected by all the officers at the station, that is with the exception of Knowels with whom Cline held a mutual dislike, going back quite a few years. It was then no surprise to Cline that on entering the incident room he was greeted with the usual welcome from his pre-selected team. The respect that the officers had for Cline had been built up during a number of years. He had never been known to reprimand anyone in public. He always took them into a private place to do that but he always praised his staff in public. That aside, he was a hard taskmaster and would not suffer fools lightly.

He was only five foot ten inches tall, and considering the normal height of six foot plus expected of policemen when he first joined the force, made him one of the smaller officers. However, when he entered a room there was an aura about him that drew people towards him and made them take notice.

Cline looked at the assembled team. At the first desk, he could see W.D.S. Wendy Baxter sitting next to D.C. Micky Poole.

Cline had worked alongside Baxter on previous cases and had recognized her as a young officer who had a great future to look forward to in the force. Poole on the other hand, had only been in C.I.D. for just over six months and no doubt, this would be his first time on a murder investigation team. Next there were D.S. Peter Jones and D.C. Garry Moore, both experienced officers. It had been expected that Jones would have sought further promotion after attaining his Sergeants stripes but he had settled in a rut and was quite content to see his days out as a Sergeant. Moore, having been in C.I.D. for two or three years was equally content, in being what he called a foot soldier. His plan being to work as much overtime as possible to enhance his pension rights then retire as early as the powers that be would allow.

A little distant away from the rest of the team, sitting in isolation, was W.D.C. Mary White. Cline hadn't seen White for some months now, she'd been off work on compassionate grounds, in order to care for her terminally ill mother.

"Good morning all, nice to have you back again Mary, I'm sure the rest of the team will join me in passing on their condolences over the loss of your mother. Pull your chair and desk up to the others Mary, we work as a team here. I don't want anybody feeling they are not a part of the team.

Now then, let's get the wagon on the road. Peter, I believe you can bring us up to date with the events so far."

Jones gave a precise update on the events to date, including the condition of the jogger, who for the moment, just happened to be the only possible lead they had.

"Now then Peter, I know you and Garry have been on duty all night and must be ready to get your heads down but you see the size of the team that Knowels has given me. Therefore, we are a bit thin on the ground. I would like you and Gary to supervise the uniform lads in a door to door on the houses near the wood where we found the body. Pay special attention to the houses that back onto the footpath. You never can tell, before it started raining last night, someone may have been having a garden party or barbecue in their rear garden. They may have heard or seen something and at the time didn't think it was anything out of the ordinary."

"Mary you'll be our coordinator, you will be responsible for the correlation of all the evidence and information passed on to you by the team. I want to be in a position to know what is happening at all times. At the moment, we have a body and no ID but we may have a witness or even the killer in St. Andrews. Mary, check to see if the jogger Graham Dawson has got a criminal record."

"Wendy, you take Poole with you and see what Dawson has to say. I'm on my way to see what the M.O. has to say. I'll meet up with you all back here, sometime after midday"

Baxter and Poole arrived at St. Andrews to find a young police constable standing outside the side entrance, smoking a cigarette.

"I hope you aren't supposed to be watching over Mr. Dawson?"

The cigarette immediately dropped to the ground and the P.C. covered it with his foot as if trying to hide it from

Baxter's view. His face had turned a very funny scarlet as he tried to put on a brave face.

"Excuse me, but who are you?"

Baxter produced her warrant card and shoved it tight up to the P.C's nose.

"Sorry sergeant, I just slipped out for a couple of minutes and a quick smoke. I've only been here two minutes."

"Then you had better hope that in those two minutes, Dawson hasn't decided to go walk about. For all we know he could be our killer."

Dawson had been placed in a private room at the end of the long main ward, well away from any prying eyes.

"Constable, stay outside the door and don't move. By the way, where's the ward sister? I didn't see her when we came onto the ward. I need to know if Dawson is fit enough to be interviewed."

"That's ok Sergeant, I have had a word with her and she said it is ok. I thought someone from C.I.D. would be along this morning."

"At least you have done something right."

Baxter and Poole entered Dawson's room, closing the door behind them. Dawson was sitting in an easy chair at the side of his bed watching the colour TV, conveniently placed on a wall shelf. Although the sound was turned down to the point where it was hardly audible, Poole walked over and switched the set off, at the same time Baxter made her introductions.

"Judging by the amount of bandages on your head, you must have suffered a serious knock. How do you feel now Mr. Dawson?"

"Apart from a blinding headache, not too bad. In fact the ward sister said I could go home later on today, after they have done a few more tests."

"Good I'm glad you are feeling much better. Perhaps you can answer a few questions for us. How much do you know about what happened last night?"

"Only what I told everybody last night or was it this morning?"

"Which was what? I would like to hear it for myself."

"Not a great deal as far as I can remember, I remember taking the short cut through the woods, because it looked like it was going to throw it down. I didn't see anything at all in front of me on the footpath. By then it had got very dark, very quickly, I suppose with hindsight I should have turned back and gone through the housing estate as I normally do.

When I fell over the body, although at the time I didn't know what it was, I must have hit my head on something hard. Everything is still hazy, I don't even know how long I was out for. After that, I don't have any idea what happened, I can't even remember ringing 999. I only know that I did, because that is what the nurses have been telling me."

"Have you any idea what time it was when you fell over the body?"

"As I've already told you, I'm not really sure about anything but normally when I go out jogging this time of year, I would normally be in or around that area for about half past ten at night. That is about as much as I can tell you. If I do remember anything more later on, I'll give you a call at the police station."

"Tell me Mr. Dawson, not being a marathon runner or a keep fit fanatic myself, it does appear to me that ten thirty at night seems a very odd time to be out training. Why don't you do you're running and training earlier in the evening or during the day?"

"For most of the year I do my training either before I start work in a morning or straight after work, about four o'clock."

"Were you working yesterday?"

"No sergeant, I don't usually work on Saturdays, it was very hot yesterday afternoon so I decided to go on my training run after it had cooled down somewhat. It wasn't a one off, I often go out late at night in the summer months, when the weather is quite hot."

"I think that will do us for now Mr. Dawson but just incase we need to contact you again, make sure D.C Poole has your home address and works address and phone numbers".

Cline couldn't help but wonder how anybody could work in the morgue, day in and day out. They must have the constitution of an ox. It wasn't so much the sight of mutilated bodies that offended Cline, it was the stench that seemed to stay with him for days after a visit. He hated it but it was after all, part of the job.

He walked briskly down the long passageway, which was lined on either side by partitioned off offices. Some he noticed, had frosted or opaque glass in the partitions, probably to provide a bit of privacy from nosy visitors, like Cline, from looking in as they passed. Most however had clear glass, which was more to Cline,'s liking.

Dr. Morgan's office was right at the far end of the passageway. Funnily enough, his office was one of those with the clear glass, which enabled Cline to see the white coated M.O. standing by his desk, shuffling papers backwards and forwards as if he was trying to get them into some kind of order.

Cline walked into the M.O.'s office without knocking on the door. "What's up Doc?" he remarked, "Having trouble with your paper work again?"

"I wish you wouldn't say that John."

"Say what Jack?"

"What's up Doc.? You make me out as a character, from a loony cartoon film."

"You must admit it though Jack, you have to be a bit loony or loopy to work in a place like this. Anyway, what's with all the paper shuffling?"

"I've just knocked twelve reports onto the floor off my desk and I was just trying to sort them all out."

"I hope one of those is not my report Jack?"

"No it's not, I haven't finished with your report yet. How come you never pop in and see us from time to time. The only time we see you down here, is when some poor sod dies or gets topped."

"Believe me Jack, this is that last place on earth I would want to visit, if I had no good reason to do so. How you put up with the stench I'll never understand"

"There's no smell in the offices. It's all in your mind. Anyway I could have sent the report to you when it is finished, that way you don't need to come down here."

"I know that Jack, but you know me, I like the personal touch and the benefit of your worldly experience that you always seem impatient to give me. I always like to hear things from the horse's mouth so as to speak."

"Now you are starting to insult me, calling me a horse." Jack was smiling as he turned to face his long time friend.

"Forget the wise cracks John, what the hell are you doing here? I thought you were off to see your sister and family this weekend."

"So did I , I was only going for one day until Knowels rang me at home first thing this morning and ordered me back to take charge of this case. There wasn't anything that couldn't have waited for me for 24 hours. The rest of the team are quite capable of managing without me."

"I take it, you two still don't see eye to eye?"

"I don't think we ever will Jack. So tell me, what will you be putting into your report?"

"First of all there was no means of identification on the body. His pockets were completely empty"

"I know that already, tell me something new."

"Don't be so impatient John. I managed to remove his wedding ring from his finger. There was no wonder the killer left it, I had to cut part of the flesh away to get it off.

Take a look at this John." Jack handed Cline a small brown envelope.

As Cline emptied the contents of the envelope onto the desk, Armstrong's ring fell out.

"Look at the inscription on the inside of the ring John, it might help you."

To Peter love Ruth.

"I suppose it's a start Jack. I wonder how many Peters there are, living in the Bolderdale area with a wife called Ruth. Why couldn't he have had an unusual name such as Rasputin?"

"Be thankful for small mercies John. If he had been called Rasputin, I doubt if there would have been sufficient room on the ring for a full inscription. You may have finished up with something like, Rasp love Ruth, or even R love R."

"We are still going over his clothes in the lab. If we get anything, I will let you know right away. As you probably already know, the body was face down when it was discovered and laying lengthways on the footpath. The victims head was towards the end of the footpath leading to the public house on the outskirt of the woods. This could indicate he was making his way to the pub, when he was struck down from behind."

"That's a lot of surmising Jack, just from the body position?"

"By itself I agree John, but when I examined the contents of his stomach I found it practically empty. Which

25

could indicate, that he was on his way to the pub for a meal before they closed for the night? I know the pub has a good reputation for its food, so it wouldn't surprise me if you found out that he was a regular diner there"

"Ok Jack, I'll go along with that for now What makes you think he was struck down from behind?"

"Take a good look at these photographs John."

Jack placed two photographs on his desk in front of Cline.

"These are close up shots of the wounds, one in the back and one on his throat. Notice the difference. This one is the wound in the back; you can clearly see the shape of the wound. The murder weapon which would most likely make a wound that shape would have to be tapered and strong. In brief, a stiletto blade. Now take a look at the other wound, the one on the throat. You can see how very thin the wound is. That would almost certainly, have been produced using a razor blade, scalpel or a craft knife."

"So are you telling me that he was attacked by two people?"

"No, I'm not saying that at all. What I am saying without you putting words into my mouth. Is that I believe two murder weapons were used to kill the victim. Take another look at the photo of the neck wound. The wound starts from a line, half way between the left ear and the centre of his throat and finishes almost directly under the right ear. I believe whoever killed him, first stabbed him in the back under the left shoulder blade.

The victim would almost certainly have tried to look over his left shoulder as soon as he felt the point of the weapon touch his back. As he did so, the killer put their right hand over the victim's right shoulder and used the second weapon to slice his throat."

"That seems hard to believe Jack. I've never come across anyone using two knives before, maybe you would get that in a pub brawl but never in a murder."

"Neither have I John but I'll wager my next month's salary that is how it was done."

Cline turned away from the M.O. and began walking over to a chair on the far side of the office. As he did so, the M.O. quickly and silently followed him and touched Cline on his left shoulder blade. Cline turned his head instinctively to the left, over his left shoulder he glimpsed the M.O. smiling at him. At the same time he felt a finger wipe his throat from left to right and heard the words "Touché"

"Ok Jack you've made your point."

"Just one more point John. Since both wounds were made almost simultaneously and both would have been sufficient to have killed the victim, I cannot say for certain which one did kill him. Not that it makes any difference; I suppose the wound in the back would be my guess. The knife blade actually struck the heart and if the heart then stopped beating, that would account for the lack of blood from the throat wound. I should know more after we have finished the post mortem."

"Have you done a blood test yet?"

"Of course we have but there were no signs of drugs or alcohol. One thing we did find that may be of interest to you, were tiny bits of vegetation under one of his finger nails."

"What type of vegetation are you talking about?

"Bits of needles off a pine tree. That's about all I've got for you at the moment John. I'll get the report out to you as soon as I can get the Post mortem finished."

I don't suppose you could fix up a photo of the victim without the neck wound showing. I could do with one for a door to door in trying to find out who he is?"

"Already done it for you, over there in that brown envelope"

Jones and Moore had lost count of the number of doors they had knocked on before arriving at No.87 St. Peter's Drive. St. Peter's drive ran parallel to the footpath that ran through the woods, with the odd numbered properties backing onto the woods. Most of the rear gardens had access through garden gates in the boundary fences right onto the footpath.

No.87 was a large five bedroom detached property with an attached double garage.

Although the house was only about thirty years old, Jones could see it had a Victorian style frontage with large gable ends and large bow windows to each room upstairs and down. The long double drive swept up to the front door which was protected from the elements by a wooden porch, which in turn was protected by two small stone lions, one either side. The lions being smaller versions of the lions guarding the entrance to the main drive. Before reaching the front of the house, the drive had cut its way through an immaculate lawn that looked more like a bowling green than someone's front garden.

The flower beds in the centre of the lawns were reminiscent of those displayed at the Chelsea Flower Show.

Jones knocked on the door several times, his knuckles red with the continuous pounding they had taken this morning. He wondered why, when it was obviously a property of wealth it didn't have an electric door bell. At last after what seemed to be ages, he could just make out the outlines of an approaching figure through the frosted glass in the front door. The door opened to reveal an attractive blonde probably in her late twenties or early thirties. She was clad in white satin silk pyjamas and a matching silk dressing gown. Jones produced his warrant card and introduced himself and explained the reason for the visit.

"I think you had better come in." She stood to one side and invited them in with a wave of her arm.

"Please go into the lounge, it's the first door on the right."

As Jones entered the lounge he couldn't help feel somewhat envious, that someone could be apparently so wealthy. The lounge was almost completely white throughout, it was almost blinding it was so bright.

On one wall stood a large white marble fire place, whilst in the middle of the lounge, there was a pair of four or maybe five seater settees and three single arm chairs, all luxuriously covered in soft white leather. The centre of the lounge was dominated by the very large white round Chinese carpet. The only colour in the room that Jones could see other than white, was the stained and highly polished wooden floor. On the centre of the Chinese carpet was a large round glass topped coffee table, large enough to seat a family of eight for a main meal. Even the coffee table had white legs. Jones felt as if he was in an operating room, the lounge was so clinical looking, he even thought perhaps they should have removed their shoes before they had entered the room.

"Please gentlemen take a seat." Again the royal wave directed them, this time to the single chairs.

"First thing first, could I have your name?"

"Of course, Mrs. Armstrong, Mrs. Ruth Armstrong. So how can I be of help to you?"

"Where you at home last night? and if so did you hear or see anything unusual at the rear of your home?"

"Well I cannot help you there Sergeant, that is not the reason I invited you into my home."

"So why did you invite us in? We really are very busy Mrs. Armstrong."

"I'm sorry about that but I was just in the process of ringing the police station when you knocked on the front door. You see Sergeant, my husband has gone missing." Jones gave a sideways glance at Moore who was busily taking down notes.

"When was the last time you saw your husband?"

"Saturday morning before he went out to work."

"Is it not normal for him to stay away from home some nights?"

"No, Sergeant, he has never stayed out all night before, without letting me know. Besides he normally works on a Sunday morning."

"What line of work is your husband in Mrs. Armstrong?"

"He owns and runs a luxury car business in the town centre. You must know of it 'Sergeant, Armstrong Luxury Motors'."

"I thought your name rang a bell. I take it from what you have already told us, that you have been in touch with the show rooms to see if he is there."

"Yes, but no one has seen him since Saturday evening."

"What is your husband's Christian name?"

"Peter."

"Can you describe Peter for me?"

"Just a minute Sergeant, at the front door you said you were making certain enquiries but you didn't give any details. So what are these enquiries about? Are they anything to do with Peter's disappearance?" "Please Mrs. Armstrong, just answer my questions for now and then I will explain things to you."

"He is about five foot ten, short brown hair and weighs about eleven and a half stones. I've got a picture here that you can take away with you; if it will help you locate him."

She walked over to the marble fireplace and picked up a silver picture frame from the mantelpiece, and removed a photograph of her husband. Having returned the picture frame back onto the mantelpiece she walked over to Jones and handed him the picture.

Jones looked at the picture of Armstrong then handed it to Moore. They looked at each other, both having recognised the picture as that of the body found in the woods.

The look of concern on the faces of the two detectives didn't go undetected by Mrs. Armstrong. "What was your husband wearing when he left for work yesterday morning?"

"Sergeant, you are starting to make me feel very uncomfortable and worried right now. I really think you should tell me what this is all about. Please" she pleaded. The two detectives looked at each other before Jones stood up and approached Mrs. Armstrong. "Please, he said in a sympathetic tone of voice. I think you should sit down, I have some bad news to give you."

As she sat down on one of the settees, Jones could see the colour draining from her face, leaving it as white as the satin dressing gown she was wearing.

"Last night a man's body was discovered on the footpath in the woods behind your home. From the picture you have just given me, I believe it to be the body of Mr. Armstrong. Mrs. Armstrong sat there in silence, taking in the bombshell that had just been dropped in her lap.

"Would you like a cup of tea?" Without waiting for a reply, he gave a quick gesture to Moore who stood up and disappeared out of the lounge to find the kitchen. "Make it strong and sweet."

Mrs. Armstrong looked across at Moore. "That's ok, just help yourself but no sugar for me." As Moore disappeared into the kitchen, Jones turned to try and calm Mrs. Armstrong, who by now was starting to shiver, not because she was cold but due to the shock which was now starting to kick in.

"Is there anything I can do to help? There must be someone I can contact to come and stay with you?"

"No Sergeant, besides we don't know for certain that it is my husband's body."

"That's true and that is why I have to ask you if you can come with us, when you feel up to it, to try and identify the body. Then we will know one way or the other."

Moore returned with a tray of tea cups and saucers and a pot of tea and a jug of milk "Whilst you pour the tea for Mrs. Armstrong, I'll go outside and make the arrangements for the body to be identified. I won't be long."

Jones made his way outside and stood on the drive away from the house so there was no chance his conversation with Cline could be heard inside the house. Not that anything he was about to say to Cline, Mrs. Armstrong was not already aware of, that is, apart from the fact she still did not know how her husband died.

"Sir it looks like we have an ID for our victim. Peter Armstrong. Address 87 St. Peter's Drive. I've asked Mrs. Armstrong to come and do an ID for us. Can you make sure the body is ready for her Sir? We should be at the morgue in about three quarters of an hour, after which I'll see you back in the incident room."

"Leave it to me. If the body is confirmed as Peter Armstrong make sure you contact Mrs. Armstrong's doctor."

Cline walked into the incident room, the only other person being W.D.C White. "Hello Mary, I was really sorry to hear of your mother's death, it must be hard for you now that you are by yourself. I suppose in one sense, it must have been a blessing in disguise when she passed away after watching her suffer for all those months."

"Before you took compassionate leave, how on earth did you cope working here and looking after your mother? I suppose you had friends and family to give you a hand?"

"No Sir, all my relatives are long dead or living miles away with their own families to look after and care for. I was an only child and my father died when I was very young. My mother brought me up by herself. After looking after me for all those years, sometimes without two pennies to rub together, there was just no way that I could put her into a nursing home for the terminally ill. What do you call it? A Hospice. The least that I could do for her was to let her die in her own home. I must admit though, it did get to be quite a strain both financially and healthwise. That's the reason I took compassionate leave to cover the last few months of illness, so I could be at home with her."

Their conversation was interrupted by the sudden ringing of Cline's phone. It was Jones calling to inform Cline that Mrs. Armstrong had made a positive ID of her husband.

"Where are you now Peter?"

"I'm back at the Armstrong's home, I've called her doctor, I am expecting him shortly."

"Good, ask the doctor to stay with her until I get over there. I should be there in around twenty minutes. I'm just hanging on until Baxter and Poole return from seeing our jogger at St. Andrews."

"Well Mary, it looks like you are going to be kept pretty busy from here on end. We've managed to identify the murder victim as Peter Armstrong of 87, St. Peter's Drive, Bolderdale. I want you to check him out. See if he has any previous record, if he has, we may be able to get a list of any known associates."

As White left the room by one door, Baxter and Poole entered by the other door at the opposite end of the room.

"Did you manage to get anything useful from our friend at St. Andrews?"

"No Sir, not a thing, just confirmation of what we already knew."

"At least we now know who our victim is, he has just been identified by his wife. He is, or was, Peter Armstrong from St. Peter's Drive. I am just off to see his wife now. I'll take Poole with me, it will give him a bit of experience."

"Have a word with W.D.C White, she'll fill you in with the day's events so far. Then, I want you to take one of the uniform lads with you and see what you can find down at the Masters Inn. That's the pub where I think Armstrong was heading on Saturday night. Check if he was a regular, White should have some photos by now, so take one with you. It was taken at the morgue, it will have to do for now. I hope Jones managed to pick a photo up from Mrs. Armstrong, at least it should show her husband with a bit more colour in his cheeks."

As Cline drove up the long drive to the Armstrong home, he noticed that Jones's car was still parked outside the house. Jones must have been watching for Cline's arrival for he was out of the house and standing at the side of Cline's car before the engine had stopped turning.

"What are you still doing here? You and Moore should be tucked up in bed right now."

"We would have been long gone Sir, but the doctor couldn't stay with Mrs. Armstrong, so I thought it better if we hung around for a while until you arrived. The doctor said it would be alright for you to ask her a few questions but if she gets too tired, he has left her a couple of tablets. You will find them near the kettle in the kitchen Sir."

"I think you and Moore had better get off home before you both fall asleep, you've had a long shift, you both look like death warmed up."

"I will just introduce you then Sir, then we will get off."

After the departure of Jones and Moore, the three of them, Cline, Poole and Mrs. Armstrong, settled down in the comfort of the lounge. Cline had the habit of being able to assess people's moods and the reactions he was most likely to get from them, just by studying their body language. It was a skill that he had acquired, with his years of experience on the force. He noticed Mrs. Armstrong was seated on the settee with her legs crossed and her arms folded across her chest. It was obvious to Cline, that any information that he was going to obtain from her, would be reluctantly given. For a women who had just identified her murdered husband, she didn't seem to be too upset. In fact, she appeared quite blasé about the whole affair.

"Would you mind if D.C. Poole was to make us all a hot cup of tea? I'm sure you could do with one after the ordeal you have had today."

"No Inspector, please feel free, I'm sure by now the whole police force will know the whereabouts of my kitchen."

Cline let the remark pass without any comment as Poole returned with the tray of tea. Cline passed a cup to Mrs. Armstrong, he didn't want a cup himself, he was just using the tea as a ploy for Mrs. Armstrong to relax and be more susceptible to his questioning. The cup of tea had the desired effect. She had to uncross her legs and arms in order to reach over and take the cup and saucer.

"I apologise if I ask you any questions that Sergeant Jones has already asked you, I like to hear things for myself first hand, I hope you don't mind?"

"Where you at home last night? Or did you go out for the evening?"

"I went out."

"What time did you get in?"

"About ten pm."

"Was your husband at home then?"

"No he wasn't, I thought he was at the pub, so I went straight to bed."

"And he never came home at all last night?"

"Not that I am aware of."

"Was there any particular pub he regularly visited?"

"Yes, the Masters Inn at the end of the woods. It's actually called The Old Masters Inn but we all refer to it as the Masters Inn."

"Who's we?"

"Everybody who uses the pub, although I must say I haven't been there for quite some time."

"Are you sure your husband never came home last night? I don't mean to be rude but do you and your husband share the same bed? If not, wouldn't it be possible for him to come to bed then leave again without you even knowing?"

"I beg your pardon, the sleeping arrangements of my husband and I have nothing whatsoever to do with you"

"I do appreciate that and I don't want to be impertinent but I just want to be absolutely sure that he never came home last night. Another thing Mrs. Armstrong that concerns me, is the fact that as yet, I don't believe you have asked how Mr. Armstrong died, whether it was natural causes or something else."

"Inspector, if I wasn't sure that my husband didn't come home last night, why the hell was I about to ring the police station, when your compatriots came knocking on my door this morning?"

"Where did you go last night? Were you with someone else for the whole evening?"

"Now just hold it there Inspector. First of all I don't really care how my husband died, he's dead and there is nothing I can do to change that fact. If you think I had anything to do with his death in even the slightest way, then you are certainly barking up the wrong tree." She had now become so agitated that she almost dropped her cup and saucer which were still perched on her lap.

"Calm down Mrs. Armstrong, please calm down. Nobody is suggesting for one moment that you had anything at all to do with his death. I must ask you these questions and they need to be answered, so I can then eliminate you from my enquiries.

Just tell me where you went last night and who you were with and it shouldn't take too long for us to check it out."

"There you go again, you think Peter was murdered and you somehow suspect that I am involved."

Cline ignored the outburst. "Please tell me where you went last night."

She could see he wasn't going to give up, he was like a terrier with a rat. She began to fidget as she hurriedly tried to come up with an answer. First she crossed her right leg over the left, then the left over the right, at the same time gripping her cup and saucer tightly in front of her with both hands, as if they could protect her from the barrage of questions.

"I went out with a friend if you must know and before you ask, no, it wasn't another man. I've never been unfaithful to Peter."

"I never thought that for one minute. Does this female (Cline emphasising the word female) friend of yours, happen to have a name?"

"Of course she does. It's Mary Duncan."

The faltering tone of Mrs. Armstrong's voice did not escape the keen ear of Cline.

"So where did you and your friend Mary get to last night?"

"We went down town and had a meal at a restaurant"

"Which one?"

"I cannot remember. Mary booked us in by phone earlier in the day. I just went with her and didn't take any particular notice what it was called or even what part of town it was in."

"Ok, can you remember what time you left the restaurant?"

"It must have been about nine forty. I drove straight home and Mary took a cab, she lives in the opposite direction from town to me."

"What is Mary's address?"

"Look Inspector, I don't really want to get Mary involved in any of this."

"I'm afraid Mrs. Armstrong she is already involved, now that you have told us you were both out together last night. If what you have told me is the truth and at the moment, I have no reason to think otherwise, then your friend Mary is your alibi for last night. At least up to nine forty."

"You still think I had something to do with Peter's death, don't you?"

"The sooner I can check your alibi, the sooner you will be in the clear. So, where does Mary live?"

"She lives at No. 23 Woodlands Drive Wheatley."

"Now that wasn't too difficult, was it? I take it that address is in Bolderdale?"

"Of course Inspector, like I said, over on the other side of town."

"I notice you are a good bit younger than your husband. How long have you been married?"

"About nine years Inspector. I fail to see why that's so important with regards to Peter's death. Unless of course you think I killed him for his money and so I could find a younger man."

Ignoring her once more. "How did you and Peter first meet?"

"Are you quite sure, that all these questions are pertinent to your investigations Inspector?"

"Yes, they help build up an overall picture of you and Peter, you can never tell which little bit of information will be the last piece of a complicated jig saw puzzle."

"Before we met, I used to be a photographic model for an agency. That's how I first met my friend Mary Duncan, she also worked as a model for the same agency.

One day Mary and I were booked to do a photo shoot, to advertise the sales of luxury cars at Armstrong Motors showrooms. That was sometime in 1985. After the shoot, Peter took me out for dinner. We were courting for approximately two years, then we got married in 1987."

"Do you know if Peter had any enemies? Had he fallen out with anyone recently?"

"Not as far I was aware. Peter was well liked, he made friends easily. If he hadn't anything good to say about anyone, then he wouldn't say anything bad about them. As far as business competitors are concerned, he didn't have any. You must know the area pretty well Inspector. You tell me, where is there another car showroom like Armstrong Motors within twenty miles of here. They don't exist."

Mrs. Armstrong produced a white silk handkerchief as if from out of thin air and gently wiped her eyes and patted her nose. It was difficult for Cline to determine whether the tears were real tears or crocodile tears, produced for his benefit.

"Did Peter gamble?"

"Gamble, you must be joking. He wouldn't even buy a premium bond from the post office. He said it wouldn't build any interest. "One of his favourite sayings was, a fool and is money is soon parted. He seemed to have a proverb or saying for every situation. Too many cooks spoil the broth, was the one he used to get out of helping me do the cooking. No Inspector, he was no gambler. He once said he wasn't working seven days a week just to give it away to some lazy sod who just happened to strike it lucky or someone who owned a betting shop."

"The only time he took a gamble, was when he price tagged one of his cars in the showroom. If he priced it too high, the car would sit there for weeks and if he priced it too low, he risked losing money on the sale, or at least reduce his profit margin."

"Would Peter normally be in the habit of carrying large amounts of money around with him?"

"Not as far as I know. I suppose he was always aware, that there was always that possibility that someone might take it upon themselves to mug him."

"Did he usually wear a wrist watch?"

"He never went anywhere without it. It's only one of those cheap gold plated digital watches, probably imported from the Far East. I bought it for him when we got married, it was all I could afford in those days. Don't forget I was only a model and not a good one at that, at least I met Peter. I had it engraved Peter love Ruth, I had his wedding ring engraved the same. I know he could well afford an expensive watch but he always said it kept good time, what more do you need from a watch?"

"Who inherits the business now? I assume it will be all yours now?" The quick change in the direction of the questions was a usual trait of Clines, used to try and put people off their guard. It also helped to stop people trying to pre-empt what question was coming next.

"Not really Inspector, I'll only get half the business."

"Why only half?"

"Because my husband had a business partner."

" Would that be a man or a woman?"

"It's a man Inspector, he's Mary Duncan's brother."

"I take it we are talking about the same Mary Duncan you went out with last night?"

"Yes, we are Inspector, I can't see anything wrong with that, can you?"

"I am not suggesting there is anything wrong Mrs. Armstrong. I just want to be sure I know who we are talking about. What is her brother called?"

"Kenneth Moss."

"I take it then that Mary Duncan is a married woman?"

"Yes, but her husband had nothing to do with the business."

"Did Peter have life assurance cover?"

"Inspector, you just can't seem to get away from idea that I had something to do with Peter's death. Now you will be thinking I have killed him or had him killed for the insurance money. The answer is still the same, I have had nothing to do with Peter's death."

"Has his life cover been altered lately, I should say increased?"

"As a matter of fact it was increased just a few months ago but that had nothing to do with me. Someone rang Peter at his office. It was one of those so called Financial Advisors. Somehow he managed to trick Peter into giving him an interview."

"How do you mean, tricked him?"

"Well you know these sales people Inspector, they all have the gift of the gab, so as to speak. He told Peter that he was in this area the following Monday morning and Wednesday afternoon and asked which of the two days would be most convenient. Peter knew he had a client to see on the Monday and mentioned this to the salesman. Before Peter could say any more, the guy on the other end of the phone said. That's alright Mr. Armstrong, I will see you at 2.30pm on Wednesday and then he put the phone down before Peter could reply. After a three and a half hour meeting on that Wednesday, in desperation to get the guy out of his office, Peter signed up to a £100,000 Whole of Life policy."

"So why didn't he cancel the policy straight away with the Insurance firm, before the cooling off period ran out?"

"He said he couldn't be bothered. Besides, he said it wasn't such a bad idea since he was slightly under covered. He also said it meant he could get a free medical check up."

"So what is the total amount of life cover now on Peter?"

"I think about £600,000"

"So he thought £500,000 was under covered? Who's the beneficiary to all the insurance money?"

"I am Inspector, so there you are, another reason for me to have had Peter killed off."

Ignoring her once again. " I think that about covers all I want to ask you for now, although there may be other questions after I have spoken to your friend Mary Duncan."

"If I were you I would take the pills the doctor left for you. Are you sure there is no one I can contact for you, such as your friend Mary?"

"No thank you I will be alright, could you please let yourselves out?"

Back in the car, Poole who hadn't said one word throughout the interview with Mrs. Armstrong, was the first to speak. "What did you think Sir? Could she have killed her husband?"

"That's a funny question Poole. It's a question I should really be asking you. So what did you make of our Mrs. Armstrong?"

"Well, I get the distinctive impression that there is something she is keeping from us. The alibi for last night sounded a bit iffy. She did seem very nervous throughout the whole interview, whether that was through guilt or not, I couldn't say Sir."

"Very good Poole, we may turn you into a detective yet."

Cline got in touch with the station and arranged for someone to be put a discreet watch on the Armstrong's home. Something just did not seem right in that household. It may be something or nothing but it would be better to find out if he could.

As soon as the PC arrived in plain clothes and had been given instructions by Cline, Poole and Cline drove off in the direction of Mary Duncan's home. "I think we'll give Mary Duncan an unexpected visit, before she has too much time on the phone with Ruth Armstrong getting her story right."

It was precisely seven pm when they arrived outside Mary Duncan's semi detached home. Cline couldn't help but take in the difference between Mary Duncan's home and that of the Armstrong's. Surely this was a sign of the different lifestyles lead by the two apparent friends. Cline reflected that in his experience, friendships like this with different social and financial lifestyles were very rarely successful. It seemed hard to believe that two photographic models with differing lifestyles could still remain good friends after all these years. Something other than being old work mates must be holding them together.

As they approached the front door, they could here raised voices from within the front of the house. Someone was having a heated argument, although it was impossible to hear what was being said or shouted. "I wonder if we have arrived just in time, do you get the feeling Poole, it may be something to do with our expected visit?" The front door bell chiming in the front hallway was the signal for the arguing and shouting to halt. It was only after the third chime that the front door was eased open by a red faced man. Whether he was normally red, or only red with embarrassment of having been caught arguing with his wife, it was impossible to tell.

"I'm D.I.Cline and this is D.S. Poole. I believe this is the home of Mrs. Mary Duncan?"

"That's correct, but why do you wish to know that?"

"I would rather discuss that with Mrs. Duncan, if you don't mind. May we come in?"

"My wife isn't in at the moment, you'll have to come back another time."

"Who's in the house now Mr. Duncan? I take it you are Mr. Duncan?"

"Yes I am, but I am here by myself."

"I will ask you again. Who is in the house with you?"

"Nobody."

"How often do you have arguments with yourself Mr. Duncan? You know you can be sectioned and locked away for good for that. We could hear you as soon as we got out of our car. Now you can either let us in or I will arrest you for interfering with a police investigation and we can spend the next twenty four hour in a police cell or interview room. The choice is entirely yours."

"We were just having a domestic argument and I thought the wife wouldn't want to talk to you with her being upset."

"That's very commendable of you Mr. Duncan, but I think I'll be the judge of whether we will talk to your wife or not. Please may we come in now? If you prefer we could still go down to the station to talk."

Duncan moved to one side. "You had better come in then, you'll find the wife in the kitchen, straight through in front of you. We've just finished eating."

"Thank you Mr. Duncan."

"Duncan followed them through and made the introductions. Mrs. Duncan was even more red faced with embarrassment than her husband had been. Cline could guess why.

It looked like they had just finished a game of throwing the custard pie, rather than having a meal. Whatever they were arguing about, it must have got quite out of hand. It seemed to Cline, that the delaying tactics at the front door, may have been nothing more than Mr. Duncan's attempt, to allow his wife to tidy up.

"Ok Inspector, what is this all about?"

"Would you mind if we sat down? We may be here for some time. It would be better if you would go into another room with D.C. Poole, while I put a few questions to your wife."

"I should tell you Mrs. Duncan that at this point, you are not obliged to answer any questions but it could save you both a lot of inconvenience at a later date."

"Just get on with it and let's get this over with. I'm sure my wife has no secrets to hide. I also think I should be here with her."

"I'm sure you would Mr. Duncan but I would prefer it if you were to go with D.C. Poole into another room." With that, Cline gestured Poole to escort Mr. Duncan out of the kitchen into another room.

By now, Mrs. Duncan was looking all worried and anxious just as Cline liked it. He guessed she was a person who always stuck to the letter of the law and someone had put her in a position, that made her feel very uncomfortable and vulnerable. All she wanted now, was a chance to clear the air and yet, she still felt a loyalty to her friend.

"Where were you on Saturday night?"

Still holding the floor mop in her hand, from her attempt to clean the kitchen floor before her husband let Cline and Poole into their home, she began to fidget. "Which Saturday do you mean Inspector?"

"Yesterday."

"Oh! yesterday, I was with my friend Mrs. Ruth Armstrong, we went down town for a meal together." The words left her mouth as if she'd been rehearsing for a play at the local drama group, they came out of her mouth so fast, that she had to draw in a deep breath in order to continue.

"We go out together most Saturday evenings."

"Why don't you go out with your husbands? Surely a foursome would have been more sociably entertaining."

"My husband doesn't like going out at night, he's a couch potato, he much prefers to stay in and watch TV all night."

"What time did you get back in last night?"

"I took a taxi from the restaurant, I suppose it must have been around nine forty pm. Ruth drove herself home in her merc."

"Which taxi firm did you use?"

"How the hell do you expect me to know that? All those black cabs look the same to me."

"Why didn't your so called friend run you home and save you the cab fare?"

"First of all Inspector, she's not a so called friend of mine, she is a friend and has been for a good number of years. It is precisely because we are good friends, that I wouldn't put on her, by expecting her to go out of her way to run me home, when she lives on the opposite side of town to me."

To Mrs. Duncan's surprise, Cline rose to his feet and told her that he was finished with her for the moment but may call back again at another time.

As cline walked past the lounge door, he beckoned to Poole that they were about to leave. They bid the Duncans goodnight and made their way back to their car.

"What did Mr. Duncan have to say, anything useful?"

"It was very strange really Sir. I thought I would ask him where his wife was last night. It was like listening to a recording of Mrs. Armstrong's statement. In fact it was almost word for word Sir. Do you think they had anything to do with Mr. Armstrong's death Sir?"

"I'm not sure but something is not right. Mrs. Duncan was acting strange. I definitely feel that they had been primed by someone, in what they should tell us."

"From where I'm sitting Mrs. Armstrong is that someone. Mrs. Duncan even gave her taxi time at nine forty pm. Why not around nine thirty or a quarter to ten, it just sounds too perfect to be true. You can bet the argument was about whether they should go along with the lies that Ruth Armstrong had told us. Armstrong must have rung them just before we arrived. What are they trying to cover up? I'm still not convinced they had anything to do with the murder but first thing in the morning I want a copy of all the telephone calls made from Armstrong's home for the past six months and especially for tonight. I also want all the drivers from the black cab firms interviewed. See if anyone can remember picking up Mrs. Duncan around nine forty on Saturday evening."

Chapter 5.

"What are you doing Terry?"

"I'm packing up and going home. We've been here all night and neither of us has caught a blasted thing, not even an old boot."

"Just give it another half hour or so, I'm sure we'll catch something soon."

"The only thing we are likely to catch is piles. We've been sat on this wet bank for over eight hours."

"I wasn't the idiot who forgot to pack the chairs.

"I know Dave. Ok I'll give it another thirty minutes and no more. I have to leave anyway, it's my turn to take the kids to school this morning. The wife's got a new job at the local supermarket on Mondays. If I make her late for work on the first day, she'll have my guts for garters."

Terry turned back to face the river, just in time to see Dave's float, bob up and down in the water.

"Dave look at your float, I think you've got a bite."

"It doesn't look like a bite to me, I think my line's got hooked up on something. Whatever it is, it isn't trying to pull back or get away. It's pretty close to the bank whatever it is, can't you see anything Terry?"

"I can see something but I cannot make out what it is."

"Don't just stand there then, get the keep net and try and lift it out onto the river bank." "Dave it looks like a bunch of old clothes. Oh! My God. Dave I can see a hand, I think you've caught yourself a real live body."

"What do you mean, live body?"

"I mean you have a dead body on the end of your line."

It took all their joint effort, to lift the body out of the river onto the river bank after which they lay there completely exhausted.

"I told you Dave we should have gone before. Let's just throw it back into the river and pretend we never caught it."

"Why on earth would we want to do that?"

"Because if we don't, we will have to call the police and I will not get away from here in time to pick the kids up."

"Ok, if you are in such a hurry to get home, let's shove the thing back into the river and we will forget all about it."

"I know, we can't do that."

"Then stop moaning and go and ring the police and ring your wife at the same time, she's bound to understand. It will give her something to talk about."

Cline and Baxter arrived at the police station together. They had just removed their jackets when the Duty Sergeant from the front desk entered the incident room.

"Sorry to bother you Sir, I think you had better put your coats back on again. We've just had a report that two fishermen have pulled a body out of the river Bolder."

"Why tell me about it Sergeant, I've already got my hands full with a murder inquiry."

"I know that Sir, but Jack Morgan the M.O. has seen the body and made strong suggestions that you should get yourself down there at once."

"Ok Sergeant, leave it with me I'll get it sorted."

"When you are ready Sir, I've got a uniformed P.C. to take you and show you where the body is."

"Looks like we are going to miss our eleven o'clock cuppa today Wendy. Get your jacket on and let's see what's so important that Morgan wants me down there. One thing about this place Wendy, there's never a dull moment."

"Pull up just over there Sir, on the bridge over the river. We'll get out there and walk the rest of the way along the old tow path at the side of the river. This is as close as we can get by car."

Leaving the comfort of the car behind, they set off walking along the tow path.

Cline was now beginning to feel just a little concerned about what was about to confront him.

Surely there is not going to be a connection between this new body and the death of Peter Armstrong. The gut pain he was feeling seemed to be answering his concerns for him. He expressed his fears to Baxter. "I was just having the same feelings Sir. I hope we are wrong. The M.O. wouldn't call you down here for no good reason."

"Exactly Wendy, exactly, that's what's worrying me."

"How much further Constable?"

"Not too far Sir, about another hundred and fifty yards past that large willow tree you can see in front. In fact Sir, you can just make out the top of the white tent, erected over the place were the anglers left the body."

The area around the tent was amassed with Forensic personnel. Cline turned to the P.C. "Who called all this lot in?"

Before the P.C. could answer a booming voice shouted, "I DID, any objections?"

There was no disguising that voice, Cline knew before he turned around that Dr. Morgan would be standing before him. Morgan was stood in the doorway of the tent, holding the flap up beckoning Cline to enter. "Good morning John. I hope I didn't get you two out of bed this morning? Not the same bed anyway."

"Oh! Aren't we the funny one this morning? Now look what you've done Jack, you've made my Sergeant blush. Just ignore him Wendy."

"Ok Jack, what's so important that you need me down here this morning?"

"Just take a look at the body, and then you tell me."

Inside the tent lay a body bag, all ready to be taken away. Cline bent down and unzipped it and took a good look at the corpse, the sole result of a night spent angling in the river Bolder. It only took one look to send a cold shiver running down his spine.

"Christ Almighty Jack, tell me there's no connection between this one and the one from Saturday night? Please."

"I wish I could John, there's even a stab wound in the victim's back just like the one in the woods. I need to get the body back to the morgue to carry out a post mortem, and then I will know for sure John, but don't be holding your breath. If I had to make a bet, I would say your killer has struck again."

"God Jack, does this mean we have a serial killer running loose about town?"

"Two trees don't make a forest John and two swallows don't make a summer but thing's ain't looking too good at the moment."

"One significant difference though, the victim wasn't robbed and he still had his wallet and identification in his pocket. His wallet contained one hundred and ten pounds in ten pound notes and his driving license." Morgan passed two see- through evidence bags to Baxter. One bag contained the money and the wallet, the other the driving license.

"Can you make out the victim's name through the plastic cover Wendy?"

"Yes Sir, Neville Preston of 29, Common Lane Bentley. D.O.B. is given as 22.05.1942."

"Jack, can you say how long he was in the water? And some idea of how long he has been dead?"

"Well John, with the state of the body, it's not started to swell up yet, I would say about thirty six hours."

"What, in the water or when he was killed?"

"When he was killed. I should have a better idea after the post- mortem that is, if I can ever get away from here with the body."

"So it's more than likely he was killed on Saturday night or Sunday morning?"

"As near as I can tell at this time."

"Well if it is the same killer, he or she must have had a very busy weekend."

Cline called over to the S.O.C.O. team. "Who's in charge?"

"I am Sir,"

"Good, I want photos of the tow-path. Just like we did in the woods over the weekend. I want to know where the body fell, was pushed or thrown into the river."

"We will do our best Sir. I would think the body was thrown in the river from the road bridge."

"You think! I don't want to know what you think. Just get out there and find where he went into the river. You are not paid to report what you think, only what you find. And I want that report yesterday."

"You know this is going to take up an awful lot of film Sir?"

"I don't give a damn if you use every film in the country, just get it done."

It was eleven thirty by the time Cline and Baxter arrived back in the incident room. Knowels was already there, getting an update of events, still unaware of the latest developments that had taken place on the banks of the river Bolder. He was only aware of a brief report stating, that a body had been fished out of the river, which he assumed was just a drunk or a suicide victim.

"Cline! What do you think you are playing at, going out wasting your time investigating a suicide case? Someone else, or even the uniform lads can sort that out."

"Well, I am sorry to disappoint you but I am afraid it wasn't a suicide. In fact it was another murder."

"Rubbish! You mean to tell me, we go years without a murder in this town and now out of the blue, we have two murders within a couple of days of each other. I don't believe it."

"Unless you can tell me, how anyone can stab themselves in the back, then cut their throat and then just to show us how ingenious he his, throw himself into the river, then it is murder."

"But that's the same as the first murder in the woods."

"Now you are telling me we have a raving lunatic running loose and unrestrained through our patch, with God knows how many knives at his or her disposal. I've just been told in no uncertain terms, that I have to reduce my expenses or risk going into overspends before the end the financial year. Then Cline, you tell me, I have a major incident on my hands."

"We are nowhere near the end of the financial year yet, what the hell have you spent it on?" Cline was loving this, Knowels in trouble with the top brass.

Knowels let the question go unanswered. "Before you ask, no, you can't have any more personnel. Get this lot sorted out as quick as you can." With an air of arrogance and pompousness Knowels stormed out of the room.

"Well that's got rid of him for the time being."

Cline walked over to the large notice board on the incident room wall and glanced at the information that had been posted by W.D.C. White.

The objects that took his interest and for that matter everyone else in the room, were the large number of photographs taken of the footpath in the woods where Peter Armstrong was killed.

They not only covered the length of the notice board, they spread almost across two full walls. Cline smiled to himself as he wondered what Knowels thought of all the photographs around the walls. So much for him cutting costs. Just wait till he sees the next lot from the river bank.

"Mary, has D.C. Poole given you any phone call listings yet, for Mrs. Armstrong?"

"Yes Sir, he brought them in and left again just before you and W.D.S. Baxter returned. He said he was going down town to check the black cab drivers and that you would know all about that Sir."

"Where are they now, Mary?"

"I've got them here Sir. I've made up a file for any information that I can't put up on the notice board." Mary opened the file and handed the telephone listings over to Cline.

He took a good look down the list. "I knew it; Ruth Armstrong had tipped the Duncans that we may be giving them a call. She made an eighteen minute call to the Duncan's home at 18.36 and finished calling at 18.54. She certainly wasted no time. The Duncans were having a right old ding-dong battle royal when Poole and I arrived at their front door Mary, have you looked through the list yet?"

"No Sir, like I said, I had only just received it before you arrived. Well I suppose I did give it a quick glance, whilst you and the Super were chatting."

"Did you notice anything?"

"There did seem to be a heavy amount of calls to the motor showrooms and to Mr. Armstrong's partner's home. Whether that means anything or not I don't know Sir?"

"Couldn't the calls have been in connection with the car business?"

"I suppose so, but quite a good number of the calls were made in the middle of the night. I can't imagine anyone wanting to talk shop about cars at three or four o'clock in the morning, can you Sir?"

"Ok Mary, I'll keep that in mind. Wendy, what did you find out at the Old Masters?"

"Nothing Sir, not yet anyway. I've got to call back again when the manager is in. He was out at the wholesalers when I called. Whether he was or not, I can't tell, but I should be able to collar him tomorrow."

Jones and Moore returned looking much brighter and fresher from when Cline had last set eyes on them.

"There's been some development since I last saw you. There was another body this morning. Two anglers dragged it out of the river Bolder. Mary will bring you up to date. Peter, I want you to get a copy of the statements given by the Duncans from Mary, and then you and Garry can go and speak to them again. Let's see if they come up with the same cock and bull story that they gave the last time. If you have any trouble with them bring them into the station, that should loosen their tongues. In the meantime Wendy, you get back to the Old Masters Inn, I want to know what they have to say, and I want to know today. Take a photo of Peter Armstrong with you just in case."

"At this stage of our enquiry, I don't want anyone outside this room, other than those with a need to know, finding out how Armstrong and Preston met their untimely deaths. The last thing that we need right now is for some copy cat killer making our job any harder than it already is. So remember, mouths firmly shut."

"Mary, I want you to find out as much as possible about Preston. As soon as Poole comes back from down town, let him take over. Somewhere there is a link between Armstrong and Preston and I want to know what it is. I believe that the robbery on Armstrong was not the reason for the attack and death. I believe it was just to slow us down in identifying him."

"Just one more thing before I leave Sir."

"What's that Wendy?

"Preston could have been mugged and killed somewhere on the towpath at the side of the river. He may have struggled and slipped into the river before his attacker could remove is valuables etc. It may have been the killer's intention to make the murders look like muggings, we just don't know. We will just have to leave all options open until we have more to go on."

"If there was a struggle somewhere along that towpath, there must be signs of it. S.O.C.O should be able to find traces where the struggle took place."

"Thank you Wendy, we'll just have to wait and see what the lads turn up."

"It was a beautiful sunny day as Cline drove onto the forecourt of Armstrong Motors.

As he locked his car doors and turned to face the showrooms he couldn't help but look longingly at the gleaming limousines, the likes of which would take at least two, if not three years salary, to pay for it. Not only had he never owned or expected to own a vehicle anywhere near the quality of those that now surrounded him, he had never had one that gleamed that much. Pulling the handle, on one of the double glass doors he entered the reception area. Immediately in front of him was a wide staircase, more suitable for a stately home, than a car showroom. To the right was the showroom full of limousines that had caught his attention from the customer's car park. To his left stood the reception desk where a young blonde receptionist was busying herself moving and sorting out coloured brochures.

"I'm D.I. Cline from Bolderdale Police Station. I would like to speak to Mr. Kenneth Moss."

"I'm very sorry Inspector but I'm afraid Mr. Moss is very busy at the moment. Would you care to make an appointment to see him?"

"Very well dear, let us say in ten minutes down at the station, it shouldn't take much longer than four or five hours."

"I don't think Mr. Moss will have four or five hours to spare Inspector, he is very busy now he has lost in partner."

"Then you had better let Mr. Moss know that I am here, hadn't you?"

"For one of the few times in her short adult life, she felt as if she was not in charge of her situation and scurried over to her desk phone, turning her back to Cline, she whispered something into the mouth piece. Try as he might, he couldn't make out what she was saying. He could only assume she was speaking to Moss.

"Mr. Moss will see you now Inspector. If you just wait there Sir, he will be along to take you to his office."

"Thank you Miss"

After what appeared to be an age, but was in fact only a couple of minutes, he could hear the sound of footsteps descending the uncarpeted staircase. Turning his head towards that direction, he was confronted by an athletic-looking bronzed figure of a man who looked as if he spent as much time on the beach or on a sun bed, than he did in his office. He would have been about five foot eight or nine inches in height and weighing in at around twelve stones. From his muscular physique, it was evident that he must also spend an awful lot of time pumping iron at the gym.

"Good afternoon Inspector, I hope Jenny hasn't been giving you too hard a time. She does tend to be a little over protective of me. She does normally have orders not to interrupt, me unless people have previously arranged appointments. These however, are not normal times Inspector. Now what can I do for you?"

"You could take us somewhere, where we will not be disturbed, so that I may ask you a few questions in private."

Moss turned towards the staircase "Please, follow me Inspector."

Cline followed in Moss's wake up the staircase and into a large and spacious office .The office was richly appointed with deep pile wall to wall carpeting. The centre piece of the room being a very large mahogany desk with a deep red leather inlay set into the top. The walls were lined with expensive looking mahogany wood panels. Mounted on the panels, were small square boxes, each box containing a model car. Most of the model cars were either gold or silver plated. Everything about the Armstrong's oozed money.

Not only would Cline never be able to afford any of the cars on the forecourt, he doubted if he could even afford any of the model cars. He wondered if this was Moss's office or whether he had quickly taken over Peter Armstrong's office since the weekend.

"Please take a seat Inspector." With a wave of his hand, he directed Cline towards a red leathered upholstered wing chair, one of a matching trio, whilst he himself had now settled into a leather swivel chair behind the mahogany desk.

"I've been half expecting you Inspector, ever since Peter's wife, Ruth Armstrong rang me with the terrible news about Peter. It is such a tragedy and so out of the blue."

"Murder usually is Mr. Moss."

"I meant his death Inspector, not his murder."

Cline was beginning to get that Déjà vu feeling all over again. Had Ruth Armstrong been doing her prompting act again?

"Tell me Mr. Moss, how did you and Ruth Armstrong get on with each other? The age difference between her and her husband was quite a bit. I believe she would be nearer to your age?"

"If that remark was meant with an ulterior meaning then I will ignore it. As far as the difference in all our ages is concerned, that's none of yours or anyone else's business.

As far as the business is concerned, the only thing that mattered is the fact that both Peter and I are, or should I say were, both fanatics when it came to cars like the Bentley and the Rolls Royce. Age difference was never an issue with any of us."

"I was thinking more of the gap between Ruth Armstrong and Peter, not you and Peter. Although I would imagine you and Ruth Armstrong would be likely to get on with each other." Cline was now testing the water, waiting for that ripple that would tell him he might have got a bite.

"I know what you are thinking Inspector but as far as I was concerned, Ruth Armstrong was just the wife of my business partner and nothing more."

"Talking about that, just how did you become business partners? You couldn't have been classroom friends because of your age difference."

"It was a good few year's back now. Peter started the business up long before I met him. He was born and bred in Bolderdale but I was born in the Midlands. Right from being old enough to walk and talk, cars like the Rolls Royce have been my dream. After leaving school imagine how I felt when I landed a job at the Rolls Royce factory in Derby. To me it was better than having eight draws on the football coupons. It was as if all my birthdays and Christmases had fallen on the same day."

"I began working as a tea boy and odd job lad. It didn't teach me about cars but it did teach me to have respect for my elders. After the first three months I was taken on as an apprentice mechanic with a five years' indentured apprenticeship ahead of me. I spent a lot of my time on the assembly lines."

"After five years I was pretty genned up on the working of the Rolls. I suppose it was as much to do with my enthusiasm as my knowledge that the management decided to transfer me to customer service. This meant visiting both private and business users of Rolls Royce cars. Just think back Inspector, I dare bet you have never heard of a Rolls breaking down in the middle of the street, that's because of people like me. By this time, Peter Armstrong had already got this business up and running. It was when, on one of those rare occasions that he had a spot of trouble with a Rolls on his forecourt, that I first met him."

"That was the start of our friendship. Six months after that first meeting at Armstrong Motors, I'd sold my home, which had been left to me by my grandparents and I went into a fifty- fifty partnership with Peter. I was lucky that my sister had moved to this area about two years previous, to a modelling agency. For the first few months, I lived with her until I had my own place. The partnership took all my money so I had to save up for a new deposit. Peter was the salesman and I was the technical man."

"So when did Peter meet your sister?"

"That was when Armstrong Motors booked the modelling agency to do some promotional work for us. That would be a good few years back now."

"Would you say that Peter had been acting his normal self over the past few days and weeks? Had he looked under pressure, worried or stressed out more than usual?"

"I can't really say Inspector, although we were business partners we very rarely saw each other. We were each so busy in our own little worlds' Peter with his paper work and book work and me with all the latest technical innovations, that we only used to really get together once a week to discuss how the business was running. I suppose Jenny on the reception desk would have been more likely to spot any changes in Peter's behaviour. After all she was also his secretary. Having said that, Peter always liked to do most of his own typing. Personally, I cannot see the point in having a dog and barking yourself."

"You mentioned that Peter did book work and paper work, I take it you meant he did the accounts as well? I assume the company still had an accountant?"

"The accounts were officially completed by an accountancy firm in Bolderdale."

"I think Mr. Moss, if I were in partnership with someone, I would want to know each and everyday what is happening with the business, especially if I had invested a large amount into the business, which from what you have told me, you did just that."

"That is why we had a weekly meeting together every Saturday night after closing. Although Peter sorted all the paper work out, I still knew exactly what was happening with regards to the business. We used to check the bank statements etc, together. That way, we both knew the financial situation every week."

"So was the business doing well?"

"Well yes, I suppose so."

"What do you mean? I suppose so. Aren't you sure?"

"it's not anything I can put my finger on, accountancy was never one of my strong points but for the past few months things didn't always seem to add up."

"Give me an instance."

"The turnover of cars has been rising for sometime now. The past few months we have been very busy. Yet the cash flow which should have been increasing has actually got smaller. Last Saturday night after Peter had left the office, I returned alone to have a closer look at the books, not that

I half expected to find anything amiss. I really didn't know what to look for, but I just had this gut feeling that I wanted to put to rest. It was the very first time that I had been in Peter's office by myself after normal hours. The only reason I had a set of keys, was in case we got called out by the Police or Fire Brigade after hours. Not that I have ever been called out. It was always Peter the emergency services used to ring first. Anyway back to my story."

"Saturday we had a bumper day, no pun intended there Inspector. I should say Peter had a good day, he sold four cars and that is exceptional in this type of market, one customer even paid cash for a Rolls."

"You mean somebody came in and dumped fifty or sixty grand on his desk and said I'll have that car?"

"It's not quite like that Inspector, but believe me there are people out there with money to burn, you wouldn't believe how many."

"You have to remember also, that most of the customers will have a trade-in vehicle which would reduce considerably the amount of actual cash handed over. We could still be talking twenty or thirty thousand though."

These people talk in thousands of pounds while people like Cline talk in pounds, it was like being on a different planet.

"So what happens to the daily takings? Do you put them into an office safe? Or do you take them to the bank night safe? I cannot see any signs of an office safe."

"We do have an office safe Inspector, it's hidden behind one of the wall panels. One of the panels is hinged and the safe is hidden behind it. We normally only use the wall safe if for some reason we have quite a large amount of cash lying about and we couldn't get to the bank at all. If at all possible we prefer to use cheques and bankers drafts. Under normal circumstances, if we did have large amounts of cash we always tried to get them to the bank or to the bank night safe whenever possible. That's about it Inspector, if ever we were to have a cheque stolen we could always have that stopped at the bank."

"When Peter made a deposit to either the bank, when it was open or to the night safe did he follow a normal and regular routine, or did he try to vary it?"

"I don't know really, I never went with him. Although I said sometimes we do have to handle quite large amounts of cash from time to time, we do deal mainly with cheques. So I don't suppose he bothered about his routine too much"

"What was different about last weekend?"

"I'm not saying things were different, it was just a worry that I had, a gut feeling after Ruth Armstrong rang me on Sunday and told me about Peter being killed."

"But you said earlier that you had concerns on Saturday night."

"I know, I just wanted to make sure the Saturday takings were ok."

"And were they?"

"I didn't look, I had second thoughts and to be truthful I felt guilty."

"When Ruth or should I say Mrs. Armstrong rang me on Sunday and told me about Peter, I just had to go back to the office and check the safe."

"I would have thought that money would have been the last thing on your mind, having just heard that your business partner was dead."

"I didn't know what to think Inspector, it was such a shock."

"So were the takings ok?"

"Not that I could tell on Sunday. The bank rang to let me know that Peter did use the night safe on Saturday night but the bag only contained cheques, no cash."

"Does that mean there could be money missing?"

"Yes, Inspector, and it could be a few thousand pounds. From my rough reckoning, I would say in the region of ten thousand pounds. I was just in the process of getting the accountants over here when you arrived, but I am fairly confident we have a shortfall of ten thousand pounds."

"I'm afraid I won't be able to let your accountants see your books just yet Mr. Moss. In fact, I must ask you to lock away all your files until my lads can look them over and if you would be kind enough to hand over all your keys it would be a big help. Now I know I could go and get a court order to do this but it would be a big help if you gave your permission. I could remain here until the search warrant arrives."

"That won't be necessary Inspector Cline. The sooner we get this mess sorted out, the sooner I can get back to running the business, although, I must say that right now, I don't feel much like working. Just do what you have to do."

"I appreciate that Mr. Moss, if you can just lock everything up and give me the keys, I'll try to be out or your hair as soon as I can. By the way, are there any spare keys that I should know about?"

"Ruth Armstrong should have a set of keys, as for Peter's keys, I don't know if he had them with him on Saturday night. Ruth said you didn't find anything in his pockets. Jenny on reception should also have a spare set."

"I'll collect the keys from Jenny on the way out, but just for the record, where were you on Saturday night? Say between the hours of eight pm and midnight?"

"I spent all Saturday evening, apart from the short time early on here in the office, at home catching up on my videos. I rang my sister Mary Duncan at her home. I usually do that on a Saturday evening, just to keep in touch."

"What time did you ring her?"

"It would have been around eight thirty or nine, that's when I usually call her."

"And was she in?"

"No, her husband said she'd gone out for the night with Ruth, that's Mrs. Armstrong. They had decided on the spur of the moment to go down town for a meal. It was then that I decided to have a shower, make myself a meal and settle down in front of the TV with my videos for the rest of the evening."

"If I remember correctly, either Ruth Armstrong or your sister told me that they usually liked to go out together on a Saturday evening. Yet you tell me, you ring her every Saturday night."

"I do Inspector, but she's not always in and I may have got the time wrong."

"How do you get on with Mrs. Armstrong? After all, you are both around the same age."

"Inspector, I think you have covered this ground before. We get on with each other, we are good friends. You wouldn't expect anything else considering that her husband is, sorry was, not only my business partner but my best friend."

"I wasn't implying anything Mr. Moss. I was just leading up to asking, if you had any idea of the type of social life Peter and Ruth lead. For instance, did they share a social life or did they go their separate ways. It's just this bit about Ruth Armstrong going out alone with your sister, that makes me stop to think why didn't Ruth Armstrong go out on a Saturday night with her husband?"

Cline could see the Moss's face become suddenly red, even the deep tan was unable to keep the redness from showing. Ha! somewhere I must have hit a chord. The thought of upsetting Moss, seemed somehow to fill Cline with a warm glow throughout his body. He knew Ruth Armstrong, Mary Duncan and Kenneth Moss had some kind of secret that it would appear, they didn't wish Cline to know of.

"I think that will do for now Mr. Moss, but no doubt I will wish to speak to you at some date in the not too distant future."

"I don't know what happened to the tea Inspector? Jenny always makes tea when I have a visitor."

"Perhaps I'll fair better next time. I'll find my own way out thank you."

As Cline strolled out of the office and then down the stairs he noticed Jenny quickly replacing the telephone back onto her desk top. He thought to himself, there's someone else with a red face, I wonder who that was on the phone. I bet I could take a lucky guess.

"How is Mrs. Armstrong today?"

"She was alr...." She stopped talking mid sentence realising that she had been caught out.

"Before I leave, I will need all the keys for the office doors, lockers, cupboards and the safe, then you can finish work for today. Mr Moss will no doubt tell you when it is ok to return in the next two or three days." An interview with Jenny would wait until later. "I'll just use the cloak room before I leave, if you don't mind."

At the same time that Cline had arrived at the Armstrong Showrooms, W.D.S. Baxter was entering the Old Masters Inn near to the first murder scene. She was armed with a photograph of Peter Armstrong which she had obtained from Ruth Armstrong on the way to the Inn. Apart from one young couple sitting in the corner, the furthest from the bar, the inn was empty of customers.

The barmaid was busying herself, washing and drying glasses behind the bar.

"Yes love, what can I get you?"

"Nothing thanks you. I'm not here on a social call." Baxter had her warrant card out in front of the barmaid's face and then back into her pocket again, before the barmaid could read it. "I'd like to have a word with your manager. Is he in today?"

"Yes, he is. Right now you've caught him at a bad time, he's in the cellar changing one of the barrels." At that she disappeared out of sight, behind the upright wine and spirit stand on the other side of the bar and returned a few moments later accompanied by a short, stocky, red faced, ginger- haired man in rolled up sleeves and a pair of dirty old jeans. As he emerged from behind the bar and entered the customer area of the pub, he beckoned Baxter over to the table in the corner, opposite to where the young couple were seated. "I think that should be private enough, although we could go through to the back if you wished?"

"No, this will do just fine, thank you. I take it you are the pub manager?"

"Yes, that is correct. I suppose this is about the body that was found in the woods late Saturday night or early Sunday morning? I don't know how I can help."

"I never left the pub nor did I see or hear anything. We get very, very busy on a Saturday evening. Last Saturday we did over two hundred meals. By the time we got rid of the last customers and got everything washed up and put away ready for Sunday morning, all I was ready for was to get my head down."

"I appreciate that Sir, but I would like you to take a look at this picture and tell me if you have ever seen this man in your pub?"

"He's not the man you found in the woods, is he?"

"Please, if you wouldn't mind, I will ask the questions. That way I won't be in your way any longer than necessary. I am sure you have more than enough work on your hands, work that you wish to get back to. So have you seen him before?"

"Yes, he comes in here but I have no idea who he is or where he lives. I guess he must be local because he comes in for a meal quite regularly."

"Did he have a companion, or did he dine alone?"

"You said did he, does that mean he is the dead man from the woods?"

"I've already told you once, I'll ask the questions, now, did he or did he not dine alone?"

"Ok, don't get your knickers in a twist Sergeant, I was only curious. When he first started dining here a few months back, he was always with a woman, she looked a bit younger than he did. From the snippets of conversation, that we can't help but overhear and pick up from time to time whilst we serve on the tables, it seemed to us that they were husband and wife."

"At first, they would come in a couple of nights a week for a drink and a meal. They always left well before closing time."

"How well did they seem to get on with one another?"

"When they first started coming here, they always seemed friendly enough. They were always holding long conversations with each other and occasionally, you would see them holding each other's hand over the table. Then gradually over the past few weeks, the atmosphere around their table seemed to slowly change. Not that they started screaming and shouting at each other, it was just little things that one tends to notice. When you've been in this business as long as I have, you can just sense the atmosphere around a table."

"What kind of little things do you mean?"

"Because they were relatively regular clients, I prefer to call all my customers, clients, you tend to notice any changes that may take place over time. When they first began to dine they seemed to chatter to each other all the time. It wasn't too long after however, that their relationship appeared to become more strained. They seemed to spend much less time talking to each other and they stopped holding hands over the table. They didn't fall out or have arguments, they just appeared to become strangers over a short period of time. During the last couple of weeks before she stopped coming here to dine with him, I didn't think they looked like a happy couple. They never seemed to smile any more." "Eventually he began coming by himself to dine. Now however, he was coming here four or five times a week for a meal instead of just at the weekend."

"Did he have any particular time of day when he ate, or did the time vary?"

"Normally it would be around the same time in the evening. I would say it would be somewhere in the region of nine to nine thirty when he would call in. Because we are normally very busy, especially at the weekends, I cannot be one hundred percent sure of the times Sergeant."

"Did he call in here last Saturday evening for a meal?"

"No, in fact one of the staff happened to comment about his absence. We just thought he was ill or something, it was the first Saturday evening he had missed for quite some time."

"Can you remember if he ever dined with anyone else, either male or female?"

"No, never. At least not as far as I can remember. The lady I have already told you about is the only dining partner I have seen him with."

"Do you know if any of your diners use the foot path through the woods to come and go to your pub?"

"I would imagine so, I should think that quite a few of our diners and drinkers would be residents of the nearby estate. Don't waste your time Sergeant, in asking who they may be, I have no idea. Whether many would have used the footpath last Saturday, is also another thing. It got quite dark just before the rains came and it would have been difficult to find your way along the footpath without a torch. After it started raining, the footpath would have got pretty muddy, not very nice to walk along, if you are just out for a drink and a meal in your best bib and tucker."

"Don't forget Sergeant, there wasn't a moon on Saturday night which wouldn't have helped matters and I can't think I have ever seen anyone come here for a drink or a meal carrying a flash light."

"I think that will do for now, thank you." Baxter was up and away and almost out of the pub door before the surprised manager realised that the interview was over. She arrived at her car just in time to receive a message to call at the morgue and pick up the M.O.'s report on Preston's body, the guy who was literally fished out of the river.

"Good afternoon Dr. Morgan. I believe you have a report for me to collect?"

"Yes, it's over there on the desk, the file with the red sticker on the front."

"Any ideas about this one Doc?"

"Well the body was dragged out of river at around 6.45am, the fact that it had been in the river at all, doesn't make my job any easier in ascertaining the correct time of death. However, I would say he'd been dead for about thirty six hours, when he was fished out of the river. Apart from that, I've been doing your job for you this morning."

"What do you mean Doc? Doing my job."

"I thought it may be of help to you and Cline, if you had some idea where the body entered the river. Now since one of my old school chums works for the River Authorities, I thought a phone call wouldn't come amiss. I've written everything down of what he said, as an appendix in my report."

"Without me having to read your report now Doc, can't you give me a quick run down on what your old chum had to say?"

"As you well know, we are in the middle of one of the longest, hardest droughts on record. This rain we are having now is the first we have had for weeks. Subsequently the River Bolder is running very low due to the low rain fall. It doesn't help either that the Water board have been pumping water out of the river upstream from where the body was fished out. The river is only moving very slowly at the moment, in fact near the river bank, the flow is virtually non-existent. The fastest flow would be in the middle of the river, where the water is the deepest. If the body had been thrown from a bridge into the middle of the river, it would almost certainly have been seen within a short period of time. It would have been quite easily visible, floating down the centre of the river.

If the body had been thrown in from a bridge near the bank of the river, the body would have remained within a few feet of the bridge and we know that wasn't so. My chum and his mates said, they are one hundred percent certain that the body either fell in or was pushed in, from somewhere along the tow-path. Because of the slow flowing river, the reeds and over hanging bushes and over hanging trees onto the water, the body would not have travelled too far from the spot where it entered the river. What is also of significance is the fact that the body, almost certainly, entered the water on the same side of the river as it was fished out."

"Why do they believe that Doc? You know what Cline's like for facts, he doesn't like guess work."

"There are two or three reasons why they think that. One, the only tow-path along the river bank, is on that side of the river where the body was fished out. The other side of the river is just fields and river bank. The killer and the victim would have had to cross a few fields, just to get to the river bank. From what I remember of the area, it is not the type of place you would go for a day out or picnic, or even a walk. Two, if the body had gone into the river on the opposite side to the tow-path, then it would no doubt have been seen by anyone on the tow-path who happened to look across to the other side of the river. It would have been spotted well before it was fished out. Three, because of the low water level, that would make the body difficult to spot from the tow-path if it had gone into the river on that side, because it would have been well below the river bank. It could have laid there by the river bank, entangled in the reeds and bushes for days, if it had not been fished out. I would say for once you had a bit of luck there. That's one of the few spots on that side of the river that anglers do any fishing. They usually prefer to tramp over the fields on the opposite side of the river where they are less likely to be disturbed by other people. Because the water level is low and the river flow is slow, the oxygen level in the water is low and the fish have been dying. It's little wonder that at the moment very little fishing is being done on the river. To put it all into a nut shell, the consensus of opinion favours you looking about one hundred yards upstream from where the body was discovered. So there you have it. That should keep Cline off my back for some time, hopefully."

"Thanks Doc, Cline will be wondering where the hell I am. You know what he's like if he doesn't know where, or what, the members of his team are up to."

"If you have any trouble with him you tell him to ring me and I'll sort him out for you."

"I might just take you up on that offer, thanks Doc. Thanks for the Report."

Outside Armstrong Motors Cline had just slammed on his brakes. "God I'm an idiot." He was almost off the forecourt, when he realised that he hadn't picked up the keys from Moss and Jenny. That was when his bladder decided it wanted to be emptied.

Abandoning the car where it had come to rest on the forecourt, he dashed over to the reception office where his unannounced entry, was just in time to witness some type of argument or disagreement between Kenneth Moss and Jenny at the bottom of the stairs.

They must have seen him dashing across the reception area just in time for them to be all sweetness and light by the time he reached them. Twenty minutes later, he had added the keys he had just retrieved from Mrs. Armstrong's possession, to those he had belatedly collected from Kenneth Moss and Jenny, and was now on his way back to the station.

"The Doc sends his regards Sir. He said if you give me any trouble I have to tell him and he'll sort you out."

"I'll sort him out the next time I see him. So Wendy, did you get anything useful from the pub manager?"

"I suppose it depends on which way you want to look at it Sir. According to what I can make out, I believe that Peter and Ruth Armstrong were going through somewhat of a bad patch. Their marriage could even have been heading for the rocks. Until a few weeks back they used to dine at The Old Masters quite regularly and always appeared friendly towards each other" She continued to tell Cline all that the pub manager had told her.

"I wonder why no one has bothered to mention to us, that they may have been having a spot of trouble with their marriage? Although I suppose if no one else is involved they may have wanted to keep it to themselves."

"I would have thought Ruth Armstrong would have mentioned it to her friend Mary Duncan, if the marriage was going through a bad patch. What's wrong Sir, you don't look very pleased with yourself?"

"Oh! It's just the usual thing. I've had another run in with Knowels. I've just been in his office to tell him, I want the area lads into Armstrong Motors to go through their books with a fine toothcomb. As expected, he blew his top again, raving on about trying to cut costs. Of course it didn't help matters by telling him I had already called them in and that they had already made a start. I just love winding him up. After I told him what I'd done, I just turned around and walked out of his office before he could say any more. To be honest I think for once, he was speechless. I think now is the time to apply a little bit of pressure on our friend Mrs. Armstrong."

"No doubt you'll tell me to mind my own business Sir, but the rest of the team and myself, were wondering why you and the Super don't seem to get on with each other too well."

"I thought everyone knew Wendy. Don't you know who Knowels married?"

"No Sir, all I know is that he his married. Is he married to someone special or famous?"

"After he left school, he actually attended a sixth form college, although you wouldn't believe it to listen to him speak. He met a girl in his class and married her just after her eighteenth birthday. He'd put her in the pudding club and it was one marriage he couldn't get out of without causing himself a great amount of grief. That was because her father was the then, Sheffield Assistant Chief Constable. After the marriage, Knowels went to University, how he got in nobody knows to this day. He was, and still is as thick as two short planks. When he'd finished at Uni he came straight into the police force on a fast track to the top. Somehow though, he got waylaid on the way up the ladder. Whether he cocked it up himself or trod on someone else's toes, I don't suppose we will ever know for sure. He is turned forty now, so with the help of his father- in- law, who now, just happens to be our Chief Constable, you would have thought he would have risen a bit higher in rank by now. Not that anyone loses any sleep over that but it does mean that if anyone here at Bolderdale wishes to rise through the ranks, they can't get any further because Knowels is blocking the way. The only way for other officers to get to the same rank or better rank than Knowels, is for them to move to another area. It is called "The Peter's Principal." Knowels has reached his maximum level of competence, so since there is no way even his father-in-law can get him promoted any higher up the ranks, he his stuck here with us."

"The only hope for the rest of us, is if Knowels was sidetracked to some obsolete post, but I cannot see that happening while we still have his in-law as the boss."

By now the team had returned to the Incident room.

"Settle down everyone. Now I don't need to remind you all, keep your paper work up to date and hand it over to White. That way we shouldn't miss anything. The last things I want are any cock ups."

The phone at the side of Cline rang out. He raised the handset to his ear and listened intently to the Duty Sergeant on the other end, then duly replaced it back on its rest.

He turned towards Baxter, "The uniform lads have just found where our second body went into the river. Get down there, S.O.C.O. are there already. See what you can pick up and make sure they take loads of photographs of the area."

"Now then young Poole. What can you tell me about Preston, if anything?"

Brimming with confidence and with a great desire to impress, he thought now is my chance to make a name for myself.

"We know from his driving licence, which was found on his body, that Preston comes from Bentley, which is a smallish village about twenty miles South-East of Bolderdale town. He works, or I should say worked, as a self-employed taxi driver operating from his home address. I've been in contact with the local Community Bobby at Bentley, to see if he had any background knowledge about Preston. I also took a trip out to Bentley to do a bit of digging myself and to speak to the Community Bobby face to face. One very interesting thing came to light, whether it means anything or not I don't know, but I am sure time will tell, Preston had another interest, other than his taxi business. He used to run the local Scout Group and Youth Club a couple of evenings each week. Not a great deal is known about him in the village other than he runs a taxi business the youth clubs and very much keeps himself to himself. If he likes a regular drink, he doesn't drink in the local pubs."

"Was there anything else?"

"Apart from what I've already mentioned not much at all. He was always seen alone, when he was seen, and he had never been seen with a female companion."

"It's not known if he had any adult friends at all. I found out who his accountants were, so I paid them a visit Sir."

"Preston was just about eking out a living, although up to about twelve months ago he seemed to be doing very well. I think a close look at his books by someone far more experienced than myself may be able to determine why. As for making a connection between the deaths of Preston and Armstrong, nothing as yet Sir. Their lifestyle could not have been more different."

"One thing has been troubling me Sir, Preston was a self-employed taxi driver with his own car. He was found dead twenty miles from home. So how did he get there? By bus?

Did the killer take him there? I don't believe for one minute that he walked there or that he hired someone else's taxi. One thing I do know, as of yet, we still haven't been able to track down his car." After relating his report to the team, at twenty words to the dozen, although without any stammering and stuttering, he abruptly fell silent hoping that what he had told them had made sense.

"Well done Poole. Have you managed to arrange for Preston's body to be identified yet?"

"Yes Sir, as far as anyone knows there is no next of kin, so I asked his next door neighbour if she would do the honours for us Sir. I took her down to the morgue this afternoon where she made a positive I.D. I think she was one of the few people who had anything to do with him. She did a bit of shopping now and again and a spot of cleaning in his house. I made sure she didn't see the neck wound Sir."

"It looks like you have been busy Poole. I hope the rest of you have too. So far we have managed to keep the lid on things, as far as the local press is concerned, and that's the way I want to keep it. If the press, be it local or national, should approach any of you, just refer them to Superintendent Knowels, he's the one responsible for all the press releases. Leave all the talking to him, he'll soak up all the attention. Mary have you checked Armstrong and Preston out yet? Are they clean or have they any past that might concern us?"

"Yes Sir, I've checked them out and both of them appear to be in the clear."

" Preston had a couple of parking infringements, i.e. Non payment of fines but nothing else. I would have been very much surprised if he hadn't any motor infringements, considering his line of business."

"Jones, what did you get from the Duncans?"

"Nothing Sir. Just confirmation of what they said in their first interviews. We didn't bring them in. I can't see them changing their stories and telling us what they are really hiding from us, unless we can prove that we know they are both telling us lies, and their statements are false. One thing Mrs. Duncan did mention was that the Armstrongs were having a bad patch in their marriage, but she didn't have a clue what the trouble was, at least she said she didn't know. I asked Mrs. Duncan if there was any chance that either of the Armstrongs were having an affair with anyone, as far as she knew. She said not and since she was her best friend, she would have been the very first person to know of anything untowards. She did say that Mr. Armstrong had been unusually moody over the past few weeks, but they neither knew why nor cared."

"Right, thank you Peter. What we need to find now is Preston's car. Has it been seen by anyone during the past few days? Mary, you get on to Traffic and ask them to keep a look out for it, it just can't disappear. Try and find out if Preston had a lock-up garage somewhere in Bentley, or anywhere else for that matter. We need to know how Neville Preston travelled from Bentley that last Saturday and finished up floating in the River Bolder twenty miles away from his home. Check the bus company. With a bit of luck Preston may have caught a bus because his car had broken down. If he had to make an important journey to Bolderdale, and couldn't wait for his car to be repaired, that could explain why we can't find his car, it could be in a garage being repaired. He may have been going to meet his killer, they may even have travelled together on the bus. Check to see if any of the bus drivers remember seeing him, and better still if he was seen with someone else. From what we have heard so far Preston didn't seem to have any friends, so I don't believe he was going visiting a friend on Saturday night."

"Poole, first thing in the morning you and I will pay a visit to the first murder site, I want to check if we have missed anything. Bring the file with you."

"That's all for today everyone, I'll see you all back here sometime tomorrow, you all know what you have to do."

Chapter 6

Tuesday morning found Poole at the first murder scene, pacing backwards and forwards waiting for the arrival of Cline. Although other uniformed police officers were present in the woods and the area well cordoned off with black and white chequered tape, he still had a very uneasy feeling, a feeling that he wasn't altogether alone. He had never been one for walking alone in the woods at the best of time, so it only made matters worse, knowing that just a few feet from where he was now standing, someone had been struck down. No matter how hard he tried to keep his mind off the subject, the cold icy shiver still ran up and down his spine. "What if the killer should return to the crime scene? They do in the films." He now realised he was thinking out loud, if any of the other officers heard him he would never be able to live it down. "Come on Poole, pull yourself together." He was still talking to himself in whispers. It was with a great amount of relief that he spotted Cline approaching in the distance .For the first time since arriving at the woods, he began to feel a little more comfortable and was no longer taking glancing looks over his shoulder every few seconds, fearful that the attacker might strike again.

"Morning Sir."

"Morning Poole, just follow me"

The following ten minutes or so were spent in silence with the pair of them walking to and fro along the main footpath, until they came to a halt at the junction of a smaller path that shot off at an angle to the main path.

"I haven't heard of anyone mentioning this path, have you Poole?"

"No Sir. I don't suppose anyone had cause to do so, I mean, it's not as if it's next to where the body was discovered."

"Maybe not Poole, but let's go and take a look anyway. Keep well over to the side of the path .When we get back to the station remind me to get S.O.C.O. down here again."

After about two hundred yards, the track, that's about all it was by now, petered out to nothing. At the end of the track, there were just brambles growing between the trees. Any sign of a track or path, had been taken over by Mother Nature.

"One thing is certain Poole, nobody came through that lot last Saturday night." Cline pointed to the brambles which were barring them from any further progress in that direction.

"Ok Poole, let's make our way back to the main footpath."

All the way back to the spot where Armstrong was discovered, Cline couldn't get rid of a nagging feeling at the back of his mind, that he had missed something. There was something out there, something that he had missed. If only he knew what it was? His gut feelings had always been right before.

"Poole did you bring the file with you?"

"Yes Sir, what do you think I've been carrying around with me all morning?"

"Now then Poole, remember who you are talking to. Being sarcastic is not becoming of you."

"Sorry Sir." Poole handed the file over to Cline, "I don't think you'll find anything in there, I went through it several times whilst I was waiting for you." The slightly barbed remark, referring to Cline's tardiness, went by without any response.

"I'm sure there was something in the M.O.'s report. Either that or it was something he said. I'll be damned if I can remember what it was."

"Eureka! That's it Poole, that's it. I knew it, I just knew it. What do you notice about the trees and bushes?"

"What is there to notice Sir? They just look like any old trees and bushes that can be seen anywhere, in any wood. A few oak trees, a couple of horse chestnuts and a few dead elms. I'm not up to knowing the names of trees, I suppose those are elderberry bushes over there to the right Sir. Nature study was never my forte at school."

"Exactly Poole, exactly. Follow me."

He handed the report back to Poole. "Read the M.O.'s report and then tell me you don't notice anything strange."

Poole found it difficult reading the report whilst he was trying to keep up with Cline. By the time they came to a stop, he had read the report from beginning to end. "I'm sorry Sir, I still can't see what's got you all excited. If it's anything to do with the trees, then like I said before, they all look ok to me. A tree is a tree as far as I can make out."

"God Almighty Poole! How on earth did you make it into C.I.D.? Haven't you just read the M.O.'s report again? Or were you just going through the process for my sake?"

"I did read it Sir."

"Then read it again, especially the bit about what Armstrong was holding in his hand." Poole read the report once again. By now he was beginning to feel a bit of an idiot. It was evident from Cline's reactions, that there must be something obvious in the report. God knows what Cli............ "I've got it Sir, I've got it. It's the trees."

"I know it's the bloody trees Poole, that's what I've been trying to tell you. So now you tell me what's wrong with them."

"There are no fir trees Sir. Armstrong had pine needles under his finger nails."

"Right Poole. So where did they come from? There are no fir trees along the main foot path through the woods. We know or believe Armstrong had come here from work, or just may have called home first, although his wife said he hadn't been home, but that's another thing. Either way, there are no fir trees at his home or at the showrooms. So that just leaves this wood. Sometime just before he was killed, he had been somewhere near fir trees, so let's find them. He may even have been killed near some fir trees then moved to where his body was found."

"We know he was dressed ready for a meal out at the pub, not a walk through bushes and bracken etc. It must have been something pretty important to have encouraged him to wander off the beaten track. Had he got a secret meeting with someone? Now then Poole, can you remember that little track we went down, which ended with all those brambles? What else can you remember about that area?"

"You're right Sir, I remember now. Fir trees."

"At last we've got there."

"Ok Poole, I'm going for another wander down that side track, meanwhile I want you to get back to the car and radio in and get S.O.C.O. back down here on the double. Tell them to bring plenty of films. You know me by now Poole, I like the area well documented. I want the side track going over with a fine tooth comb, with loads of photographs. I'll meet you back at the car when I've finished here."

At that Cline spun around and was gone, leaving Poole to make his own way back to the car.

As before, Cline stayed to one side of the path, taking care not to disturb any would-be forensic evidence that still may be available. He had preceded approximately two thirds along the length of the track, when he noticed that the types of trees suddenly changed from deciduous to coniferous. Gone were the Hawthorns and the English Oaks only to be replaced by tall spruces and Christmas- type firs. It was at this point, when he spotted the fallen tree, partly covered with moss and ivy. Now it was Cline's turn to start talking out loud to himself. "I must be getting as bad as Poole, how the hell did I miss that the first time I came down here? I wonder how many courting couples have whiled away their evening nestled behind that?"

The ground around the fallen tree was well worn, most possibly by the same people that he had just been reflecting about. One end of the tree looked as if it had rotted away, creating a hole in the end. Looking into the hollow, all he could see were rotten pieces of wood, pine needles and bits of fir. Thrusting his arm into the hollow he searched the void in an attempt to find anything that may have been left in there. His only reward for his effort was the resulting mess left under his finger nails, a mess of bits of pine needles and fir. It was just like the matter taken from under the nails of Peter Armstrong. Using an old, small pocket penknife, which had been given to him when he was a child, he scooped the debris from under his nails, placed them in a small plastic bag which he marked up, before placing it in his pocket. Poole was waiting for him when he returned to his car. "Have you called it in to S.O.C.O.?"

"Yes Sir, all done and dusted. They should be on their way here as we speak."

"Good, we'll hang on here until they arrive. You should have learned something this morning Poole. You can't afford to miss a thing. I should have picked that up in the report, about the stuff under Armstrong's nails. I shouldn't have got onto you like I did. I suppose I was really mad at myself for not spotting it. Let's hope we haven't lost vital time and evidence, or next week I might not be in charge."

"I very much doubt that Sir, besides we've had the woods cordoned off since the body was discovered and we know that no one could get down that side track from the other end, due to all those brambles etc. They were just too thick."

"Let's hope you are right Micky Poole."

"I must admit Sir, I was a bit embarrassed and felt a bit of an idiot myself. It just shows, we don't always read or take in what our eyes actually see. I once read Sir, that when we read, our brain tends to recognise words rather than letters. For example, if you were to read a sentence, with all the words spelt wrong, but each word still containing the correct letters, you would have very little difficulty ready it. The brain is a funny thing Sir. That's why we sometimes see optical illusions."

After a twenty minute wait, S.O.C.O. had arrived, received orders from Cline, and Cline and Poole were in the car heading towards Bolderdale. "Do you fancy a cuppa Micky?"

"Not half Sir. I feel like my throat has been cut in half, it's that dry. It must be in the eighties already and it's not even midday yet."

"Good I think we've earned one this morning. We'll call in at a little café in the town centre, the one opposite the Post Office."

As they drew up and parked outside the café, Poole was thinking more in the terms of a pint of ice cold beer than a hot cup of tea. I suppose I should be thankful for small mercies. I've had one rollicking today, there's no way I'm going to risk another by suggesting we have a beer whilst on duty.

Cline placed a hand written note, "Police On Business" on the facia of the car, so as to be visible from the outside. The last thing he wanted was a parking ticket, from an over zealous Traffic Warden for parking on yellow lines.

As they entered the café, Cline pointed to a vacant table by the window. "You grab the table and I'll go get the teas in. Do you fancy a bacon butty?"

"Yes please Sir. Any chance of some brown sauce?"

"Ok Poole, sit down and I'll bring it over."

As Cline approached the counter, an oldish looking woman in a flowered apron, came through the open door from the kitchen at the rear of the café.

"What can I get you Sir?"

"Two teas and two bacon butties please. Oh! and a bottle of brown sauce for my friend over there. The old lady scribbled the order down on her little note pad "You can pay now Sir, I'll fetch the food over to you when it's ready. You can take the brown sauce over to the table with you if you wish."

Miraculously he successfully managed to transfer the bottle from the counter to their table, without covering his hands with the brown sauce which was plastered around the neck of the bottle.

"I don't know how you can eat that stuff, it's a wonder you don't catch something you cannot get rid of."

"Don't worry about that Sir, it all adds to the flavour."

"By the way Sir, whilst you were ordering the teas, I have just seen Superintendent Knowels coming out of the Post Office."

"Was he alone?"

"Yes Sir, Why do you ask?"

"Well, I could have sworn the Super had a Press Conference, pencilled in for sometime this morning."

The little old lady came hobbling back across the café from behind the counter with the tray of food and drinks that Cline had ordered. Cline thought she seemed too old and frail to be carrying heavy trays of food. She placed the tray on the table and was just about to remove the food. "That's ok love, we'll see to it now." Cline felt sorry for her, he thought this is no job for a woman of her age. There's no way I would allow my mother to do this for a living.

"I think we can safely say we've made at least some progress this morning. We know from the M.O.'s report that Armstrong's stomach was almost empty and according to the manager at The Old Masters Inn, Armstrong usually ate there on a Saturday night, but failed to do so the night he was killed. I am sure he was on his way to the pub for a meal. For some reason yet unknown to us, he made a trip down that side track towards that fallen tree. At this stage, my guess is that he either took something out of the hollowed out end, which I found when I looked at the tree, or put something in the tree. If he had collected something from the tree, I would have expected to have found it on his body, since there was no time or place for him to put it elsewhere. Of course, the killer could have taken it from him. Everything else was missing. Personally, I believe he left something in the tree for someone else to pick up. I cannot see him picking something up from the tree and then going to the pub for a meal."

"If Armstrong did collect something from the fallen tree and the killer took it from him, then that doesn't make sense to me Sir. The killer could just have taken whatever it was, if there was something, straight from the tree. Don't forget Sir, we are just hypothesising at the moment. There was no need to kill Armstrong unless that was the killer's intention all along."

"Perhaps the killer didn't know about the fallen tree. Let's hope S.O.C.O. can come up with something. I think we can safely say the time of the murder was in the region of nine thirty to ten pm. whatever was put in and taken out of that tree couldn't have been kosher. My guess is it must have been drugs or money, or both. Either way I can't see Armstrong picking up a packet of drugs or money and then coolly strolling down to the local pub for a drink and a bite to eat, it doesn't make sense. It's more than likely he placed something in that tree, most probably for the killer to collect later on in the evening. Again it's all guess work, and then we come back to the question, why did Armstrong have to die? We know it wasn't an accidental death by virtue of the way he was killed."

"Perhaps things may become clearer, if and when, we can make a link between the deaths of Armstrong and Preston. From the wounds they both suffered, I would say the same killer murdered them both."

"You might be right Poole, you just might be right. There is another scenario that we haven't looked at yet."

"And what may that be Sir?"

"According to Kenneth Moss, Armstrong's business partner, it would appear that there could be about ten thousand pounds missing from last Saturday's takings. What if Armstrong was being blackmailed and that is where the money went to, into the hollow of that fallen tree. It could be that Armstrong had decided he'd had enough of the blackmailer and threatened to go to the police. One thing we do know about Armstrong, from what we have gathered from the people we have interviewed so far, is that he has not been his self for the last few weeks. The killer could probably see that Armstrong was near to breaking point and so decided to cut his losses and do him in."

"If blackmail is the only motive Sir, then we haven't discovered anything to suggest a blackmail connection to Neville Preston."

"Maybe not Poole, maybe not. It could be that we just haven't found the connection yet. If there is something murky in their past, I assure you we will find it. It's all just a matter of time and, of course, a large amount of footwork."

It was then, as Cline looked out of the café window that he saw the Traffic Warden approaching his car, pen and book at the ready, and a grin on her face that would have made a Cheshire cat proud.

"Quick Poole let's get out there. I think I'm about to get a parking ticket." They arrived at the car at the same time as the Warden was about to start filling out the ticket.

"Is this your car Sir?"

"Yes it is. Well it belongs to Bolderdale Police actually, I just happen to be the one using it. Does there appear to be a problem?" Cline waved his warrant card in the air.

"No Sir, it's quite alright, there's no problem at all. I just thought someone was trying to get one over on me whilst they went into the café for a cuppa. It's surprising what notes some folks put on their car fascias and windscreens, just to try and get a bit of free parking time."

Cline thought to himself, little does she know, as he and Poole got back into his car.

Poole threw Cline a crafty grin as they closed the car doors, at the same time the warden tapped on the driver's side window. Cline opened the window to face the warden. "They really do make very good bacon butties at the little café, I must admit, don't they Sir?" She stood up as they drew away from the footpath edge. This time she was the one wearing that Cheshire cat grin once more.

"Well Poole I don't suppose we will ever win them all. I've had a change of plans, I'm going to drop you back off at the woods again, make sure S.O.C.O. do their job right. Don't forget about the photos of the complete length of the track. When they are through, go back to the lab with them, and get them to develop the photographs at once. Get them back to the incident room as fast as you can. If you get any hassle from anyone, give me a ring and I'll sort it out. When you are ready to come back to the station give us a call and someone will come over and pick you up."

"That's no problem Sir, I'll find my own way back."

"Like hell you will. I don't want you using public transport whilst you have those photographs with you."

"Just think of the hue and cry from the press if you got mugged and lost what may, or may not, be important evidence. The press would have a field day and it would be all at my expense. I'd look like a proper prat wouldn't I?"

Cline went straight back to his office where he was greeted with one of those little coloured memo stickers. The sticker had been affixed to the centre of his desk top so that he couldn't fail but notice it. "I WANT TO SEE YOU AS SOON AS YOU GET BACK TO YOUR OFFICE (PLEASE) KNOWELS"

"The sarcastic sod doesn't know how to be polite." Cline slammed his office door shut, as he reluctantly made his way down the corridor towards Knowels's office.

Knowels was ranting and raving before Cline had time to sit down.

"What's being done about the prostitutes? They are still operating along the Boulevard, I thought you had someone down Turpin Road sorting things out."

"We cannot be in two places at once. Jones and Moore were down there, now they are on the murder enquiry. Don't blame me; you picked my bloody team for me."

"Look Cline I don't really give a shit about your problems, I'm getting flak in the neck from upstairs. So get it sorted out before we speak again. Before you ask, NO YOU CANNOT HAVE ANYMORE MEN."

For once Cline was lost for words, well at least he never replied to Knowels's outburst and that was due solely to the inner rage that was bursting to explode outwards. Released, his outburst would almost certainly cost him his job. So it was in silence, that he left and made his way to his office, still fighting the urge to yell out some indescribable insult at the only boss he had, who didn't have a father.

He'd hardly sat down when there was a knock on his door and W.D.S. Baxter entered.

"I've just returned from the second murder scene Sir. I thought you may want to know what I've got so far."

"I hope it's something interesting, I need some good news to get my day back on track again. I've just had another run in with Knowels. "It does look like we have found the spot were Preston was murdered and fell into the river. The ground's hard again now, the hot sun soon got rid of the water from the weekend's rain."

"However we found skid marks on the tow-path as if someone had been fighting or struggling. There were also marks down the steep river bank, all the way to the water level. Anyone falling or slipping off the tow-path and down the banking would have no chance of stopping themselves from landing into the river, especially if it had been raining like it did last weekend. Because we know that it started raining just after Armstrong was killed, the dry patch on the footpath under his body told us that; and the fact that the skid marks were made on wet ground on the tow-path, which must have been some time after it started to rain, then I would say Preston was killed after Armstrong."

"Anything else?"

"Only that if the killer or killers murdered Preston and then, because of the very wet conditions, lost a grip on Preston's clothes, before having a chance to search his pockets. That would explain why he slipped into the river, before his pockets could be emptied, and why Preston's I.D. was still on his body. We also found a bus ticket at the murder site. It was issued by "The Easy Travel" bus company, which just happens to operate the service between Bentley and Bolderdale. I know almost anyone could have dropped that ticket, but it seems too much of a coincidence that it should be found at the spot where Preston was most likely killed, and the fact that Bentley is his home village.

S.O.C.O is checking the bus ticket to see if they can get a match for Preston's prints. Meanwhile I'm going to pay a visit to the bus station in town. With a bit of luck someone may be able to tell us something. Perhaps someone can even remember Preston getting on the bus. The ticket should be a big help. I'll pick it up from S.O.C.O. on the way to the bus station."

"Ok Wendy, but first you'd better call in at the incident room just in case there have been any further developments. Don't forget to give White what you've just told me."

"I've already left a copy on her desk Sir, but I'll pop in, just in case there is something she doesn't understand."

W.D.C.White was already in the incident room when Cline and Baxter entered. She was busying herself updating the wall map with the information that Baxter had left for her.

Looking at the wall map, a map that showed times, of the different events which had taken place. Cline was now beginning to get a clearer overall picture.

A single pink pin represented Armstrong's home, three miles to the North West of the town centre. A red pin, very close to the pink pin, indicated where Armstrong's body was found. Cline wondered about the colour coding Mary White had chosen.

Was the red pin used to indicate blood? A bright blue pin was positioned to the right of the red one indicating "The Old Masters Inn." The inn was roughly five hundred yards East of Armstrong's home and about one hundred and fifty yards due East of the murder scene. Two further pins, both pink, were used to show the location of Mary Duncan's home one and a half miles to the North East of the town centre, and the other showing the location of Preston's home, which was about twenty miles South East of Bolderdale at the village of Bentley. A further red pin was now being added showing the position where Preston's body fell into the river, which was about three miles South West of the town centre. It looked like red pins were for blood after all.

"Why haven't we got a pin for Kenneth Moss's home?"

"I didn't think he was involved Sir."

"Mary, until we get this case solved, everyone is a suspect and I'll be the one who decides when someone is, or is not, a suspect. So get a pin and get the map up to date." Cline pointed to the map, "that's where he lives, on the river-side wharf near the town centre. It's a bachelor pad, number seven. Also, find his secretary's address, at the moment we only know her as Jenny, so get her surname as well. As I said earlier, everyone is a suspect. From the map we can see that the river bisects the town in two at forty five degrees, as near as damn it. Whatever means Preston used to get to his final resting place, he would have had to have gone through the town centre. There is no other way for him to have got to that side of the river, unless he made a thirty mile detour South West of the town. I don't believe that for one moment. There are no bridges unless you go miles out of town. From what we know to date, it is my guess Preston caught a bus from Bentley to Bolderdale on Saturday. Don't forget, just because he was killed late Saturday evening or sometime on Sunday, he may have travelled on Saturday morning. Hopefully after S.O.C.O. have confirmed by fingerprint analysis, that the ticket was issued to Preston, the bus company should be able to tell us when the ticket was issued. The one thing I cannot get my head round yet."

"If he caught a bus from Bentley into Bolderdale, he would have had to walk at least three miles in the rain to where he was killed.

Now, if you look carefully at the map, you can see that running along side of the river on the tow-path side, there is a small lane. It runs parallel to the river for almost four miles after leaving the town. It looks like it is used by the local farmers as a service road to the farms and market gardens on that side of the river. You can see that, even though the lane is a few miles long, it is still a cul-de-sac, since it stops as a dead end in a farm yard. So surmising once again, Preston must have had some transport to take him out there. I doubt if that lane is on a bus route, which means he either took a cab or the killer took him there. Wendy before you and Poole get off to the bus depot, pop in or ring S.O.C.O. and ask them to check that lane, you never know they may strike lucky."

"Where is Poole Sir?"

"He won't be long; he's gone to pick up some photographs from S.O.C.O. If he's still there when you call them, tell him to stay there, then you can do two jobs at once and pick him up at the same time."

Baxter then left Cline and White alone, as she left the incident room.

"How's it going Mary?"

"Very well Sir, I'll soon be back in the full swing of things as they say."

"I didn't mean work wise, I meant in general after losing your mother."

"Oh! That's ok Sir, you know, I'm just starting to get used to having the house all to myself again, for the first time in months."

"Have you always lived with your mother?"

"Yes, apart from when my father left home, my mother went to pieces and had problems coping, so I was put into a children's home for a few months until she felt better and could manage on her own again."

"I suppose the house feels empty now there is only you living there?"

"It does. When mother was sick, there was always someone, like a nurse, or social worker in the house. When she first took to the bed, I asked Social Services if they could help in any way. They sent me a night sitter and a care nurse for a couple of nights and days each week."

"The main trouble with that however, was the fact that even though they were of help, it wasn't always the same personnel that came every day, a different face every day."

"As mother's cancer slowly worsened, and the pain became more intolerable and more unbearable, she became more demanding. She couldn't understand who all the different strangers were, coming and going. The Social Services said there was no way they could send the same staff to attend my mother. In the end, I decided to employ private carers, nurses and night sitters to look after her when I was out shopping or at work. Since I was now paying for my mother's care, I could have qualified nursing staff day and night as required. The night sitters sent by Social Services weren't nurses, they were just ordinary folks who wanted to earn a bit of pocket money, and had a bit of time on their hands. When things go wrong at night, all they can do is call for help. It did turn out to be very expensive, employing all that qualified staff, as you can well imagine. My mum's house was mortgage free, so whilst she was still mentally capable and able, she signed the house over to me, which meant that I could re-mortgage, to help pay for the nursing costs."

"Look Mary, there's not a great deal for you to do today, take the rest of the afternoon off, and recharge your batteries. There's no doubt, that before much longer, as the investigation warms up, you could be spending more time here than at home. I'll see you back here in the morning at nine sharp."

Chapter 7

At precisely nine a.m. Cline entered the incident room, to find the team already hard at work swapping notes and ideas.

"Morning everybody."

"Morning Sir."

For one awful moment, he thought he was back at school at the early morning assembly.

"Right, we've had three full days on this case and we don't really seem to be any further forward, than we were when we first started. We need a break and we need it quick. Has anyone got anything new to report?"

White was the first to speak. "Traffic has been on to us this morning Sir, it would seem that on Saturday afternoon one of the Traffic patrol cars was passing through Bentley when it nearly ran into Preston's car. Preston was trying to reverse his car into a lock up garage. At the time the patrol driver just gave Preston a severe reprimand and told him to watch how he drives in the future. It would appear that Preston had only just started renting the lock up last week, and still wasn't used to reversing into the garage. The garage was situated on a blind bend, so Preston thought it would be easier and safer to reverse into the garage, rather than reversing out onto the road."

"Have we got a warrant to search his garage? Do we know if his car is in the garage?"

"Yes to both questions Sir. S.O.C.O. is already in there. In fact, the car is back here in the lab, being given a good going over. One very interesting point Sir, we have found a few M.O.T. certificates in the glove compartment of the car. In fact they sent them over here, along with accounts, books and a load of petrol receipts. We've had a quick look at them and something quite interesting as come up."

"Such as?"

"According to the accounts, Preston seemed to be doing very well over the past few years, that is, up to about a year ago, when for no apparent reason his takings seemed to take a nose dive. Now when we checked his M.O.T. certificates, the last one being dated June this year, we found that the car mileages are much the same. So why, if the business was going through a bad patch, were the mileages, and remember these were recorded by the M.O.T. station not Preston, all very similar, within a thousand miles per year?"

"Was it because he had more time on his hands, and so he did more private mileage? I doubt it. If he went off on private trips, he would not have been available if any work turned up. A friend of mine is a self employed electrician. I remember once he told me, that being self employed is very much a "Catch Twenty Two" situation. When you have plenty of work, you have no time for holidays or leisure time. When you have no work, then you don't have the money to go away. I would think that for some reason Preston was fiddling his books. Which then brings up the questions, if he was on the fiddle? What was he fiddling? Why was he fiddling? And where is the fiddle money? Now we have to ask the question, were both Armstrong and Preston being blackmailed? If so, then as we have said before, there must be a connection from their pasts. When we find that link, no doubt we will have found the killer or killers. We know that apart from Preston being involved with the scouts and the youth club at Bentley, he appeared to have no other interest and means available to him, to disperse of any fiddle money."

Having listened with interest to what White had just told them, Cline proceeded to recap what he and Poole had discovered in the woods.

"From all the evidence we have gathered to date, it does appear to me that blackmail is very much at the heart of these murders. If blackmail is not the main reason for the deaths, I still believe it has had a great part to play in the events up-to-date."

"Mary, have we anything back yet with regards to Armstrong Motors accounts? I reckon we should have had something back by now."

"Yes Sir, that's the next thing I was going to mention. The report was just handed over to me before I came in here."

"Good then let's get on with it."

"Whilst in the process of going through the accounts and receipts etc, the lads found that some of the customer deposit slips had been altered. The normal procedure practised at Armstrongs is not one that is usually practised in the run-of-the mill car showrooms.

For instance, as soon as a prospective customer takes an interest in a particular vehicle, that customer is encouraged to leave a deposit."

"The deposit entitled the customer to first refusal for a period of seven days, during which time, no one else was allowed to purchase that vehicle. You would be amazed at the number of people who have the ready money to put a few thousand down as a cash deposit. It's usually money that should be destined for the VAT man or Tax man. If the customer did not eventually purchase a car, then his deposit was returned. When the deal went through however, this was when it looked like a fiddle was in progress. It was the deposit slips that had been altered. After the deal as gone through, a copy of the deposit slip was altered; let's say by five hundred pounds. Then on paper, the price of the car was reduced by the same amount, nobody is any the wiser. On top of that, the business saved a little bit of V.A.T. on the selling price. So if nothing else, there is a V.A.T. scam and I suppose a Tax scam as well. So it wouldn't be too difficult to fiddle a few grand every month without your partner knowing what was happening. Our lads got Moss to ring a few of their clients on the pretence of offering an after sales courtesy call. Without raising any suspicion from the clients, it was soon confirmed that some of them had paid more for their cars, than the sales book indicated."

"Sir, we have also checked with Mrs. Armstrong if they, that is the Armstrongs, have made any expensive purchases of late, such as holidays abroad, maybe a Caribbean cruise. Had she been aware of any unexpected increases in cash floating around the home? We know the money never went through the bank accounts. As far as she was aware, everything seemed to be normal and she had no reason to believe otherwise. To sum things up Sir, it is believed that roughly twenty to twenty five thousand pounds are missing from the business."

"Thank you Mary. I can't see why or for what reason, Mrs. Armstrong would blackmail her own husband but I think it is time we had her in here to answer a few more questions and whilst we are at it, let's have Mrs. Duncan in here as well. I know that pair have not been telling us the truth, and fetching them in here and exerting a bit of pressure on them just might loosen their tongues a bit. Mary you organise it with uniform to bring them in."

"As for the rest of you, we need to find out what the connection is between our two victims. Whatever links them together must be pretty heavy, you don't fork out thousands of pounds to someone, for no good reason. And another thing, we need to set up the surveillance again on Turpin Road. This time, I want answers. I need a description of the mugger. You cannot tell me, that with all the muggings that have taken place amongst the prostitutes, that not one person can give you an I.D. Pull the other one. Get down there, threaten to pull them all in off the streets. I want this sorted and I want it sorted out quickly. Make them more afraid of you, than they are of the mugger. I want that description, better still, I want the guy behind bars, then we can all concentrate on the murder investigation. Jones and Moore you can deal with that."

"But Sir........."

"No buts Jones. The sooner you catch the guy, the sooner you get back here on the team. That should be incentive enough for you to pull your finger out, besides, you two know the Toms and which one might be best to pressurise, to get the info that we want."

"Baxter and Poole will take the bus station. In the mean time, I'll be talking to our friends Armstrong and Duncan."

It was two p.m. when Armstrong and Duncan were escorted into the station by two W.P.C.s. "Where would you like us to take the two ladies Serg?"

"Take them to interview rooms one and two and stay with them until D.I Cline gets to you."

Ten minutes later, Cline walked into interview room number one. The W.P.C. was standing near the door as if on sentry duty. Mrs. Armstrong was seated on the far side of the room behind a metal table. It looked like the experience of being brought in to the station by police car and then having made to wait for Cline to appear, had the effect of making her very nervous and somewhat frightened. She had no idea why she and her friend should have been carted off like a couple of street villains. She wondered how her friend was doing, in room number two. Her fingers started turning white, as the white satin handkerchief tightened around her fingers, the more she nervously twisted two ends together.

"I don't know why you've brought us down here like a couple of hardened criminals; we've told you all we know."

"Are you both criminals, Mrs. Armstrong?"

"How dare you suggest that Inspector, of course we aren't criminals. Shouldn't we have our solicitors here before you start asking questions?"

"Why, have you something to hide? You see I know you are criminals. You may not think so but as far as the law is concerned, lying to a police officer in the course of a murder investigation is an offence. Believe me when I say, I know you are lying,

I know your friend is lying, what about, I have no idea, yet. I will tell you and I will be telling your friend exactly the same thing; if because you have both been lying to us, wasting our time when we could have been looking elsewhere, someone else his murdered, I will have the book thrown at you."

"At this time I have no intention of charging you or your friend with any crime. Neither of you are under caution as yet and you are free to leave whenever you wish. Having said that, I am conducting a murder investigation into the death of your husband and it would surely be to your advantage to start telling me the truth. The next time I call you in here you will be asked to bring your solicitor, if at that time you do not start answering my question truthfully you will be charged. The choice is now yours."

"Now where were you last Saturday night? Who were you with? What time did you go out? What time did you get back? Who else can vouch for your whereabouts? NO BULL SHIT, this time, I want straight answers."

The look of disgust on her face was enough to make milk curdle. "There's no need to take that attitude Inspector. I've a good mind to report you to a senior officer."

"Answer my questions truthfully and you can go straight home and write or phone to anyone you wish, from the comfort of your lounge. Tell me more lies, and you can make your complaints from a police cell."

"Neither of us, has done anything wrong or anything to be ashamed of."

"So far, you have not shown one iota of sadness or loss, since your husband's death. You have continued to lie to us. Give me one good reason, why I shouldn't think that you had something to do with your husband's death. After all, you will be financially better off, if we can prove you had nothing to do with his murder. You see, it can only be in your own interest to clear your name. There will be no insurance payout until everything is cleared up."

For the first time, she seemed to be getting some idea of how serious the situation had become. The mountain of mascara around her eyes now started to run down her cheek, as she dabbed the tears away from her eyes.

"I went out with Mary Duncan's brother."

It was like a shot from the blue. Cline could see why she had lied about her date, it's another motive for getting rid of her husband.

"You mean you were out on a date, with your husbands business partner Kenneth Moss?"

"Yes Inspector, what's so wrong with that? I know how it must look to you, but I assure you we had nothing to do with Peter's murder."

"Then why tell lies about it?"

"Because I knew you would automatically point a finger at us."

"Because of your deceit, you have put yourself into the frame for Peter's death."

"Now then let's have the truth about last Saturday night and don't leave anything out."

"I suppose it started much the same as any other Saturday. I went down town, did a bit of shopping for food and odds and ends, then went back home. I rang Jenny, she's the receptionist at the showrooms, to ask her to tell Kenneth Moss to meet me at the Kings Head public house down town. It must have been around three thirty in the afternoon when I left home, had another good look around the shops and then called in one of the cafés for tea and scones. I then met Kenneth later on, in the Kings Head as prearranged. We had a couple of drinks, then made our way over to the "Blue Lady Night Club" in Foster Street where we had a meal, a few dances and the left at about 1.30am. Sunday morning. So you see Inspector, we couldn't possibly have killed Peter if he was killed on Saturday night."

"That's the truth Inspector. Having fallen in love with Kenneth, I soon began to realise that I probably was never in love with Peter. I hate to admit it, but I suppose I fell in love with his lifestyle."

"Did you begin to hate Peter?"

"Of course not Inspector. If I did hate him, and I assure you I did not, you would be the last person I would tell. That would give you another reason to put my name on the top of your suspect list. I've told you where Kenneth and I were on Saturday evening, why don't you check it out, then we can put a stop to all this nonsense?"

"Don't worry Mrs. Armstrong, we will check it out. From what you have told me today, you realise that you have put Kenneth Moss right up there on that list with you?"

"Of course, that's why we kept quiet about it."

"You do realise, that if you and Kenneth Moss decide to get married and for some inexplicable reason you should die, Kenneth will finish up with everything, lock, stock and barrel as the saying goes?"

"You are the most suspicious man I have ever met in my life Inspector. First you think I killed my husband, now it sounds like you think Kenneth killed him and is now about to kill me. You've been watching too many films Inspector, I really feel sorry for you."

"It must be the job I do."

"I've told you everything there is to know Inspector, you've no reason to keep Mary Duncan here now. She was just being a good friend. If I hadn't been out with her brother I doubt if she would have lied for me."

Cline wondered if there was still something else that Ruth Armstrong had not told him.

"You are not out of the woods yet. It may be that your alibi proves to be ok, but that doesn't mean you didn't hire someone else to kill Peter. We know someone had been fiddling the books of a few thousand pounds, I thought it was Peter but it could have been you and Kenneth, to raise the money to pay the killer."

"God you are so paranoid Inspector."

"As I have already said, it must be the job and the company that I keep."

"As you already know Peter did the books, he would have known at once if Kenneth had been doing any fiddling."

"Maybe he did notice and that is the real reason he was killed."

"You are twisting and turning everything I say into making me look involved in Peter's death. I'm not saying another word unless I have my solicitor present. I'd like to ring my solicitor, RIGHT NOW PLEASE."

"At this time Mrs. Armstrong, if what you have told me today checks out to be the truth, for a change, then you will not be in need of your solicitor at the moment. If on the other hand, you still have something to hide and you are not being one hundred percent honest with me, then that could be another matter. Before you leave I will ask you once more, are you sure that you cannot think of any reason why someone would wish to blackmail Peter?"

"No, if he was being blackmailed, then it must have been for something he did, long before we became acquainted."

"Ok, I want you to remain here for a little while longer whilst I have a word with your friend Mrs. Duncan. Would you like a drink or something?"

"No thank you Inspector. I just want to get the hell out of this place as quick as I possibly can."

Leaving Ruth Armstrong to ponder on the events of the past fifty minutes or so, he left her with the W.P.C. and strolled casually into interview room number two. Mrs. Duncan was by now, in a very agitated state. The long wait in a room, with only a W.P.C. for company had given her ample time to reflect the events of the past few days. The delay in the start of her interview, could only mean that things weren't going too well with Ruth's interview. She wondered if Ruth had told the truth about her relationship with Kenneth.

To keep us this length of time, we must be in big trouble.

"Sorry to have kept you waiting Mrs. Duncan but it couldn't have been avoided. You've been a very silly woman lying to the police, just to protect your friend and of course your brother. I have told your friend that I could charge you both for wasting our time but I have decided not to at this time."

"She has cooperated fully, I hope, and if things check out there will be no problems. She has told us about the affair with your brother Kenneth Moss. All I need now is your version of what happened on Saturday night."

It was obvious to Cline, that as soon as she had the chance to clear the air, there would be no stopping her until she had utterly exhausted every word that she had created in her mind, whilst waiting for Cline to come into the room to interview her. Her statement confirmed that which had been stated by Ruth Armstrong. It didn't provide any indication of any guilt or innocent by any of the parties involved, but it did confirm Ruth Armstrong's statement.

"I really am sorry for wasting your time Inspector. I would not have lied to you, if I had any thought in my mind, that either Ruth or Kenneth had it in themselves to be killers.

None of us have slept a wink since we made our first statements. I've been dreading your knock on the door ever since, I'm glad it's now all out in the open."

"Ok, you can be on your way, you can tell your husband I won't be wanting to interview him, at least not for the moment. Mrs. Armstrong will join you in a few minutes."

Having watched Armstrong and Duncan leave the station he made his way to the incident room. "Mary, have Baxter and Poole returned from the bus station yet?"

"Not yet Sir."

"Ok, if anyone wants to get hold of me, I'll be down at the bus station."

He parked his car some distance from the bus station. The thought of a short walk wouldn't do him any harm, at least that is what he told himself as he realised he had parked further away from the bus station than he had intended.

Walking from his car to the bus station, he had time to think and reflect that if he had gone to his sisters Saturday morning, no one would have been able to contact him and someone else would most likely have been given this investigation. I would have been breathing fresh air all weekend. Now the air was full of diesel fumes, and the closer he got to the bus station the stronger the smell of the fumes.

As he walked past the left luggage area, he could see Baxter in the distance talking to one of the bus drivers. It was the bright blue uniform of the driver that first attracted the attention of Cline to that area of the bus station. "Everybody seems to wear coloured uniforms now a days. Lucky for me but unlucky for some other poor sod, I only wear mine for funerals." Anyone passing would think he was a nutter, talking out loud to himself.

He waited until Baxter had finished with the bus driver before approaching her.

"Any luck at all Wendy?"

"Not yet Sir."

"What have you done with Poole?"

"He's knocking around somewhere Sir. I sent him over to the other side of the station with a couple of uniformed lads; it's a bit busier over there. Let's hope they're having better luck than I'm having."

"Let's nip into the station café and get a drink and you can tell me what you haven't got so far."

"It won't take me long to tell you what we haven't got Sir."

They collected their drinks and sat down at the only free table, which happened to be just inside the door. They soon realised why that was the only table unoccupied. It was a lovely warm day outside but, for some unknown reason there was a force ten gale blowing through the door. To the dismay of the other customers, who were not sat in the draught, Cline stood up and closed the door.

"So far I've had no luck with the drivers, but something did cross my mind. Can you remember a few weeks back we had all that trouble with the drug pushers and users, using the left luggage lockers as drop off points? I got to thinking, if blackmail is behind these murders, could the lockers down here be used as one of the dead drops for the money from Armstrong and Preston. Uniform are down at the lockers now, asking the regular users if they could recognise Armstrong and Preston from their photographs. As yet they've had no luck."

"You just might have something there Wendy, good thinking."

"I saw the Super down here earlier on. He's the last person I would expect to see using Public transport."

"Did he see you?"

"No, at least I don't think so. I was talking to one of the drivers at the time and I just caught a fleeting glimpse of him in the distance."

"I don't think he would have been catching a bus, least of all at this time of day. It's more than likely he's come down here to see if we are doing our job, he probably thinks we spend all our time here in the café." A sly grin appearing on Cline's face as he spoke. Cline was not known for his joke telling, but he could be very sarcastic at times.

"I take it the drivers have had nothing to tell you yet, that is, anything of interest?"

"Because the drivers all work shifts, and change their routes pretty regularly, it is difficult trying to get hold of the driver who was on the Bentley to Bolderdale run last Saturday, however our luck might just be taking a turn for the good. I am due to meet one of the drivers who did the Bentley to Bolderdale run last Saturday. Let's hope he can remember something useful for us."

"In that case let's get out of here and go and meet him. I don't want him doing a runner before we get the chance to speak to him."

As usual, the bus kept faith with the public belief that buses never run on time, by arriving ten minutes late. As the bus came to a stop, Baxter, with warrant card in hand stopped the driver in his tracks, before he could run off to the staff canteen for his break. She introduced herself and Cline to the driver and suggested they all go to the staff canteen together. The driver could eat his sandwiches and drink his tea during the interview.

"Would you like to lead the way?" They followed the driver up a flight of metal stairs at the side of an office building, until they entered the staff canteen. The canteen was partly occupied, so Cline looked round until he saw a table where it would be unlikely that they would be overheard.

"First, can you confirm you drove the bus on the Bolderdale to Bentley route on Saturday?"

"Yes, I was on that route on Saturday p.m. I must tell you though, I can only talk to you for fifteen minutes, that's when I am due out again."

"Don't worry about that, arrangements have already been made for someone else to take over your next run. That should give us sufficient time to discuss what we have in mind."

"I hope I'm not going to get my pay knocked because of this."

"I don't know about that, you will have to take that up with your bosses after we have finished here. I feel sure, because they know you are helping us with our enquiries, you should have no problems."

I hope they don't think I've been in trouble with the police, I'd soon lose my job then."

"Don't worry, as I have just told you, you are only helping us. Besides, you are not the only driver we've been talking to."

Taking his snapbox out of his bag, the driver was soon tucking in to one of his sandwiches, "So what do you want to ask me?"

"You'll have plenty of time after we've finished with you to eat your snap. For the record, can you tell us your full name?"

"William, William Tomkin but everybody calls me Billy."

"You said you were on the Bolderdale to Bentley route on Saturday."

"Yes, I started my shift at 6.00pm and continued right through until the last run."

"Good, can you remember seeing or picking this man up in Bentley, anytime at all during your shift?" Cline handed Billy the photo of Preston.

He took a long hard look at Preston's face in the photo, at the same time he subconsciously put his hand on the part eaten sandwich, lifted it to his mouth and took a giant sized bite of ham and cheese. "Yeth, I picked him up." His mouth was now that full it was difficult for him to speak clearly.

Cline reached over and grabbed the half eaten sandwich and the snapbox, and moved it out of the driver's reach. "I said that can wait until after we have finished with you, if you don't mind."

"Sorry Inspector, it was just automatic."

"What time did you pick him up? Are you sure it was the man in the photo?"

"Positive, it would have been the nine thirty from Bentley arriving in Bolderdale at roughly ten forty five pm."

"What makes you so sure it was this guy?"

"A brain surgeon I'm not, but two things I am very good at. One is being a bus driver and the other is remembering faces. I cannot always remember names but faces, now that's a different thing altogether. There's another reason why I remember him so well, and this may well seem queer to you, but he was a stranger. When you drive buses to the outlying villages you get to know the regular passengers, they tend to catch the same bus on the same day at the same time. This guy, last Saturday night, I had never seen before. That's why I am sure he was the guy I picked up."

"Can you remember if he was alone? What kind of mood was he in? Did he have a season ticket or did he have to buy one on the bus?"

"Yes he was alone, and yes he bought a ticket but how the hell do I know what kind of mood he was in? I suppose though for a Saturday night, he did look more like he was going to a wake rather than to some social function."

"Why would you think that?"

"Most people who travel from Bentley into Bolderdale on a Saturday night are going out drinking or clubbing. In other words they are going out to enjoy themselves. This guy looked like he'd found a penny and lost a fiver. He sat at the rear of the bus so I never saw him again until we reached the town centre bus station where he got off."

"Do you know if he spoke to anyone on the bus?"

"No, not as far as I can remember. He was the only passenger to get on the bus at Bentley. I think that was the first time that as happened with me on a Saturday night. I believe the weatherman had forecast a dry night until around ten or eleven o'clock so people stayed at home and had a barbecue, instead of going down town."

"Did you drop him off somewhere before you got to Bolderdale?"

"No, I've just said, he came right here to the town centre bus station."

"So when he got off the bus, that would have been the last time that you saw him? Were there many other people in the bus station at that time?"

"No, the station was empty, at least I can't remember seeing anyone else knocking around. Don't forget Inspector, this is Bolderdale, not some great metropolis which only wakes up at one o'clock in the morning. My bus was the last bus into the station that night, so I wouldn't have expected to see too many people."

"So you say you didn't see him again?"

"Well to be honest Inspector, I cannot be sure. I can only guess it was him. After leaving the bus, I walked over to the office and cashed up, gathered my gear from my locker and went over to my car. I always park my car round the back of the bus station in the staff car park. As I turned the corner at the rear of the building and walked towards my car, I saw this man with a woman on the opposite side. I couldn't make her out, but the guy who was with her could easily have been the guy on the bus, the same guy in this photo. He was actually standing between me and the woman, so there was no way I was able to get a good look at her, not that I was taking too much notice of them anyway."

"What time was this?"

"Don't mention it to my boss, but I arrived back at the depot ten minutes before my scheduled time, that was because there were so few passengers, I could get into big trouble if he found out. I was also rushing back to catch a night movie on tele. It must have been about eleven twenty by the time I'd cashed up and got to the car park, give or take five minutes."

"So from what you've said so far, you cannot give us any description of the woman? Was she tall? Was she thin or fat?"

"I'm afraid not Inspector, although the car park is lit, there are too many dark spots and it just so happened that they were standing in one of them."

" I think you've told us as much as you can. We'll leave you to get your sandwiches in peace. Oh! there is one more thing, did you notice how many cars were left in the car park?"

"Only two or three Sir."

"Did you recognise any of them?"

"Yes, one was naturally mine and the other two belonged to two of the office staff."

"Ok Billy, thank you for your time, you've been a big help."

Jones and Moore had questioned every prostitute plying their bodily wares along Turpin Road. The threat of at least one night in a police cell, followed by a good sound thrashing from their pimps for not having earned any money prompted a few of the girls to reluctantly answer a few questions. By the time the two detectives had returned to their car they had a good description of the mugger.

He was described has being six feet two inches tall, weighing in at around fourteen stones. He was clean shaven and well spoken and always wore a suit, not the usual run of the mill mugger. Another odd thing about this mugger, he never sought the prostitutes' services in order to get them into some private location, where it would have been a lot safer for him, he always mugged them on the streets in the open. Perhaps the mugger thought there was more of a chance of bumping into the girls' pimps back at their place of work.

They'd only just seated themselves into the car when Jones tugged Moore's jacket. "What the hell is going on over there? Christ it's the bloody mugger, quick get over there, don't let the bastard get away or we'll both be pounding the beat again."

"Don't worry Sir, he's mine, you see to the Tom."

The mugger must have heard Moore pounding down Turpin Road towards him. Like a shot from a gun he raced off trying to get away from Moore. Moore's mind was working overtime. "There's no way this guy is going to outrun me. I'm not the Northern Area Police 400 metres champion and the town's local rugby hero for nothing, I'd never be able to live it down. Christ, I must admit though, this guy can certainly go a bit, he must train every day." At the end of Turpin Road, Moore was still twenty metres adrift and beginning to feel the leg muscles tighten up due to lack of oxygen in the blood. He remembered the words of his sports trainer, "Open your mouth wide, take large gulps of air into the lungs." At long last the gap was slowly closing, he knew if he didn't catch him soon he was going to lose him, and that just wasn't an option he could afford. Moore willed his mind, body and his legs for one last push, which took him to within a couple of feet from his prey. Moore was back on the rugby field, "I can't let him score a try, no way." He flung himself forward towards the pair of legs in front of him, his right hand caught hold of one of the flying legs, both men were now on the ground sliding along the road surface. The left foot of the mugger, whether by accident or intention, hit Moore under his chin. It was all he could manage, to hold on to the leg with his right hand, already out of breath and weakened from the chase, the blow to the chin had knocked him temporarily unconscious. How he held on to that leg he will never know.

His saving grace, was the fact that Moore was heavier than the mugger and had fallen on him when they both hit the ground, knocking all the wind out of him. It was Moore who recovered his senses first, forced the mugger's arms behind his back and slapped on a pair of handcuffs. Moore then collapsed on top of his prey, utterly exhausted from the chase. After a couple of minutes he stood up, lifted his catch to his feet and marched him back to the car in Turpin Road.

"What took you so long, I thought you could run?"

Moore ignored the remark and dumped his catch into the rear seat of the car. Before he could shut the car door, the Tom who had just been saved from a mugging, hurled verbal abuse at her assailant and at the same time flinging herself at him, sharp finger nails clawing at his face. By the time Moore had pulled her out of the car, the muggers face was covered in blood, although it probably looked a lot worse than it actually was.

"I want her charged for assault?"

"Assault, what assault? I didn't see an assault did you D.C.Moore."

"No Serg, I thought he hurt his face when we fell down on the road surface during the chase, or it might have been when one of these fine ladies was defending herself during one of the attacks he made on them."

"You get in the back with him and I'll drive up front with our Amazon warrior here."

"I'm not going to the station with you, I've got work to do."

"Look, be careful we don't change our mind about the assault. We still need your statement to get this guy off the streets. What's your name by the way?"

"My street name is Rosie."

"Look Rosie, it won't take long to make a statement down at the station. I'll even make arrangements to get transport to fetch you back." "Now that's got to be a first."

Two hours later the mugger was charged and locked up, and Rosie had made and signed her statement and was back on the streets.

Jones dropped in to see the duty Sergeant.

"The mugger we have locked up in cell number five still refuses to tell us his name, he doesn't want to phone anyone and he said he doesn't need a lawyer."

"So Sergeant, leave him to stew for a while, you can see if he wants anything to eat or drink. We'll talk to him again in the morning"

It was eight a.m when Jones and Moore met up again on the police station steps.

"I wish I hadn't gone home this morning, no sooner had I got to bed, it was time to get up again."

"I know what you mean Serg. My eyes feel like sand paper. I think I'll go and give them a swill under the cold water tap."

"Ok, while you do that, I'll nip in and see Cline for a few minutes. When you've seen to your eyes, ask the Duty Sergeant to transfer our mugger from cell five to interview room number two. I want to start the interview at eight fifty."

Jones gave a courtesy knock on the door to Cline's office and walked in, without waiting for the customary, "Enter" "Good morning Sir, I thought you might want to hear the good news. We nabbed the mugger last night, we actually caught him in the act of carrying out a mugging on one of the Toms. With a bit of luck that should get the Super off your back."

"Yes, I had heard, well done. The duty Sergeant on the front desk told me when I walked in this morning. I heard Moore gave a good account of himself."

"Yes, he did Sir, but for God's sake don't tell him I said so or I will never hear the last of it."

"Any idea who our mugger is? I believe he isn't one of our regular Bed and Breakfast visitors."

"We have no idea who he is at the moment Sir, he is just refusing to say anything. Moore and myself are just getting ready to interview him in a few minutes time Sir, did you wish to do it?"

"No, that's ok. You and Moore have done all the hard work so far, the pair of you may as well see it through to the end."

"I'll let you know how we get on then Sir, thank you."

When Jones entered interview room number two, Moore was already seated at a table diagonally across from the as yet unknown assailant and a uniformed officer was standing inside the door.

Seating himself next to Moore, Jones gave the formal introductions to the twin decked tape recorder and got the interview underway.

"The last time I saw you, which was the early hours of this morning, you were reluctant to give us your name and address, in fact you would hardly speak to us at all. So I have to ask you again, do you wish for a solicitor to be present during this interview?"

"No thank you."

"It would make things a hell of a lot easier, if I had a name that I could use to address you. After spending a few hours in your cell, do you feel that you want to change your mind and tell us your name? You will get out of here a lot quicker, I assure you"

There was quite a long pause before Jones heard a faint whisper. "James Rothwell, James Peter Rothwell to give you my full name."

"That's better Mr. Rothwell. Now I'll ask you again, can we contact anyone for you, a relative for instance. Surely someone will be concerned that you never went home last night, don't you think they would be worried about you?"

"No, no one thank you."

"Mr. Rothwell, as you can see, this interview is being taped, a copy of which you will be given at the end."

"Last night, Wednesday the 11th of July 1996 at 10.55pm D.C. Garry Moore interrupted you whilst you were in the process of attacking a female prostitute, with the unlawful intention of robbing her and, in the process maybe, to cause her body harm. The alleged Offence took place on Turpin Road, Bolderdale. After chasing you along Turpin Road and subsequently apprehending you, you were arrested and placed into custody. How do you wish to plead to the charges made against you?"

"Guilty. What can I say, I was caught with my hands in the till so as to speak."

"You are a man of very few words Mr. Rothwell."

"Call me Peter if you wish. There is not a great deal to talk about is there Sergeant? Why don't you just charge me and get it over with."

"It isn't quite that simple Mr. Rothwell. Over the past few months there have been numerous muggings on the prostitutes along Turpin Road."

"I need to know if you are the one responsible for all the muggings and if so why."

"I cannot tell you that for certain, but I can tell you, I have robbed and mugged between twenty five and thirty girls over the past few months. Whether anyone else has been doing any muggings down there, I have no idea."

"I must admit Mr. Rothwell you did take us all by surprise. We don't tend to get too many muggers running about in pinned striped suits, with collar and tie to boot. What's with the smart clothes?"

"I didn't know there was some sort of dress code for muggers. I suppose you would have been happier, had I been running about with my arse hanging out of my pants."

"True Mr. Rothwell, it is somewhat unusual all the same. Where do you work Mr. Rothwell? I assume you do work."

"I work as an accountant for 'Goodfellow, Flint and Rothchild's', they are one of the largest accountancy firms in town."

"Surely you must be on a decent salary, why the hell do you need to go out mugging and robbing prostitutes? I just don't understand."

"What may seem like a good salary to one bloke might be as poor as piss to another. It's not what a person earns these days that matters, it is more to do with what he spends. My top line is about £14,000 per year. Not over the top when you think that I have a wife, two grown up kids and a £80,000 mortgage to support."

"Is that the reason you went out mugging the prostitutes?"

"What do you think Sergeant?"

"It seems strange to me that you went out dressed like you did. In that area, you were more likely to get mugged yourself, we get some rough characters down that end of town"

"Oh, I didn't worry about that, I am quite capable of looking after myself. I spent a good few years in the Army."

"Did you do the full stretch?"

"I joined when I was eighteen, did a few years then left. I have been out now for three or four years."

"So how did you become an accountant? Were you in the offices in the Army, or a fighting unit?"

"Three years before I left the army they put me through an accountancy course, and then they backed it up by putting me in the offices at the 'Catterick Army' camp. At that time the Army was in the middle of a cost cutting exercise, they were looking for people to volunteer to demob. You know what they say about volunteers in the army. There was no way I was leaving the army, to become another low paid security guard, on a couple of quid an hour. So I let the army retrain me, and then I left to join the firm where I work now. The army actually found me this job."

"Don't you get an army pension, as well as the salary you are getting from your employer?"

"I've elected not to collect that until I retire, that way, it will be building up into a nice little nest egg for later in life."

"That just doesn't make sense to me. You have the option of an army pension, but you prefer to go out risking everything to rob and mug prostitutes. It is more than likely that now you could even lose your freedom."

"Why waste my pension? The pension and my salary still wouldn't cover my outgoings. Both my kids are grown up and at college and they don't receive any government grants, so I fund them any way I can. What happens now? I've coughed up to the crime, I couldn't do otherwise since I was caught in the act, why don't you charge me and bail me and let me go home?"

"That won't be for a while yet. We have to check a few things first, and get your statement written down and signed. Then we may start thinking what we should do with you. Are you still sure there is no one we can contact for you? Your wife will surely be worrying where you are. I'm surprised she hasn't been in contact with us by now or do you make it a habit to stay away from home all night on a regular basis?"

"No, it's alright, she won't be at home anyway, she goes to stay with her parents every few weeks, just for a few days at a time. They haven't been keeping too well of late, nothing life threatening, but the wife likes to help and fuss around them now and again when ever she can, usually when the kids are away at college or on holiday with their friends."

"Is that when you used to go out and carry out your muggings, when your wife was away?"

"Yes, that way, I never had to answer any embarrassing questions such as, where have you been all night? I didn't want my wife to think I had another woman, now did I?"

At that Jones brought the interview to a conclusion, he stopped the tape recorder removed the two tapes, signed and dated one of them and handed it over to Rothwell. Turning to the constable on the door, "would you escort Mr.

Rothwell back to the cells please. I'll let you know when, or if, he will be released on bail."

After Rothwell had left the room Jones turned to Moore, "well, what did you make of all that Garry?"

"To be honest Serg, I think he is a right fruit and nut case. Surely he can't be all there?"

"I think you might be right, but for God's sake don't say that outside this room or the sod will most likely plead insanity, and I definitely wouldn't put it past him."

"There was one thing that I thought was very strange Serg."

"What was that Garry?"

"Well, at first he wouldn't say a thing, and then this morning we couldn't shut him up. All he wanted to do was to get out of here as quickly as he possibly could. Why? Is the wife due back today from her parents? and he only remembered this morning, so now he wants to go back home before she gets there and starts asking awkward questions. All the trouble he is in and all he can say is, he didn't want his wife to think he had another woman. If I hadn't heard him with my own ears, I don't think I would have believed it."

Cline was still in his office when Jones sought him out. "I've finished with the mugger Sir, we managed to get a full statement from him this time." Jones relayed to Cline all that had been said during the interview.

"If he's signed his statement bail him, with the condition he is not to go within five hundred yards of Turpin Road. Make sure you dot all the i's and cross all the t's. I want your report up-to-date and everything signed and sealed. I want you and Moore back on the murder case pronto."

Cline decided against another face to face confrontation with the Super, instead he picked up the phone and gave him the good news. Half an hour later, Poole who was still working in the luggage area at the bus station, spotted the Super walking briskly through the station concourse.

Chapter 8

Cline awoke to the sound of the teas-maid, he opened his eyes and stared at the clock face. It always appeared to be grinning at him, teasing him to turn over and have another ten minutes in bed. No wonder they call it a teas-maid. "I should have thrown it out years ago," he'd bought it over eight years ago, when his wife upped and left him. He could still remember the good times, even though they were heavily out numbered by the not so good times. The bad times had been more memorable because they were more frequent and usually highly emotional.

He had been so much in love with Grace, he had never anticipated what life would have been like without her by his side. She used to be so loving, and understanding but slowly the obstacles that had previously broken many a policeman's marriage, began eating away at their relationship. Too many overtime hours, irregular hours, working weekends, and sometimes not coming home at all due to pressure of work. They both missed not having any children, whether or not that would have made the situation any better or worse he would never know. Eventually Grace couldn't stand the unstable lifestyle and one day packed her bags and walked out. Two years later they were divorced, since then he'd never been romantically involved with anyone, besides there was no way he was going to endure the same emotional turmoil that he had gone through with Grace.

By seven o'clock he'd had his shower, two cups of tea and four slices of burnt toast. "That's another thing, that's got to go, the toaster." After ringing his sister, which he liked to do has often as possible, he set off walking to the station.

It was another beautiful, warm sunny morning, not a cloud in the sky. He had plenty of time to reflect on the events of the past week. Two murders and no further forward in identifying the killer or killers, at least we've caught the mugger. By the time he had arrived at the police station, he was feeling refreshed and invigorated and, thankful that after his marriage break up, he had decided to purchase the two bedroomed town house about three quarters of a mile away from the station. It was only small, but it fulfilled its purpose.

The duty sergeant welcomed Cline with a welcome smile and a "Good morning Sir. Today you have a choice, would you prefer to receive the good news first or the bad news first?"

"That depends on how bad is the bad news?"

"Pretty bad Sir, I'm afraid."

"In that case I will have the good news first." "Now the muggings in Turpin Lane have stopped, we've heard that the Chief is no longer on the Super's back, which means the Super will no longer be on your back."

"I wouldn't take any bets on that one Serg, what's the bad news?"

"We've got another body Sir."

"I don't suppose you know if it is connected to the other two?"

"No Sir I've no idea, all I do know at the moment is that it was found on some waste ground behind the 'Blue Lady Night Club'. Baxter was here when the call came through, she's taken Poole with her and should be down there now."

"Have S.O.C.O. and the M.O. been informed?"

"Yes Sir, they should also be on site by now."

"Have you any idea if it was a male or female body?"

"Again, I've no idea. You know as much as I do now, if I hear any more, you will be the first to know Sir"

"Thank you Sergeant."

What a start to a Saturday morning. Another body was the last thing he wanted. If he was to get marks for planning, then he wouldn't be getting any today. Because Jones and Poole had worked extra hours on the mugging case, he had told them to have the day off. He knew things could soon get very hectic if things started to develop, and he didn't want them burning themselves out. From what the duty sergeant had just told him, that time when things begin to get hectic, had already arrived. In one way, he thought to himself, it might not be such a bad thing if this latest body was in some way connected to the previous two murders, it could make it easier to find the connection. There I go again, jumping the gun, nobody has said the body is a murder victim. It could be a natural death, or the result of a street fight, after all it is supposed to be outside a night club.

Now that's another weird thing, where have I heard that name before? The Blue Lady Night Club.

"Serg, if Baxter rings or calls in, tell her she can contact me in the canteen"

He entered the canteen only to find it completely empty of diners. "Blast that Knowels, I'd forgotten about his budget cuts, one of which was to order the canteen closed at the weekends. He said the Saturday canteen staff was a non essential expense, looks like the vending machine again." He was still muttering to himself, as he looked at the choices on offer to him from the glass fronted machine. Cheese and onion, that should be ok, at least they looked fresh. Having inserted his coins and pressed the required buttons, he stood there staring at the cheese and onion sandwich, which was soon to become his morning snack. There again it might not be, first the machine gave a shudder as if it had just been disturbed from a deep sleep. Then the spiral coil, holding his sandwich, began to turn slowly, edging his morning snack slowly to the drop to the bottom of the machine. He put his hand into the receiving slot, palm turned upwards ready to catch the sandwich. It was then that the machine decided it wanted to return to its deep sleep by giving another shudder and the spiral coil stopped suddenly, leaving Cline's sandwich hanging precariously half in and half out of the coil. No manner of thumping, kicking or verbal abuse was going to make the vending machine give up it's load... He was just on the verge of leaving the canteen, when the duty sergeant walked in with a cup of piping hot tea and a bacon butty.

"Here you are Sir. I remembered after you had left that the canteen was closed, so I sent one of the lads over to the café. You owe me 95 pence Sir."

"Cheap at half the price Sergeant, thanks."

It was almost midday by the time Baxter and Poole returned to the incident room, where Cline was waiting.

"Well Wendy, tell me the worst."

"It looks like another one, throat cut and a stab wound in the back, right behind the heart. White male, about early to middle forties, no I.D."

"Where exactly was the body discovered?"

"On the waste ground between seventy and one hundred yards behind the Blue Lady Night Club."

"Where have we heard that mentioned before Wendy?"

"That's where Ruth Armstrong and Kenneth Moss went last Saturday night Sir, the night of the first, and probably the second murder as well."

"What had the M.O. have to say?"

"He said it looks like the same as the first two deaths, but he won't know until after he has had the body on his work table, as he calls it."

"Any clues at the site near the body?"

"Not yet, S.O.C.O. are going over the area right now, I don't think they've ever been this busy before Sir. Poole tried to get access into the 'Blue Lady' to see if any one in there was causing trouble last night. No luck though, we'll have to come back again tonight when the place is open."

"That's ok, we'll give them a call later on. You and Poole go and get your lunch, don't forget the canteen's shut. I'll see you both back here later, I'm going over to see the M.O. he should be able to tell me something by now."

There it was again, that smell of death. It was always the very first thing that Cline noticed whenever he called here at the morgue. Whether the smell was there, or it was just that he so expected to experience it, it was all in his mind. Either way, he still didn't like it. Dr. Morgan was doing the post mortem on the latest victim as Cline entered the laboratory, so he made himself at home in the M.O.'s office.

After thirty minutes or so Morgan returned to his office and it was obvious to Cline that not all was well.

"What's the matter Jack? You look troubled."

"John, who's privileged with the modus operandi of the first two murders?"

"Only the people in my team and you and your lads down here, including S.O.C.O. of course, why do you ask?"

"All three victims have had their throats cut and all were stabbed from behind, but there's something different about this latest one John."

"In what way Jack?"

"Here take a good look at these photos of the wounds on the latest victim and compare them with the other two cases." Morgan laid the photos on top of his desk so that Cline could compare them more easily.

"Right John, lets start with the back wounds."

"In the first two cases the attacker used a stiletto, about a quarter of an inch wide and not too sharp. In the latest attack the blade was half an inch thick and very sharp, but it was still double edged. Now look at the throat wound, in the first two attacks, I would say the attacker used a craft knife, the neck wounds were too thin for any other type of weapon other than a surgeon's scalpel. But as you can see here on the latest victim, the attacker must have used something more akin to a hunting knife, very sharp but much thicker to give it strength, nothing like a craft knife. This knife also had a serrated edge, that's another reason I believe it to be a hunting knife."

"Anything else Jack?"

"Yes, this guy is quite a big fellow, yet the stab wound in the back was made with a downward thrust, unlike the first two murders where the knife wounds were almost horizontal. The strength used in this latest murder to stab the victim, was so forceful, that it left an impression of the knife's hilt on the victim's back. The knife went straight through the victim's heart. This guy was dead way before his throat was cut."

"God Jack, I don't suppose you have any more bad news?"

"Not bad news as such, but the victim had scratches on his face. I don't think the scratches had anything to do with the murder, I think they were caused a good few hours before."

"What do you think caused the scratches?"

"I can only guess, some look like he's been pruning the garden roses. Some look like they were made by a cat, and the newest, look like somebody had a go at rearranging his face with their finger nails. That's about as good as I can make out."

"Any I.D. on him Jack?"

"If there is, we haven't found it yet John. I'll let you know if we find anything else."

"Let me have your report as fast as you can Jack. It looks like we have a copy cat killer out there. God knows where they are getting their info from."

By two thirty p.m Cline was back in the incident room. "Hi Wendy," picking up his phone he called the duty sergeant, "who was the last person to have the pool car before me?"

"I've no idea, but I can soon find out for you Sir, Why, is there a problem?"

"Why! A problem! I should think so, I picked the car up this morning and it was an absolute disgrace. There were fish and chip papers, Chinese take-away trays, and empty cigarette packets strewn all over the inside of the car and the car stunk to high heavens. If Knowels had seen that, we would all have been for the high jump. I don't really want to know who's responsible, I will leave it to you to sort out, and I've enough on my plate at the moment."

"Leave it with me Sir."

"What's the latest then Sir? Have we got number three, or is it a copy cat killing?"

"Well, unless the killer has changed the knives, and has been taking steroids to increase his or her strength, I would hazard a guess that we have ourselves a copycat killer out there. Don't ask me how a copy cat killer could have got hold of the modus operandi, not even the newspapers know exactly how the first two victims died. Let's hope the forensic boys can come up with some thing, at the moment we are still clutching at straws."

"We at least have one link between the latest murder and the first murder, that is, 'The Blue Lady Night Club'"

"Agreed, and here's what we are going to do next. By now, there should be someone at the club, we'll call at the morgue and pick up a photo of our latest victim and go and give the club a quick visit. We'll get a couple of uniform lads to pop down there as well. Just in case they are still closed, get Poole to contact the key holder and tell him to get his backside down there straight away. The key holder's name should be on file in case of a fire or a break in. From now on Wendy, nobody talks to anyone outside this team, and I mean no one, not even other police colleagues. If we do have a leak at the station I want to be sure we are not doing anything to assist them. Tell the others when you see them."

The three detectives arrived at the night club to find two uniformed constables already waiting outside the main entrance.

"Is there anyone in there?"

"Yes Sir, the key holder arrived about ten minutes ago. Somehow he doesn't look too happy."

"Good, that's what I like to hear, get them on the back foot to start off with."

Cline turned and shoved the club door open. "Constable I don't want to be disturbed, so let no one in until we come back out."

"No problem Sir."

It took a few moments for their eyes to get accustomed to the difference, between the bright sunshine outside, and the very poorly lit interior of the night club. To call it a night club was really going over the top somewhat, it was just a glorified pub with a dance floor and a few table and chairs scattered about here and there.

The club had been built about three years ago on a piece of waste ground, just outside the main shopping precinct in the town centre. His eyes, now accustomed to the darkness Cline could make out two figures seated at a table on the far side of the dance floor. The two figures, which at first appeared only as silhouettes, rose from their seats and turned towards the approaching trio.

One of the men was about six foot tall and nearly as wide, he must have weighed in at around twenty two stones, Cline guessed he must be the club bouncer, or at least one of them.

The second man was much smaller at around five foot eight inches tall and no more than ten stones in weight. Whereas the large guy was dressed in a black vest and black jeans, the smaller man was more dapper, sporting a silver grey double-breasted three piece suit, white shirt and a bright pink tie. His hair was plastered back with some kind of gel and the long ends of hair at the back of his head were tied with a narrow ribbon creating a pigtail. His attire was completed with the addition of a pair of pink socks and a pair of snake skin shoes. He looked like a throwback from one of those American gangster movies from the so called roaring twenties. Careful to avoid shaking hands, Cline made his introductions.

"I'm the owner of the night club. What do you want? I've more to do with my time than waste it talking to the likes of you."

His voice was high pitched but with no volume to it, this only added to the overall weirdness of the man, to whom Cline took an immediate dislike. Come to think about it, he wasn't too keen on the ape impersonator either. The remark was like waving a red flag to a bull, and would do nothing to help Cline endear himself to the club owner.

"So far I have not had a very good day, you might even say, that it's been a shit of a day and so I am not in a mood to stand here and take a load of bull shit from a short arse like you and your pet gorilla. From here on, I will be asking all the questions, understand?"

"Now look here Inspector, we came here of our own free will, if we had known you were going to be heavy handed I would have had our lawyer down here as well."

133

"Heavy handed, you don't know the meaning of the words. For a start, I don't think your pet monkey had an invite to this party. I can't imagine even you would allow him to be a key holder. As to being heavy handed, how does this sound? Baxter, make a note that the main door opens inwards and not outwards and could be a hazard in case of a fire. This place could be a death trap. Don't forget to mention that the emergency exit signs are broken, I bet they don't light up anyway. I wouldn't be at all surprised if one word in the right ear, couldn't get this place shut down within the hour. Now what do you have to say to that Mr. Club owner?"

"You can't do that."

"Maybe I can and maybe I can't, but by the time that all the services, such as the Fire Brigade, Health and Safety, the police and anyone else I can think of, have completed their inspections and investigations and made out their reports, say in about three months time, all that bureaucracy just drives one mad doesn't it, I wouldn't be surprised if you weren't bankrupt. So do we talk? Or do we play games?"

"Ok, what do you want to know?"

"During the early hours of this morning, a man's body was found on the waste ground behind your club."

"We no nofink about no body, we dint put im there"

"I'm talking to the organ grinder not the monkey. Baxter take this oaf out of my sight, see if you can find a few bananas to keep him quiet for half an hour or so."

"Now then let us try again, this time you can start by telling me your name."

"Gene Simmons Ford."

Cline burst out in laughter. "Jean, What kind of name is that for a man?"

"Not Jean as in a woman Jean. Gene as in man. You know like Gene Kelly. Everybody used to laugh at me when

I told them my name, why do you think I employed the gorilla, it certainly wasn't for his good looks."

"Ok Gene, what can you tell me about the murder last night. Did you have any kind of trouble in the club last night?"

"You never mentioned anything about this geezer being murdered. How the hell do you expect me to know what goes on outside these club walls, and no we didn't have any trouble last night. What time are we talking about Inspector?"

"Sometime before seven thirty this morning."

"Christ Inspector, you must be joking, the club was closed along time before that and at that time I was back at home in the land of nod. I don't live here you know."

"So then, what time did you leave the club?"

"The usual time, about four thirty a.m. It takes me a couple of hours or so to get cashed up and make sure the place is cleaned down, ready for re-opening at night."

"You are sure you had no trouble last night? Would it have been possible for you to have trouble and you not know about it, after all, you do employ the gorilla, and probably some of his mates, to sort out any trouble before it gets to you."

"Dead sure Inspector, as you say, the gorilla sorts the trouble makers out but I didn't get any reports back, that it had been any other but a fairly quiet night."

"What do you mean by, fairly quiet?"

"Well there was one geezer in his early forties, wanting a bottle of champers but he had no money, kept going on that he had loads of money at home and he would be getting a lot more tonight. He said if we let him have the champers, he would pay whatever price we wanted to charge him and he would fetch the money tonight. He was pissed as a newt."

Cline took a photo from his jacket pocket and passed it to Ford. "Is this the geezer you are on about?"

"Yes, that's the guy, although he doesn't look too good in that photo, I thought he looked like death warmed up last night, but he didn't look THAT bad."

"Probably that's because when this photo was taken a few hours ago, he was dead, having said that, he still looks better than your gorilla friend." Cline shouted across the dance floor for Baxter to fetch the gorilla back. "By the way, what's the gorilla's name?"

"Kev."

The gorilla waddled over the dance floor, his arms hanging down by his sides.

"Gene has just told me you had some trouble last night with a guy over a bottle of champagne, is this the guy?"

"Yes, dint giv me no trouble though, I frew im out."

"But this is the same guy?"

"Yep, that's the same geezer. I'd know him even if he was dead."

"That's just what he is, dead. Have either of you seen him before last night?"

""No, but that doesn't mean he's not been in here before last night. We can't remember everyone that comes through the door, especially when we are packed out to the rafters."

"When you threw him out of the club, was he able to walk by himself, or did you have to help him to a car?"

"I'm only paid to either let them in or fro em out, besides, he wos too pissed to dwive. Wot they do when I fro em out of ere, is up to them. He wos back outside the door arf a our later when I went out for a breever and a fag."

"You have such an eloquent way of speaking Kev, it must come with the looks. What do you mean, he was still outside? Surely you weren't expecting him to come back into the club?"

"Wots up you fick or sommat? When I say he wos outside, I mean he wos outside, he wos sat down on the ground, just outside the door. When I fro em out they stay out."

"They certainly do when they are dead."

"Now look ere Inspector, I ad note to do wiv the geezer's deff, all I did wos to fro im out."

"When you found him outside again, did you speak to him?"

"Yeh, I told him to shuv off. He said he wos waiting for somebody. It wos nearly chucking out time so I just left im there and went back into club."

"Was this guy still outside the club door when you both left it early this morning? I believe you mentioned four thirty, is that right Gene?"

"Not as I remember, no definitely not. When we leave the club we have the night takings with us, which we always take straight to the night safe at the bank. Kev always goes outside first, to check if there are any suspect characters out there, I'm sure if he had seen the guy again, he would have mentioned the fact."

"That's right, I didn't see no one Guv."

"Are you sure he was alone in the club? It's hard to believe he intended drinking a full bottle of champers to himself, you are sure he didn't have a lady friend?"

"As far as we know he was alone, but don't forget when Kev saw him outside later, he said he was waiting for somebody, perhaps somebody was going to give him some money."

"Ok, that will do me for now, but we may be back later. We'll find our own way out thank you."

Outside the sun was still very bright and it took almost as long getting their eyes accustomed to the light, as it did, getting them accustomed to the darkness when the entered the night club.

Cline handed the photo of the latest victim to one of the uniformed constables standing outside the club door. "I want everyone stopped before they enter this club. Ask them if they have seen him, or know of him, and especially if they saw him last night and, if they did, was he with anyone? If you get any hassle from within the club, just remind them of the outside main door, they will know what you mean. Nobody goes into the club without first looking at that photo. I don't give a damn if the queue to get in the club ends up two miles long."

"Just as you wish Sir."

We know this guy was still here near to closing time, so try and concentrate on that time to start with."

"Someone may have seen car headlights as they left, they may even have gone over the waste ground behind the club, for a bit of hanky panky. Surely, somebody must have seen something."

The trio were soon back in the incident room, throats parched from the hot sun outside. "Poole how about putting that kettle on and making us all a nice cuppa?"

The tea arrived in double quick time, "that's not a bad cup of tea Poole, you'll have to be muver all the time." The remark brought a laugh from Baxter."Ok, let's look at what we know. Our latest victim was seen outside the night club at closing time, or near enough closing time, but there was no sign of him at 4.30 when the owner, with his gorilla, left. From what Kev said, our victim could have been waiting for someone, and that someone, may just have been his killer. Or did the person he was waiting for, arrive, hand over money and then leave? Then we could be looking at a simple mugging gone wrong."

"I doubt that Sir. If that was the case, why was the attack made to look like the first two murders?"

"True Baxter, I was just being hopefully cheerful."

"This is beginning to look like another blackmail case, in which case, who was blackmailing who, and why?"

"In the first two murders, it looks like the blackmailer killed the people being blackmailed, but in this latest killing, it looks like the blackmailer has been killed. Everything is now arse over tits."

"It would appear to me that we don't know very much at all Sir."

"Thank you for that observation Poole, I feel a lot happier now."

"Sorry Sir."

"Wendy, have you anything to add?"

"Only that we cannot be certain if he met anyone or not. He could have been killed by anyone coming out of the night club."

"No way Wendy, from the way he was killed there has to be some connection to all three killings and, when we find out what that is, then we will find the killer."

"Wendy, first thing tomorrow morning, I want you and Poole, to chase up the forensic reports on the clothes of the first two victims. There might be clues there. As yet, no ones knows of the difference in the murder weapons used on the latest victim and that's the way I want it to stay. When we get the M.O.'s report, it comes straight back to me, no one else, understand."

Chapter 9

Cline's first port of call was the duty Sergeant's desk. "I take it your lads came away empty handed from the Blue lady last night?"

"I'm afraid so Sir."

"Thanks Serg, I was just living in hope that something may have turned up."

It was during his talk to the duty Sergeant that Cline had a glimpse of a petite red-headed female, who had just walked into the room, strolled past Cline and disappeared out of the door at the far end of the corridor beyond. The only indication that what he had seen was not a mirage, was the lingering remains of her perfume, not one of those cheap obnoxious ones bought from a market stall, but one with a delicate bouquet that titillated the senses, just sufficiently enough to arouse attention of the opposite sex.

"Who or what the hell was that Serg?"

"That Sir, was Samantha. She's a civilian typist temp, on loan to us from area whilst we have staff shortages during the staff holiday periods. She started here last Friday and I can tell you that, apart from looking good and smelling good, she's a bloody good worker."

"She may well be, but I bet the lads don't do much work with her to distract them."

Back in the incident room, W.D.C. White was waiting for the latest update from Cline.

"I've not got much for you yet Mary, you can put this photo of our latest victim on your board though."

Ten minutes late the whole team was in the incident room.

"Sir, I think you had better come over and take a look at this."

"Why, what's up Jones?"

"I think Moore and me can identify this guy in this latest photo."

Cline walked over to the wall board. "Why, is he a friend of yours?"

"I wouldn't say that Sir, he's the guy we caught and pulled in for questioning for those muggings on the prostitutes."

"Are you sure?"

"There's no doubt Sir. What clothes was he wearing, a pin striped suit?"

"No, he was dressed in a pair of brown trousers, black polo neck jumper and brown shoes and socks, why do you ask?"

"I was just wondering if he'd been out mugging again, he was always dressed in a pin striped suit before."

"I take it that means we have a name for this guy?"

"Yes Sir, Rothwell. Moore, can you go and get a copy of his statement and fetch the audio tape from his interview."

"Moore get Samantha to give you a hand, I'll square it with the duty Serg."

"Oh! you've seen her then Sir?"

"Yes I have, thank you Poole."

"Now we know who he is, that answers one of my questions."

"Which question is that Sir?"

"The M.O. remarked on the scratches on the victim's face. If I remember correctly Jones, didn't you say that one of the 'Toms' attacked this bloke after you arrested him?"

"Yes Sir, she really dug her finger nails into his cheeks."

"Right Jones, you and Moore try and get hold of his wife, didn't you say she was away at her mother's home?

We need S.O.C.O. to go over his home, see if we can get something from there. He may have been done in, by one of the 'Pimps', but I doubt it. I'll leave you to sort out the search warrant."

"Jones, did you say Rothwell had been in the army?"

"Yes Sir."

"Ok, you get off with Moore. Wendy, first thing this morning, you take Poole and have a word with Rothwell's employers. I believe I saw something in Rothwell's statement, I think they are accountants. When you've done that, I want you both to go over the photos taken at the first murder scene in the woods. See if we have missed anything. Meanwhile, I'll see what I can find out from our army friends."

Having been transferred from pillar to post, Cline eventually found himself speaking to the Commanding Officer at Aldershot Army Camp. After thirty minutes fighting his way through army bureaucracy, he was finally rewarded with an appointment with Major Brian-Lee-Forsyth for the following day.

White, entered his office and placed a copy of Rothwell's statement along with Jones's report on his desk.

It was beyond Cline's comprehension to understand why someone with the stability of a normal family life, and an apparently good job, would wish to resort to mugging prostitutes, surely there must be more to it than trying to get a bit more money. No doubt he would have a good army pension to go along with his wage from his everyday job.

If Rothwell was waiting for someone to pay him some money, where was it? Perhaps the answer could be found in his home. His thoughts were interrupted by the intrusion of Baxter's voice. "I think Poole and I have found something Sir, I think you should come and have a look."

"I'll be with you in five minutes."

Baxter and Poole were still examining the photos when Cline approached them. They'd managed to acquire, from

God knows where, one of those magnifying glasses set in a round fluorescent light, like the ones used by medical staff for looking for foreign objects in patient's eyes or when they are looking for splinters.

"Ok, don't tell me where you got the magnifying glass from, I'd rather not know. So what have you found?"

Baxter stood up and offered Cline her seat at the table, a table that just happened to be completely covered from end to end by the photos taken in the woods. "What am I looking at?"

"Right Sir, if you start with photo number one which was taken at the end of the footpath closest to the pub, and then work westwards towards the murder scene, now bear in mind Sir, that we know from the M.O.'s report and S.O.C.O., along with the jogger's statement that it started to rain at, or just after Armstrong was killed. Remember the dry spot on the ground underneath the body; if you look very carefully at the photos taken from near the pub, up to where the body was found, the only footprints that can be seen, are those of the jogger and those of the flat footed P.C."

"How does that help us Wendy?"

"Well Sir, just bear with us for awhile. Compare the photos taken to the west of the body and those taken around the body; can you see anything that you didn't see in the first set of photos?"

He took the magnifying glass and took another look at the photos, this time hoping and praying he could see what he was meant to see. He'd feel a right idiot if he failed to see what both Baxter and Poole could apparently see, especially after giving Poole such a hard time for not spotting the different trees in the wood.

"Your eyes must be a lot better than mine Wendy, all I can see are scuff marks where the jogger fell over the body and the prints of our flat-footed friend. The only other marks seem to be those roundish black spots."

"Exactly Sir. Now look about one to two inches away from one of the black spots, what do you see?"

"What do I see? Not a lot really, just that very faint outline of a shape that does look a bit like a shoe sole. It's very small though Wendy."

"That's because Poole and I think it is the print of a woman's shoe. They are far too small for a man's footprint and besides, what type of man wears that kind of shoe with that type of heel, unless he is a transvestite? They look like stiletto heals Sir. We believe a woman was on that footpath at the same time Armstrong was killed. The prints would not have shown if the ground was still bone hard from the sun, if the woman had gone down there after it had been raining for some time, then the heels would have gone deeper into the softer ground. Besides that Sir, we know Armstrong was found by the jogger, not long after he was killed, and the footpath was closed off soon after to the general public. If an innocent female member of the public had gone down that path before the jogger, then she would have been the one to have reported finding the body. Before you make your own mind up Sir, continue checking the photos westward. You can see those same black spots and small shoe prints and they show that the wearer walked in both directions down the footpath. At this point, we come to the path that shoots off to one side of the main footpath. Again you can see those prints in both directions, but this time they are slightly deeper impressions. They can be seen all the way down that side tract, as far as the fallen tree stump and then back down to the main footpath where they turn westward, away from where Armstrong's body was found. Eventually the prints leave the wood at the west end of the footpath."

"That's very good Wendy, so what are your conclusions?"

"Not yet Sir, there's more."

"If we look more closely at the photos taken four or five yards west of the body, note the prints are moving eastwards. At this point they leave the path as if the woman, and I firmly believe they do belong to a woman, walked onto the grass at the side of the path. Now if you look at the path two yards to the east of that point you can see where she stepped back onto the footpath again. I know the prints are very, very faint and we were lucky to see them at all; I believe they were made before the rains came, when the ground was very hard. There could have been a slight sprinkling of rain before the main rainfall, which was just enough to make the prints visible, but I'm just surmising. It looks like the woman was waiting in the bushes for Armstrong, in fact you can see that some of her prints are on top of Armstrong's. We think the woman waited for Armstrong to come along, stepped out behind him and then killed him. She then went to the fallen tree to collect whatever he had left for her to pick up, that would also explain how the killer knew that Armstrong would be walking through the woods at that time."

"Well done the pair of you."

"There is another thing Sir."

"This is starting to become a good day, go on excite me some more."

Poole produced more photos and shoved them over to Cline, "take a look at these Sir, they are from the second murder scene."

It didn't take too long before Cline noticed the same tell tale black spots and the faint outline of a woman's shoe sole print. He checked the prints against the first set from the woods, they were the same size.

"The ground on the river bank was very hard Sir, that's why the prints are only very faint, too light in fact, to make a plaster cast of them. I really think the photos are conclusive enough for me to say that we are looking for a woman killer Sir, at least for the murder or Armstrong and Preston."

"You have certainly done well but as you yourself fear, we may have another killer out there. I don't think a woman could inflict the kind of stab wound that was used to kill Rothwell; the M.O. said a significantly amount of force was used to push the knife into his back for the knife hilt to have made an impression on the victim's back. Don't forget the victim was wearing clothes, so the force used must have been quite excessive."

"Don't forget Sir, there are some mighty big and powerful women out there."

"Maybe, but I bet they don't wear shoes with prints as small as the ones we've got, what size would you think they are Wendy?"

"It's not that easy to tell Sir, but if you are pushing me for some kind of an answer, I would say size 5 or 6."

"Could we be looking for two murderers, working together Sir?"

"It's possible Wendy, and to be honest, I don't know whether that would be a good thing or a bad thing. If they are working together that could mean we only have one motive behind the killings, where as with two separate killers, we are going to have more than one motive."

"Sir, if you are trying to keep our findings secure within our team, is it such a good idea to have Samantha, the new temp helping W.D.C. White?"

"Very good point Poole, I'll go and have a word with her now. I want you two to go over to Armstrong Motors and interview the receptionist Jenny, I think that's her name. You can let me know tomorrow how you get on with her. I'll see you, all being well, after I get back from Catterick Army Camp. I shouldn't be too late back, sometime after lunch."

Chapter 10

Walking was always more pleasurable to Cline than driving, although in this instant, the drive up to North Yorkshire, at least brought him some sanctuary and thankful relief from the rigors and tensions of the past week. He was beginning to feel the heavy burden on his shoulders, that a murder investigation such as this, always seems to create. The trip also kept him out of the reach, or should that be the clutches, of Knowels.

The A1 road that he was travelling ran virtually over the same course as the Old Roman Road and was now called The Great North Road, and the best thing about it, was the absence of reporters clambering for statements, no senior officers demanding that he pull his finger out. Apart from the traffic, all he had to contend with was the Yorkshire countryside. He felt cocooned and protected from all the pressures of the outside world, even the occasional whiff of diesel fumes was a pleasant reminder that he was away from his office.

The weather was almost perfect, with clear blue skies and no forecast of rain for the foreseeable future and the radio tuned to one of those easy listening stations, he found himself talking out loud, "why can't all the days be like this?"

He could not help but think about the investigation, at least here there was no one to disturb his train of thoughts. He thanked the Gods that they had been lucky enough to keep the lid on things, as far as the press were concerned, but for how much longer, he daren't even hazard a guess. No doubt the shit will hit the fan when the Rothwell murder gets out, someone from the night club will no doubt have been doing their public duty by ringing the press with their story. He then remembered that Knowels had taken a few days off, but couldn't remember whether it was for sickness or a small break. That's what happens when you are not interested, and don't really listen when people talk to you, especially when you hate the person's guts. I suppose I should have sent Baxter and Poole up here, and then I could have stayed and taken the flak when it hits.

The journey was all too short for Cline, by 10.45 he was at Catterick with forty five minutes to wait until his appointment. At 11.25 he was being ushered into the office of Major Brian-Lee-Forsyth.

The major held out an inviting hand. "Good morning Inspector, did you have a pleasant journey? I know at times, the A1 can be a nightmare of a road to travel on."

"Yes, thank you Major, it's very good of you to see me on such short notice, no doubt you must be a very busy man."

"You sounded as if it was most important that you should see me as soon as possible when we spoke on the phone yesterday, besides I must admit my curiosity got the better of me and I cannot wait to hear what this is all about."

"One thing I must stress Major, whatever we discuss must not be repeated to anyone. I would prefer that only you should be aware of the details of my visit here. I am sure you will understand why, after you have heard what I have to say."

"First things first Inspector, please take a seat. Corporal Jenkins, tea and biscuits in five minutes, and knock and wait when you return. Now then Inspector, what's all this about?"

"I mentioned to you yesterday that I am interested in one of your old soldiers, I don't mean old in the true meaning of the word, I should have said one of your soldiers who has now left and is now in civvy street, Sgt. Rothwell."

"Yes, I drew his file out as soon as I came off the phone with you yesterday. I hope you realise that I am very restricted in what I am able to tell you. I don't want Rothwell's solicitor suing me for passing on privileged information about him to the police."

"I don't think it will come to that Major, in fact I know it won't, and I don't think Rothwell will complain either. You see Major, Rothwell was murdered outside a night club in Bolderdale."

"You didn't mention that on the phone yesterday Inspector, I think you had better let me hear what you have to say before I give you any information from our files. I take it you are sure he was murdered and it wasn't an accident or natural causes?"

There was a knock on the office door.

"Come in Corporal." The tea tray with tea and biscuits was placed on the Major's desk and the Corporal left without another word being spoken.

"Help yourself Inspector whilst you tell me your story and then I will see if we can be of any help to you."

"Naturally I am also limited in what information I can reveal to you, be it for different reasons, yours for personal reasons, and mine because of a need to know basis. Rothwell was brutally murdered outside a Bolderdale night club, not long after he was released from police custody. He had been arrested on a mugging and an assault charge the previous night. I need to know what kind of a man he was. If I knew more about him, about his character, his likes, his dislikes, whether he was prone to outbursts of temper, anything that might help me to discover why he was killed. He was in the army for a good number of years, why did he not progress up the ranks? Was there a flaw in his character?"

The Major took a long hard look at the file in front of him, it was after a few moments of silence that he raised his head and looked over his desk towards Cline.

"Rothwell never exhibited any real initiative towards promotion and, any promotion that he did get, mainly for years served, was thrust upon him by the army. When he first enlisted he actually signed on for the full slog, twenty one years. Men usually only do that if they are trying to run away from something in civvy street, whether that was the reason Rothwell signed on for the full term I don't know. From his records I can tell you that, unlike the rest of the squad, Rothwell was pretty much an introvert. I know quite a few of the new recruits tend to be that way inclined at first, but after just three or four weeks of basic training and square bashing, they are usually knocked into shape. Not Rothwell though, he was always on the outside, always the outsider, in fact some of the lads used to nick name him the Lone Wolf. I'm surprised he lasted so long without being chucked out of the army. He was caught on several occasions fighting other members of his squad for no other reason than they were there. It got so bad he was sent for a psychiatric assessment."

"According to the Medical Officer all the inbuilt aggression was a result of once being very badly bullied at school, he was beaten so badly he spent quite some time in hospital.

The M.O. said his desire to get revenge was so powerful, it didn't really matter who it was on the receiving end of his temper, and he just wanted to inflict pain on others. He wanted the world to experience what he had gone through when he took that beating. He blamed the authorities at the school and the system in general for allowing it to happen. Surprisingly, after a few counselling sessions with the psychiatrist, he was deemed fit to continue his service in the army. After that, he seemed to settle down, but it must be said he was still much a loner, preferring his own company to that of the other members of his squad. What he was like with his wife and family, that is something I am not able to help you with. There isn't a lot more that I can tell you Inspector, I hope you haven't had a wasted journey."

"No, Major, I appreciate the fact that you've been able to spare me the time to see me. One thing about my business, you can never tell which bit, of sometimes apparently useless information, is the bit that puts the villain behind bars. It's my job to sort the wheat from the chaff, so as to speak."

Cline arose from his chair and shook the Major's hand, and bid him good day.

"I'll get Corporal Jenkins to walk you back to your car, that way the M.Ps won't stop you, they are still wary about strangers on the camp."

"Corporal"

Jenkins must have been close to hand, the Major had hardly finished calling his name and he was in the room. "Walk Inspector Cline back to his car, we don't want him wandering off, now do we Jenkins?"

Walking back to the car, Cline thought the Major must have been joking, they must have been walking at the same pace as the Gurkhas on a forced march, 180 steps per minute. After thanking Jenkins, Cline collapsed into the driving seat of his car, thankful for the rest. It was 12.55 as he passed through the camp gates, "with a bit of luck and no traffic hold ups, I should be back in the office by 15.00hours."

Once safely back in his office, he removed a file from his brief case and studied it very carefully, before placing it in one of his desk drawers. Although the Major wouldn't allow Cline to read any of the army files on Rothwell, he did provide a copy of Rothwell's original application form, which at least provided additional information with regards to his education and the schools he had attended.

"Afternoon Sir, hope you had a good day."

"Not too bad Wendy, how about you?"

"Do you want the good news first or the bad news?"

"Oh! no, here we go again, give me the good news first."

"The good news is there have been no more murders, and the bad news is that the local press have got hold of the story." Baxter threw a copy of the local rag onto Cline's desk.

"SERIAL KILLER ON THE LOOSE IN BOLDERDALE"

"Before you blow your top Sir, it wasn't any of us that leaked the story, we are just as mad about it as you are."

Cline quickly read through the report in the paper.

"I leave the office for one lousy day and, by the time I get back, all hell breaks out. How the hell did they get all this information, it must have come from within this station. Christ, now we will most likely get every loony from within a twenty five miles radius of Bolderdale ringing up or dropping into the station claiming to be the serial killer. That's all I need."

"They have even reported the manner in which the murders were committed Sir." "That's true Wendy, one thing may be in our favour though, they don't seem to know the victim's names, or at least they haven't printed them."

"I would think that if they don't have the names yet Sir, if the leak did come from this station, it shouldn't be too long before they do have them."

"How did you get on with Jenny at Armstrong Motors?"

"She's too honest to be in any kind of trouble with us, she's just been in the unfortunate position of having privileged information and trying to keep faithful to all her bosses at once. She's just been the piggy in the middle. She did tell us that it was Ruth Armstrong who rang her the day Kenneth Moss was interviewed."

"Did she say why Mrs.Armstrong had phoned her?"

"Yes, she said that Mrs. Armstrong had rung to warn Kenneth Moss that it was more than likely that we would be calling in on him and she wanted to ensure that he didn't mention their affair since, as far as she was concerned, it had nothing to do with her husband's murder."

"As it happened, her call came too late to have a difference, Moss never even mentioned the affair, so the call was just a waste of time and only helped make her position in all this, very suspect. Did you manage to call in at Rothwell's employer, what's the name? Goodfellow, Flint or whatever."

"Goodfellow, Flint and Rothchilds and they aren't as stuffy as their name might imply.

We managed to get hold of Mr. Rothchild, one of the partners in the business. He confirmed that Rothwell had worked for them and had done so since he left the army.

He was a good solid worker, very orderly, which was probably a product of his army experience. However, he was every bit an introvert, always kept his own council, never went to office parties and, unless it was work inspired, very rarely spoke to any of his fellow work-mates. They knew from his application form that he was married with a family, but they were never mentioned. He was a very peculiar man, but he was a very good worker, and so he was tolerated. One strange thing came out of the interview though, Rothwell never ever worked overtime, nine till five man, through and through. I thought he said he was hard up and that was the reason he gave for mugging the prostitutes. We may never know Sir, whether Rothwell was a blackmailer or was being blackmailed."

"Can't anything be straight forward in this case?"

The ring from the desk phone seemed so much louder than normal, it must be due to the warm weather, at least that's what Cline was thinking as he walked over to pick it up.

"Cline here."

"It's me Sir, Sergeant Jones"

"I know that Jones, I am able to remember voices, I'm not ready for the knacker's yard just yet."

"We've been sat outside Rothwell's home all day, there's just no sign of Mrs. Rothwell. The next door neighbour said that Mrs. Rothwell is due back to day because she was asked to buy her fresh milk and fresh bread ready for her return. Do you still want us to stay down here Sir?"

"Yes, I doubt that, unless Rothwell's death has been picked up by the National Press, Mrs. Rothwell will still be unaware of her husband's death. So I need you to be there, to break the news to her. Sorry about that, but it will be better coming from you rather than the next door neighbour. If she does come back, try and find out if his pin striped suit is at home, I need to know whether he actually called at home after he was released on bail, I'll see you when I see you."

"Wendy, have forensic returned the clothes yet from the first two murders?"

"No, not yet, I did give them a ring earlier this morning, all being well we should have them by six tonight."

"Ok, get a bite to eat and we'll meet back here at six thirty."

"Six thirty and the forensic lab still hadn't sent the clothes over. Cline was in the process of ringing the lab when a uniformed officer walked into the room, carrying two large brown parcels. "I believe you have been waiting for these Sir."

"Thank you just put them on desk." With the two parcels there were two lab reports from which Cline read out the highlights aloud. Well you all heard that. The only thing of any significance that the forensic lads have detected, were traces of a cheap brand of lipstick smeared on the back of the collar of Armstrong's jacket and on the shoulder of Preston's coat. They say there is no way they can identify the lipstick, it's just one of hundreds of cheap brands on the market, unless of course they had a sample to compare it with. Now I happen to think that is brilliant, instead of forensic helping us to find the killer, we have to find the bloody killer first, so they can then get a match for the lipstick. Sometimes I wonder why we bother."

"It does more or less prove our killer is a woman, and the lipstick could just be the icing on the cake when we need forensic evidence that she was at the murder scene."

"Icing on the cake! We still haven't got a bleeding cake yet, Wendy"

"I believe the lipstick tells us one thing Sir."

"And what's that?"

"I think that puts Ruth Armstrong out of the frame for the murders, I can't see her wearing cheap lipstick, can you Sir?"

"You may well be right, but there could well be a few twists and turns before this case gets sorted out. Don't forget she could have paid somebody else to do the killings, but then we have to ask ourselves, why did she have Preston killed?"

The door to the incident room burst open and a young P.C partly walked and partly ran into the room.

"Is it alright to come in Sir?"

"NO WAIT OUTSIDE"

Cline was furious, "here we are trying to keep things between ourselves, and we have people dashing in here as if it's Kings Cross Station. Wendy find a key for that door, before every Tom, Dick and Harry makes it into a thoroughfare." The young P.C did a quick u-turn and was back outside the room as quick as his face had turned bright red.

Cline shouted across the room. "OK, YOU CAN COME IN NOW"

"Now then young man, what's so urgent, that you haven't time to knock before you enter the room?"

"I'm sorry I burst in like that Sir, but something has come up that I thought you might be interested in. It's to do with the Preston murder."

"How come you are involved?"

"I'm the Community Bobby on the Bentley beat."

"Ok then, let's hear what you have to say."

"This morning I was walking my usual beat around the village when I was stopped by the caretaker of the village Scout Hall. Apparently they've just appointed someone to replace Preston as the Scout Master."

"They haven't wasted any time have they? But why should that be of any interest to me?"

"Well, that fact by itself doesn't Sir, but what may interest you is that fact that the new Scout Master wants to get into Preston's old locker but nobody knows where he kept the key to the padlock. The caretaker wanted to know if the police would have any objections if they were to smash the padlock; I told him to leave it for now and that I would get back to him later. I thought if you didn't know about the locker before, you may wish to have a look inside it, before they throw away all Preston's things."

"Too right Constable, well done. Why didn't we get to know about this locker before?"

"Nobody bothered to ask Sir."

"Will the Scout Hall be opened tonight?"

"I don't really know Sir, but I can get over there and make sure the caretaker is on hand, if you want to have a look at the locker tonight."

"You bet I want to look in the locker tonight, you make your way back and I will see you outside the main church, two hours from now."

"Why the church?"

"Because I don't know where the Scout Hall is situated, but I do know where the church is."

"Ok, I take it that it will be alright for me to be present Sir?"

"No problem, I'll see you at Bentley later."

"Sergeant Jones rang a few minutes ago Sir. He said there's still no sign of Mrs. Rothwell at her home. He said he and Moore will stay until ten o'clock then call it a day." The duty Sergeant disappeared as quickly as he arrived.

"Wendy, I know it's going to be late, but I would like you to come with me to Bentley. There's a little job we have to do when we get there, I'll fill you in with all the details as we go."

The young Community Bobby and the caretaker were both waiting at the lich-gate outside the Parish Church.

"The caretaker doesn't seem to pleased to see us Sir."

"He's probably missing Coronation Street or some other stupid soap on the tele. At least it will give him something different to talk about, over his pint in the local tonight."

Whether the waiting pair was in some kind of a hurry, but Cline and Baxter had hardly got out of the car before they were both hailed, "This Way! It's just up the road from here."

"We'll have to wait here a bit constable. S.O.C.O. is on the way, I asked them to meet up with us, here at the church."

"Don't you worry yourself about that, once we are inside the Scout Hall, you can leave the keys with us, and get yourself back home."

"I can't do that Inspector; I'm responsible for everything in the Scout Hall."

""Once you've pointed out Preston's locker to us then you can get off. If you can't trust the police, who can you, trust?"

"That's just it Sir, you don't know who you can trust these days."

"I'll pretend I didn't hear that."

It was only a matter of a few minutes before S.O.C.O. arrived and they were all marching through the main door of the Scout Hall. The caretaker pointed out Preston's locker, then handed the keys to Cline and walked off chuntering obscenities in his wake.

Preston's locker was not situated with the other lockers but was at the far end of the locker room in a secluded corner.

"Before we open the locker, I want the outside of the locker and the padlock dusted for prints and also a photo of the outside of the locker before you cover it in dust."

"Ok Sir, we've done with the outside, do you want the honour of smashing the padlock off?"

"We'll let Sergeant Baxter have that pleasure." Cline handed Baxter the seven pound lump hammer that he had earlier taken out of the boot of the car. "Here you are, do your worst."

"After three almighty swings with the hammer, the padlock lay in pieces on the locker room floor."

"I see you must have had your Weetabix this morning Wendy. Ok, let's see what the inside holds in store for us. Again, plenty of photos and fingerprints before and after we touch or remove anything."

The locker was divided into two parts by a horizontal shelf, the top section being about one third the size of the lower section.

The lower section contained nothing of great importance as far as Cline was concerned, just the expected scout uniform and shoes. From the top section he removed a mug, a jar of instant coffee, a knife, a fork and a spoon. Each item was carefully placed onto a table which stood next to Preston's locker, and then photographed before they were placed into a plastic bag and then identified. The last remaining item in the locker was an A4 size brown envelope, which looked the worse for wear due most probably from constant use.

After the usual procedures, Cline, now wearing protective gloves, slowly removed the contents of the envelope. "Christ Wendy, these are disgusting," he turned the photos so Baxter could see them without having to touch them herself. "Wendy, they seem to be photos of naked boys between the ages of six and thirteen. There I was, thinking things just couldn't get any worse and along comes this lot. Now it looks like Preston could be a member of a paedophile ring. God I hope not, I hope this is just an individual case involving Preston. We really need to keep this lot under our hats, or there will be a right hue and cry if the general public get any inkling of what we have found here. Thank God I sent the caretaker home. There must be nigh on two dozen photos here, what the hell was he into? Whatever it was, at least he won't be at it again, let's hope he was just a looker and not a doer."

"These photos do appear to be very old Sir."

"Precisely, that's why we don't want to go upsetting people if we don't have to."

Outside the Scout Hall Cline turned to the Community Bobby, "I'm sorry but I should have asked you before now, what is your name?"

"P.C Watson Sir."

"Right Watson, I shouldn't need to remind you how important it is that what we have discovered here tonight goes no further than us, having said that however I need you to make very discreet enquiries around the village. I'll leave it to you as to how you go about it, but the last thing I want is for the villagers to suspect something is seriously wrong. If Preston was playing around in Bentley, then I want to know all about it."

"I doubt it myself, Bentley is a close knit community for something like that to be taking place and nobody knowing about it. If he was up to no good, then I believe he was playing away from home. Here's my card with my mobile number, if you manage to get anything, ring me straight away, but make sure you cannot be overheard."

"There's not a lot we can do tonight Wendy, there's a little pub out in the country on our way back to town. How do you fancy a nice meal and a glass of wine? My treat of course, that is if you haven't anything else planned for tonight."

"That sounds fine to me Sir. I didn't know what time we would be getting away from Bentley, so it would have been pointless trying to make any arrangements."

By the time they had made themselves comfortable at the 'Rose Cottage Inn' it was already 9.15pm.

"Choose whatever you wish, this one's on me. It makes a nice change to eat out and have someone to talk to, instead of a quick take-a-way by myself at home with only the tele for comfort."

"I know exactly what you mean Sir."

"I think now we are off duty, I cannot see any harm in using my first name, as long as you feel comfortable with that. Tell me to mind my own business if you wish, but I've never understood why a good looking woman like you has never got married and settled down."

"That's ok Sir, sorry John, I suppose for the same reason you had a divorce, long irregular hours with no time to really call your own. I used to live with a boy friend for about eighteen months, but it didn't help the situation with him being a fireman. He used to work odd shifts and I worked long hours, so we were like ships that passed in the night, we would sometimes go days on end without seeing each other. In the end we called it a day. We are still good friends, but that's about all. Since then, I haven't bothered dating, I just can't see the point, any relationship would only end the same way."

"What do you like to do if you ever get any time off to yourself?"

"I love to get up to the Yorkshire Dales or over to the Derbyshire Peak District with my sister and family, I was about to have a few days off when this case broke out."

"You can get away from the madding crowds, it's so peaceful if you know where to go, have you ever been there?"

"No not really, I once passed through the North Yorkshire Moors on my way up to Whitby with some college friends. We went up there one summer to see the Whitby Regatta. We didn't get much of a chance to see much else, it never stopped raining from the moment we arrived there, and it was still raining when we left two days later. Mind you, we shifted some ale between us."

"I know Whitby pretty well. When the weather is fine there are lots of nice places to visit such as, Runswick Bay and Robin Hood's Bay. Then you have Goathland and Grosmont with the steam railway, and then there's the. 'Falling Foss Waterfall'. Don't get me talking about Whitby, you won't be able to shut me up. Did you know that nearly all the world's black jet comes from Whitby? It's the fossilised remains of the 'Monkey Puzzle' tree, also known as the 'Chile Pine' "

"It sounds like you are well genned -up , you'll have to take me with you the next time you go up there and show me around. Oh! I didn't mean for that to sound the way it did. I...." "It's ok, I know what you meant, and I think it would be a good idea. We could get a party of us to go all together, it would make a really good weekend break. When we've finished with this case I'll get it arranged, that's if we'll ever get the case sorted, we seem to be going around in ever decreasing circles"

"That would be great, it would be something to look forward to for a change."

The next thirty minutes or so were spent in relevant silence, with only the casual comment on the quality of the meal.

Cline and Baxter had no way of knowing that in the not too distant future, their investigation would take a downward turn, by the discovery of a fourth body, a body again, seemingly unconnected in any way to the previous victims. That information alone would be sufficient to cause Cline more sleepless nights, but the future chase to save and rescue a kidnapped victim would certainly test Cline's ability to withstand pressure to the very limit of his endurance.

A pause between courses brought an opportunity for Cline to ask Baxter what her thoughts were on the murders.

"So far it looks like the main reason for the murders is blackmail, although at this stage it isn't clear whether it is the blackmailers or the blackmailer's victims who are being killed off. We could spend all evening surmising this and that, who's blackmailing who? And we still wouldn't be any nearer getting to the bottom of things. We've checked the background of all three victims and there doesn't seem to be any reason for either blackmail or murder to be committed. That was before we found the photos in Preston's locker, but how they tie in with Rothwell and Armstrong, still remains a mystery."

"One thing we do know now is that Rothwell could not have murdered Armstrong or Preston on Saturday night because he was out mugging the prostitutes on Turpin Road. It was just a pity Jones and Moore weren't at the other end of the estate, or Rothwell may well have been arrested on that Saturday night, and may even, have been alive today."

"That's right Sir, but don't forget, now we have the evidence of the footprints, we said we are now 99% certain that the killer of Armstrong and Preston is a woman."

"I must be getting tired, just forget my mutterings, I must be getting old."

"What's up now?, was Cline's exclamation to his mobile phone ringing. "I thought I'd turned the blasted thing off." The rest of the diners looked towards Cline, the looks they gave him for having the impertinence not to have turned his phone off, was enough to turn milk sour. "It's Sergeant Jones here Sir. We've managed at long last to get hold of Mrs. Rothwell. I've informed her of her husband's death and the circumstances surrounding it. She's pretty damned shocked about it all, but didn't seem too shocked or distressed about her husband's death. It was the mugging of the prostitutes, and possible blackmail business that seemed to have shocked her the most. She even let us search her husband's room, luckily they had separate sleeping arrangements, and so it was no hassle to her for us to search his room. She said she never went into his room, not even for cleaning or decorating, no one was allowed in, only Mr. Rothwell. We searched his wardrobes and his pinstripe suit was hung up in one of them. I'm sure it is the only pin striped suit that he had, I asked his wife if she knew how many pinstriped suits he had, and she said, as far as she was aware, he only had the one. In the bottom of one of his wardrobes we had an interesting find, it was a wooden box and within the wooden box was a shoe box."

"Go on now, surprise me, what did you find in the shoe box? Not shoes I hope?"

"I'm coming to that Sir. Inside the shoe box we found a wad of money, all in old used notes."

"Are we talking hundreds or thousands, here Jones?"

"Thousands Sir, I reckon there's around ten grand in fivers, tanners, twenties and fifties."

"What had Mrs. Rothwell have to say about the find?"

"She almost fainted, it was obvious from the look of disbelief on her face, that this was the first time that she had seen the money, least of all touched it. She was actually very angry, all this money just lying there in a shoe box, she was raving on how she'd struggled and scrimped and saved to make ends meet, when all the time there was so much money in that shoe box."

"Have you taken her to I.D. her husband?"

"Yes Sir, I know it's late, but I thought we had better get it over with as soon as possible. Mrs. Rothwell is going to be staying with her neighbour until we have finished going over her house with a fine tooth comb. The house is all locked up now, ready for an early start by S.O.C.O. first thing in the morning. In the meantime I have also arranged for the uniform lads to keep an eye on it for us".

"Good work, in the morning send Moore straight back to Rothwell's home, so he is there when S.O.C.O. arrive. You come back to the station first thing, and with a bit of luck, we may be able to start to put things together at last."

Chapter 11

It took the best part of two hours for W.D.C.White to up-date the records with the recent turn of events.

"Mary, check again and make doubly sure that Rothwell hasn't a criminal record."

"Jones, you get over to Rothwell's home, check with Mrs. Rothwell if she knew her husband may have taken out any type of loan, or even remortgaged their home. Check with their mortgage company, they should be aware if any additional loans have been taken out. It could explain where the money came from but I doubt if that 10 grand is legit."

"Poole you get on to S.O.C.O., see if they've managed to come up with anything from the country lane down by the river. In the meantime Baxter and I are going back to school."

"Why Sir, and to which school?"

"Because......" Cline touched the right side of his nose with his right index finger as if to say "Wait and see." I will tell you where we are going though, to Rothwell's old secondary school, if the present cannot provide us with any answers, let's see what the past can tell us. White, don't forget if you want a hand with anything, get Samantha to help you out. In fact, get her to go through the old files in the basement, all the old records may not have been transferred to the computer yet; or something may have been missed, it's got to be worth a try, you explain to her what we are looking for. Right, you all know what you have to do, get on with it."

It was mid-morning break time when Cline and Baxter walked up the main drive to the school, in a cacophony of screaming children, all intent on producing more decibels than anyone else.

They arrived at the main school door only to find it locked, admittance being gained by inserting a numbered code into a newly installed security lock, or by requesting access, via the intercom system at the side of the door. Naturally, not being armed with the initial means of entry, the numbered code, they had to resort to pressing the intercom button and wait for some one to call.

Cline had expected someone to ask for their identity and then operate the release mechanism of the lock from some distant room, but was surprised to be face to face with a middle aged man, with only the double glazed glass panel on the door separating them. After getting the proper identification from his visitors he then opened the door and introduced himself as Mr. Berkely the school headmaster. After a fairly lengthy walk through long twisting corridors, they found themselves in the headmaster's office.

"Now in what way do you think I can help to you Inspector Cline?"

"I'm interested in one of your old boys, a James Peter Rothwell, I believe he attended at this school about the 1970s."

"Give me a few moments and I will see what I can find out for you."

Taking a large bunch of keys out of his coat pocket, Berkely walked over to a door behind his desk, unlocked it, and then opened the door to reveal stacks of shelves covered with files and books. "You know Inspector, in this room, we've still got all the records of every student who ever attended this school from the very first day of opening. Here we are Inspector Cline, I think if there is anything here that will help you, it should be here in this file. It starts 1969, around the year Rothwell came here."

"Was he a good student? Did he ever give cause for concern? Were there ever any incidents which were out of the ordinary?"

"Give me a minute, I'll have a look, you need to understand I wasn't at this school at that time, in fact, non of the present teaching staff were here then. So like yourself Inspector, I need to look in the files to answer your questions. Ah! here we are, this could be it, around the late 60s and early 70s there was some trouble with bullying. In fact, according to this report, there was also quite a bit of trouble with regard to drugs. Now then that rings a bell, although I wasn't at this school then. I believe one of the older member of staff told me sometime after I arrived here, about the time when three or four lads were beaten up, and it was all related to the sale of drugs. Here it is, 'referring to the report' Rothwell was one of the lads who was beaten up, he was beaten so bad that he had to spend quite a lengthy time in hospital."

"Did they ever find out who carried out the beatings?"

"Not according to this report, the lads who had taken the beating were too afraid to give either the school or the police any names."

"Does that report happen to have the school register for all the boys attending school from 69 to 70? Not just for Rothwell's class, but the whole school."

"It should be here somewhere, here we are." The head handed the register over to Cline, "here take a look for yourself, you know what you are looking for."

"That's the trouble Mr. Berkely, I don't really know what I'm looking for. Probably something that doesn't seem right, something that sticks out like a sore thu....mb. Do the records show if that lad ever caused any trouble?" Cline

169

pointed a finger to one of the names in the register. Now then that's strange Inspector, when we first started to talk about bullying and drugs, I seem to remember that was one of the names that was floating about when the staff were talking about events that happened before I came here. Let me just make sure." Berkely again scanned the report. Yes, he was the main suspect for both the bullying and the selling of drugs, but they just couldn't prove it at the time. I suppose it was too much of a coincidence that, after he left the school, both the bullying problem and the drug problem stopped. When I say the trouble went, I mean the more serious stuff. This report still records the odd bullying and drug problems, but neither were organised as they were whilst he was at the school. Would you like to tell me what all this is about Inspector?"

"I would love to, since you have been a great help to us, more than you will ever realise, but I simply can't."

Berkely walked with them back to the main exit, and then bid Cline and Baxter good day.

They walked back to the car in silence, the playground was silent and so was Cline, being in deep thought.

"Sir, who's name was it that aroused so much interest in that school register?"

Cline touched the side of his nose with his fore finger of his right hand. "That would be telling Wendy, that would be telling. You drive, make your way over to the forensic labs, I want to check if they've managed to come up with anything from the Scout Hall."

"Morning Inspector, we've just about finished." It was the same pair of S.O.C.O. who had been at the Scout Hall. "I'm afraid there's not a great deal that we can tell you, the photos that we found in Preston's locker weren't new. In fact they appeared to be quite old, all the corners were dog-eared and the pictures themselves were all discoloured with age.

The only prints we managed to lift from them belonged to Preston, it was the same on the inside of the locker. The outside of the locker did have other prints, but that was only to be expected. I think it is pretty obvious that the photos were for Preston's personal pleasure and gratification. I can't even guess, what type of person he was to own such filth."

"Did the photos have any printer's names on them, or anything to tell us where they were developed?"

"Nothing Sir, the photos are just photo-copies of the originals and could have been made anywhere, I doubt if the originals would have gone to a High Street developer, otherwise the police would no doubt have been informed. They would have been made in some seedy back room, in some perverts home."

"Ok, what about the envelope the photos were in?"

"Again no luck, just an ordinary standard manila A4 envelope which can be purchased from any High Street Post Office or Stationery Store, anywhere in the country."

"Ok, if you do get anything else let me know at once. Do you know if D.C. Poole's been here today? He was supposed to call here this morning, to see if your lads had anything further from the second murder scene."

"Yes, he was in earlier, he left about 10 minutes before you arrived, you can check with those two over there, that's who he was talking to. They'll tell you if he took anything with him."

"Hi guys, I believe you've been talking to D.C. Poole, did you have anything for him?"

"As a matter of fact we did. We had a good look at that service road to the farms, the road that runs parallel to the river for a short way. We found a set of car or van tyre prints, that looks like they belong to a car that parked at the spot near to where we believe Preston fell, or was pushed into the river."

"We also found foot prints leading from where the vehicle was parked, up the banking, and right up to were we think Preston was killed."

"Could you tell if the footprints were male or female?"

"Both Sir, male and female. We couldn't really have missed the woman's prints, it looks like she was wearing stiletto heels."

"Were the prints good enough to make plaster casts?"

"Yes, well some at least, D.C. Poole has taken copies of the prints with him."

The search at Rothwell's home was well underway, by the time Jones and Moore arrived. Mrs. Rothwell was also present, having witnessed the arrival of S.O.C.O. from the window of her neighbour's home where she staying until she was allowed access to her own home again.

Jones explained he wanted special attention given to Mr. Rothwell's bedroom, "that's the one on the right, at the top of the stairs."

Two cups of coffee and half a packet of biscuits later, "Sergeant Jones, I think you may wish to take a look at this. We found this taped to the underside of one of the drawers in his bedroom." He handed Jones a black diary and then left the room to continue his search upstairs.

With gloved hands, Jones briefly flicked through the diary. He could see at once, that most of the pages had been left blank, although entries had been made at intervals throughout the book. Still in the plastic bag, where the diary had been placed by S.O.C.O. Jones handed the diary to Mrs. Rothwell. "Have you ever seen this before?"

"No Sergeant, I don't believe I have. In fact I'm damn sure I haven't. I didn't know my husband kept a diary, come to that, there seems to be a lot of things I didn't know about my husband. Even whilst he was in the army, I was always the one to remember birthdays and anniversaries etc."

"I take it from that, you keep a diary yourself?"

"Yes I do, but I don't fill it in every day, it's mainly used to put dates of birthdays etc. I do put some notes in, they act as memos, but not too many."

"Do you mind if I take your diary with me? I will make sure that it is returned to you in due course. I would like to compare dates between your diary and that of your husband."

"Take it by all means, if it will help you sort out all the sordid mess. All this is beyond me Sergeant, the muggings and all that money and now a diary. I honestly thought I knew my husband through and through, but it's obvious from all this, I don't. I've never seen so much money before, to think how we have struggled putting the kids through uni, if he wasn't already dead, I'd kill the bastard myself, sorry about that, I don't normally swear. I'm beginning to wonder just how long he's had all that money upstairs. I still can't believe its all illegal, there's just got to be a logical reason for it."

"Don't forget Mrs. Rothwell, he was caught red handed mugging prostitutes, and I can safely say that is illegal, can't you?"

"Yes I know, but it is just not like him, I know he was funny most of the time, but dishonest, I would never have thought that in a million years."

"Did your husband ever talk about his childhood days or how he got on at school?"

"Not often, although there was one incident with Christopher, that's our son when he was 13 or 14 years old that springs to mind. It was whilst we were up at Catterick in North Yorkshire, my husband was still in the army. Chris came home from school all covered in blood, he'd been badly bullied. When his dad came home and saw the state he was in he hit the roof. He ranted and raved about bullies always getting away with blue murder and it was about time someone should teach them a lesson and give them a piece of their own medicine. He demanded to know the names of the bullies, he said he would bloody well go out and kill the, believe me Sergeant Jones, at that moment I wouldn't have put anything past him. He went out for a drink at the local pub and when he returned, it was as if the previous incident had never taken place, after that, it was never mentioned again. Thinking back to that moment, that's when I did see a change in him, he became restless and started going on about leaving the army and getting back into Civvy Street. He had been training as an accountant in the army, but I was still surprised how easy it had been for him finding a job."

"I thought the army found him the job, but I believe he said he knew someone outside the army, who owed him a few favours and would be only too pleased to help him find a job. I must admit, I did think it was a bit strange at the time, how did he know someone well enough outside the army who would want to help him. He was never sociable with the army lads, so how he knew someone in Civvy Street really does amaze me. I have no idea who this someone was, but he must have helped, my husband was demobbed on the Friday and he started work on the following Monday."

"I noticed when I just skipped quickly through his diary, that he had quite a few meetings with somebody simply identified as 'B', or could it have been a place, have you any idea what or who 'B' may refer to?"

"Can I just have a look at his diary? I want o check something against my diary."

She flicked through both diaries; it didn't take her long to find what she was looking for.

"I've just checked all the appointments with 'B' against my diary. All the appointments with 'B' were made for when I was away at my mother's home. That's why I had no idea what was going on, whenever he wanted to get up to no good, he just waited until I was away. Now that's another thing, he never used to give my parents a thought or even the time of day, and then all of a sudden, his attitude changed. It was actually his idea, that since they were getting on a bit in age, I should see them more often and even go and stay with them for a few days each month. The devious sod. God I must be so thick."

It was as Jones took the diaries back from Mrs. Rothwell, that he detected a slight bulge on the rear cover of Mr. Rothwell's diary. It was only a slight bulge, but it is surprising how sensitive the human fingers can be. Still wearing a pair of plastic gloves, he carefully removed the dairy from the plastic bag and ran his fingers around the edge of the bulge. It was then that he noticed that part of the cover over the bulge wasn't perfectly stuck down. Taking a small penknife from his coat pocket, he proceeded to remove the lining that covered the bulge, until the culprit for producing the bulge was removed. In this case the culprit was a key.

He turned and showed the key to Mrs. Rothwell, "please don't touch it, but have you any idea what this key is for?"

"No, as far as I can tell, that's something else of my husband's which I haven't seen before. I didn't know about the diary, so there was no way I would know about the key."

"We've finished now Sergeant Jones, there's nothing more we can do here." "Ok, let's have your report ASP, I can't see why you cannot move back in here now Mrs. Rothwell, sorry for any mess we may have made."

"Don't worry too much about that, just keep me informed if you find anything else that so called husband of mine has done."

"I'll do my best, but it may be after we have finished our investigation, before I will be able to tell you anything."

Chapter 12

"For she's a jolly good fellow, for she's a jolly good fellow." It seemed to go on for ever and ever but eventually it did stop thankfully for Ann Buxton, who was becoming more and more embarrassed with every rendition. At six o'clock that morning when she jumped out of bed, to be welcomed once more with the sight of another fine summer's day on opening her bedroom curtains, did she in her wildest dreams, think anyone would make a fuss at work. All this, just because it was her last day at work.

It had been her intention to drop in at work, finish off any unfinished paperwork, tidy up her desk ready for the next occupant, say her goodbyes and leave without any fuss or commotion. However, it was obvious to Ann as soon as she entered her office that morning that someone else had other ideas on how her last day at the office was going to pan out. She never realised, that she was liked and respected enough to warrant such a retirement office party. Her work mates here at the Social Services Office, were always looked at, by outsiders, as being very staid and reserved and unable to let their hair down. Today, Ann knew that myth had been laid to rest, the empty wine and champagne bottles were a tribute to that. Instead of the customary sandwich and a cup of coffee for lunch, it was a full three course meal plus all the trimmings. On her return to the office, she had been swamped with presents, by that time, her delicate laced handkerchief was no more than a sodden piece of cloth. It was to be hoped, that no senior member of staff from Head

Office should make an unscheduled visit, or they could all be celebrating their last day at work. By 6.00 pm, everyone was much the worse for drink none more so than Ann, who had come to the realisation that there was no way she would be able to carry all her presents home. She would have to call back the next day and pick them up, when she would be sober enough to drive her car. The presents were all collected and taken to the storeroom, where they were locked away for the night.

After one of the most memorable days at work that she could remember, Ann began to make her way home. The weather was perfect, far too nice to be sat on a bus, besides, the fresh air would help to clear her head. Life now felt perfect, the weather was fine, the birds were singing and she had never been so content with life, retirement was to be the icing on the cake. So deep in thought, oblivious to the rest of the world and it's problems, that she was unaware she was being followed, had she been aware, she may not have been so happy with her lot.

Ann lived in a small tree lined mews. The trees were on both sides and had been planted in round plots which had been excavated out of the concrete road. There wasn't a footpath as such, the road stretching from the houses on one side of the mews to the houses on the opposite side. The area between the houses and the trees was used as the walkway, leaving the area between the trees, to be used by the few cars that used the mews. All the properties had built in garages with up and over doors for easy access.

Ann had only just closed her front door behind her, she hadn't even had sufficient time to remove her bright yellow lightweight summer jacket, when the door bell rang. She turned around wondering who on earth it could be, it was very rare for her to have visitors. She opened the door as far as the safety chain would allow and peered through the small three inch gap between the door and the door-jamb.

"Oh! hello."

Ann closed the door in order to remove the safety chain, then opened the door wide and invited her surprise visitor into her home.

The visitor walked passed Ann without uttering a word. It's been said on many occasions that the hand is quicker than the eye, and this time was no exception. As Ann turned her back on the visitor, so she could close the front door and put the safety chain back on, she felt the sharp point of a knife under her left shoulder blade and then momentarily became aware of an arm over her right shoulder. Just like Armstrong before her, she was dead before the knife sliced the flesh around her throat. The wound through the heart, had already accomplished the required effect, which was the demise of Ann Buxton.

There would be no more parties, the yellow summer coat would never be seen again in the mews, it had now in part turned orange, where it had been covered in red blood from Ann Buxton's throat wound. There would have been much more blood, but for the fact, that the heart had stopped pumping before the carotid artery and jugular vein had both been laid open for all to see. It wasn't a pretty sight, poor Ann didn't even have sufficient time to reflect on the most wonderful and now, the most devastating day of her life.

The killer pulled Ann's now limp and pitiful body away from the door, just sufficiently enough to allow it to be opened and an escape to be made. One quick look up and down the mews to check if the mews was clear of people, and the killer was gone, the front door being left closed, hiding the body of Ann Buxton.

Chapter 13

"Ok everybody settle down, let's have a bit of brainstorming, Jones you go first, share your worldly wisdom with us, it cannot be any worse than mine."

"What can I say Sir, we seem to be going round in circles. One minute we think we have the reason behind everything worked out, and then bang, something else happens and we are back to square one again. Take Armstrong and Preston, we now know they were killed by a woman, but according to Dr. Morgan, Rothwell was killed by a man. We also know from the owner of 'The Blue Lady' nightclub that it appeared that Rothwell was in the process of receiving a wad of money the night he was killed. If we didn't know that the first two were killed by a woman, I would have sworn Rothwell had killed them, and he was the blackmailer trying to cover up his tracks. If there is a connection between all three of the victims, then it must be something that happened a long time ago. Let's check with the Inland Revenue, they must have copies of their P45s or P60s, lets see if they ever worked for the same company, at the same time. The National Insurance people up in Newcastle may also be in a position to help. If we have two different killers, are they working together? I don't think so, and if that is the case, how did the copycat killer know how the first two had died? From the papers, no, he knew first hand. How? That's for us to find out later."

"So Jones, I take it you believe we have an informer amongst our mist?" "Not amongst our team Sir, I can't believe any of us would tell anybody about what we find. Before you started locking the door, any Tom, Dick or Harry could have walked in here."

"There is one very interesting thing that's come to light, we know a key was found hidden in the back cover of Rothwell's diary, now I have checked with the duty Sergeant, that the night Rothwell was arrested for mugging the prostitutes, the key in question, was fastened on his key ring when his belongings were checked in. So I have to ask myself, why did he need to have the key handy the night he did the muggings, but not on the night he was killed? He must have hid it in his diary immediately he was released from here. The others appeared to be a house key and his car keys."

"We've shown the key to one of the town's locksmiths, and he reckoned it looks like one of the keys used for the left luggage lockers at the bus station. It might also be a good idea to see if it fits Preston's locker at the Scout Hall, I know he had a padlock on it, but the locker does still have its own built-in lock. I am going to check with all the town's banks, and see if any of their security boxes use a similar key, just to be on the safe side."

"Very droll Sir."

"Since you raised the matter Jones, you and Moore make the checks with the Inland Revenue and the National Insurance people and see what, if anything they can tell us. You may as well check with the Motor Vehicle Licence Office at Swansea and the V.A.T office, somebody must be able to tie them together. Check their passports, if they have them, see if they ever went abroad at the same time as each other, and if they went to the same country."

"Baxter, I want you to call at Goodfellow's Accountancy Firm, by some stroke of luck, or it may just be another coincidence, it would seem that not only did Rothwell work for them but they just happen to be the Accountants for Armstrong Motors. Check if Rothwell every did the books for Armstrong Motors, if he did, then we might just have got our first positive link between them. However, whether that will help or not, is another one of things that only time will tell."

"The Super is back today after his short break, so he will be expecting his match report as soon as he sets foot back in his office. So if you want me, and you can't find me, you will know where I am. I don't know where he's been for the past few days, I wonder if he's brought me a present back? I doubt it. I'm going to try and see Kenneth Moss again, hopefully sometime this morning. With a bit of luck, I may be able to gather a little bit more knowledge about Armstrong's background. Surely they must have talked at some times about old times. Poole, you can come with me."

For some particular reason, Cline had taken a shine to young Poole. It may be that he reminded him of his own early days in C.I.D, full of eagerness and anticipation.

He was also aware that Baxter also got on well with Poole, at least she had never said anything to the contrary. Given the right kind of help, he believed Poole would make a good detective, time and experience would do the rest.

Cline was correct, he didn't get a present from Knowels, fortunately, at least that was Cline's first thought. His briefing with Knowels had only been underway for a matter of a few minutes, when it was interrupted by the duty Sergeant entering Knowels's office. "Sorry about this Super, but we have an important call at the custody desk for D.I. Cline."

"What's wrong with just transferring the call to my phone Sergeant?"

"I would normally Sir, but there's a fault with the phones, the engineers are sorting the problem out now."

Cline followed the duty Sergeant out of Knowels's office. "Any idea what the call's about?"

"I think it's from Dr. Morgan the M.O. He did say he wished to talk to you direct Sir." Lately, just the mention of the name Dr. Morgan sent shivers down Cline's spine, it was with baited breath he picked up the phone. "Cline here."

"Hello John, it's Jack, Jack Morgan, I think you would want to be down here right away, I'm at 21, Pinetree Mews. I'll hang on until you get here."

"Don't tell me we have another one Jack."

"I'll tell you when you get down here."

His hands were shaking, his legs like jelly, his stomach muscles tightened up and beads of sweat rolling down his face, "God will it ever end? There must be another one, or Jack wouldn't have called me."

"Are you ok Sir? You look like death warmed up."

"That's just the way I'm feeling at the moment Sergeant." At that Cline made his way back to the incident room to collect Poole.

"Poole, come on, change of plans, unless my gut feelings have got it all drastically wrong, I think we've got ourselves another murder victim."

The end of the Mews had been taped off and was being guarded against uninvited entry by two uniformed P.C.s. The tape was lifted to allow Cline's car access to the vicinity of number 21, where it parked close to a white screen that had been erected around the front of the house.

Jack Morgan was waiting for them on the other side of the screen.

"Ok Jack, tell me it's not what I hope it's not."

"I wish I could John, go and take a look for yourself."

"Do we have a name for the victim Jack?"

"Yes, Miss Ann Buxton. She's a social worker with the Social Services, well she was until yesterday when she retired. At least she won't have the worry of knowing whether her pension will be sufficient to live on. They had a leaving party for her yesterday, she left the party as far as anyone can tell, at about 6 p.m., give or take 30 minutes either way. She was a bit under the influence when she left, from all accounts, so were all her work mates. I'll know how much she's had to drink, when I have the results the blood and urine tests back."

"We aren't doing bad Jack, how many is that? Four bodies in about ten days, I think you are trying to get into the Guinness Book of records."

"Very good John, don't throw your abacus away, at this rate you might not have enough fingers to keep count."

"Oh! aren't you the witty one, I just hope it doesn't get any worse. Is there anything else you can tell me?"

"She was due back in at work this morning, after she had sobered up, not to work, but to pick up all the leaving presents that she had left behind last night. If nothing else, according to her work mates, she wasn't someone who changed her plans without good cause. So when she failed to call in at work to pick up her presents, they tried to contact her with no success. They were so concerned about her, mostly because of the large amount of booze she had taken in at the party, they sent one of the office girls over here to check up on her. As soon as she approached the house, she could see the bright yellow jacket on the floor through the glass of the front door."

"She tried to get in the house, but the Yale latch was on, so she rang the police. The rest you know. Are you ready to take a look at the body?"

"Lead the way Jack."

Cline and Poole followed Morgan into number 21.

Buxton was still lying in the same spot, where the killer had left her the previous day.

"I take it she died the same way as the others?"

"Just the same, stabbed in the back with the knife penetrating her heart, and then followed by the slicing of her throat. From what we can make out so far, she was facing the front door when she was killed, you can see the blood stain on the glass of the door, that would have been from the throat wound. The reason there is only a small amount of blood, is the same as in the other cases, the heart had stopped pumping. It looks like she was killed whilst she was either opening the door to let someone out, closing the door after letting someone in, or opening the door to let someone in. I don't believe in the latter, because that would mean the killer was behind her whilst she was opening the door for a caller. That would have been risky for the killer, to have a witness, would have been out of character and stupid."

"You know Jack, you should have been the detective on this case, and I should have been the M.O."

"There is no sign of a break in John, so I don't think the killer was already in her home waiting for her, I think it is like I just said, she let the killer in. Which then induces the question, did she know her killer? She still has her jacket on, I believe she had just got in from work, hadn't even had time to remove her jacket, when she had a visitor who she let in. Her work mate confirmed that Ann was wearing that Jacket when she left the office after the party. It all ties in with a time of death being at 7 or 8 o'clock last night. This is the first time the murder has taken place indoors. I hope this doesn't mean our killer is getting more confident, and here we are, absolutely no nearer to finding the killer."

"Thank you for that vote of confidence Jack, I needed to be reminded of that. It may just be that our killer is either getting careless, don't forget anybody could have seen the killer walking in the Mews, or they could have been in a hurry. Things could just be starting to turn our way."

"So do you think Miss Buxton is another blackmail victim Jack?"

"You should read your local papers more often John, it's surprising what little tit-bits one can pick up."

"God knows how they found out about the blackmail side of things, it certainly wasn't from any press release that we have given out." Cline turned to one of the S.O.C.O. "Have you got anything for me?"

"Yes Sir. If you look over here, you can see where the body's been dragged back away from the door, probably to let the killer out the front door. You can see the trace of blood on the floor and that could be a mistake by the killer. The killer had to walk in the blood in order to get out the door. You can clearly see the impression of a woman's shoe on the floor, between the body and the door. We've taken photos of the print and I'll see you get a copy as soon as possible. As we first thought, there are no signs of a break in. These Mews houses are actually back to back houses, so this is the only door leading to the outside."

"I want everything to be gone over with a fine tooth comb, accounts, tax forms, bank statements, diaries, phone records, in fact, anything that you think may be of any help to us. If you get anything let me know straight away."

It wasn't until Cline was leaving the house that he realised Poole was nowhere to be seen. He found him, discharging his breakfast of bacon and egg and diced carrots, (funny how most people seem to have a meal of diced carrots before they are sick), onto the base of one of the pine trees outside the mews cottage.

"Are you alright Poole?"

"I am now Sir, I suppose I should have expected that, but it's not every day you see a woman laid out with her throat sliced open."

"I don't know about that Poole, it seems to be a bit of a regular occurrence at the moment. Come on let's get back to the station, you can get some fresh food inside you, you'll feel a lot better then. You'd better get a good wash as well, you stink like a cesspit.

When you've had that wash, I'll see you in the canteen."

No sooner had he sat down at his desk, when the bellowing voice of Knowels could be heard reverberating along the corridor. "CLINE, MY OFFICE NOW"

"What the hell are you doing about these murders? I've just got back from a short break and I've got everybody on my back. How the hell did the press get all their information, sounds like you have a leak in your team? Then to top all that, I've just heard we have another body."

Cline had taken about all he was going to take. "You two-faced pompous prat, you sit there on your arse in this office, for hours on end, shuffling paper work backwards and forwards pretending to be busy. When in fact, you know as much about police work as you do about brain surgery, BUGGER ALL. You were the person responsible for all the press reports, you were so good at it you decided to take a short break right in the middle of the investigation. Since the press couldn't get hold of you, they obviously went elsewhere for their story. Just remember, now your father-in-law has retired, there's no one looking after your backside. The grapevine has it, that the first chance they get, your bosses will have you out of here faster than you can say 'Unemployed', if I were you I would keep my nose clean and my head down." The last thing Cline remembered, as he left Knowels's office slamming the door behind him, was the sheer stunned expression on Knowels's shocked face.

"God does that feel good or what? I've waited years to do that, I should have done that ages ago."

It wasn't very often that Cline got to eat in the canteen, and the plate in front of him, filled with all the ingredients of a full English breakfast, looked more than just a little appetising. This time, he knew his lunch would not be interrupted by the incompetent Knowels. Poole looked at Cline's lunch, "I think I might just give lunch a miss for now. What are we doing after lunch Sir?"

"We'll go and see Kenneth Moss and see if we can throw a bit more light on Peter Armstrong's past."

Jenny recognised Cline as soon as he entered the reception area. "I've already given my statement, there isn't anything else that I can tell you."

"That's quite alright Jenny it's not you that we've come to speak to, is Mr. Moss in?"

"Go straight up Inspector, you know your way now, I'll call him and let him know you are on your way up."

As they entered Moss's office, they were just in time to see him pick up a silver framed photo off his desk, and place it in one of the desk drawers.

"Please Inspector, take a seat. What can I do for you this time?"

"You could try telling the truth this time"

"I'm sorry about that Inspector. I knew Ruth and I were together at the Blue Lady night Club, which meant she couldn't have killed Peter. I just thought there was no reason for it to become public knowledge that Ruth and I were having an affair, it would only look like we had a motive for killing Peter."

"What makes you think that you and Ruth Armstrong are off the hook, why shouldn't you both still be my number one suspects?"

"Because, as I said before, we were together all night."

"Because Peter Armstrong is dead, the financial reward to his wife is more than sufficient reason for her to have employed someone else to do the dirty deed. She could also have been using you and your sister as her alibi, what a cosy affair."

"No way Inspector, no way."

"Ok Mr. Moss. I know about the insurance on Peter Armstrong's life and what Ruth Armstrong will profit from his death, but what about you?"

"What do you mean, what about me?"

"I would have thought, that with a successful business like you have here you would both have taken out Partner Protection Insurance. How much was that for?"

"I can't remember, in fact, I had forgotten all about that until you just mention it."

"Pull the other one Mr. Moss, I may look stupid."

"We were both insured for £250,000 each."

"So now it turns out that Ruth Armstrong is your alibi."

"Ok, let's change the subject. Did you know of anyone called James Rothwell or Neville Preston?"

"No, I've not even heard of them."

"What else can you tell me about Peter's past, other than what you have already told me?   I got the impression that Peter went straight into business as soon as he left school."

"As I told you before, we very rarely sat down and had a good old natter like mates usually do. From what I do know, I believe he started on a part time basis, at the same time, he was working for a pharmaceutical company as a rep, I suppose Ruth should be able to tell you more about that, he must have talked with her about his past."

"She did say that Peter didn't appear to have too many friends, were you ever aware of any of his friends?"

"I don't think anyone got close enough to Peter to ever get to know much about him. I would think Ruth, would be the best person to be asking those types of questions to."

"Did he ever say where he was born or where he lived as a child?"

"I know he went to school in Bolderdale, he didn't speak much about his parents. I remember that once, I did ask him if his father had ever helped him financially with starting up the business, he got very upset and said he would never take a penny or a brass farthing from his father, even if his life depended upon it. He told me never to mention it again, and so I never did."

"I think that's about all for now Mr. Moss, we'll show ourselves out, thank you."

Cline and Poole called in at the morgue on the way back to the station. "Are you sure you'll be alright? I don't want you being sick again."

"I'm ok now, it was just the shock of seeing her throat slit open."

"Good, then let's see what the Doc's got for us."

"If you spend much more time here John, they'll be giving you a desk next to mine."

"It's conclusive now, that Armstrong, Preston and now Miss Buxton were all killed using the same knives. Rothwell on the other hand, as we said before was killed with different knives, but made to look like the other murders. From all the evidence we now have, I would say Armstrong, Preston and Miss Buxton were all killed by a woman and Rothwell was killed by a man. Four murders, two murderers."

"Thank you Jack, you always make me feel happy, now I know for sure that I have two separate investigations but they are somehow connected."

"Come on Poole, let's go and get a breath of fresh air, I can't stand it in here any longer."

Chapter 14

"Morning all, Baxter, how did you get on at Goodfellows, or whatever they are called?"

"We spent five hours going through Rothwell's complete work load, from the day he started until the very last day he was at work. On no occasion did he work on Armstrong Motors' accounts. If Rothwell did know Armstrong, then the connections not at Rothwell's place of work, it must just be a coincidence."

"What did you come up with Jones?"

"I followed up the lead you got from Moss about the pharmaceutical company. I checked with the Inland Revenue and the National Insurance Offices and, sure enough, he worked in this area as a rep for a London firm called P.F.C. Pharmacy. I've arranged for their present rep for this area to call in the station today to see you. In fact he should be here in about thirty minutes. I've ask him to bring a record of all his customers, past and present in this area. I didn't actually speak to him, I spoke to someone at his head office in London, but they said they would contact the rep, no problem. One thing I didn't do and that was to get the reps name, so I suppose the rep may be a woman."

"Anything more about Preston?

"Again we've struck lucky Sir. Before Preston became a self employed taxi driver working from home, he used to work for the Social Services at, wait for it, a Children's home. That could be where the photos, we found in his locker at the Scout Hall, came from. At last Sir, we seem to be getting somewhere. It was during this time that he trained as a child welfare worker, he worked in children homes that provided short term care for children at risk or children waiting to be placed with foster parents. He did move about a bit from place to place, and department to department during his training, until he qualified and eventually he became the night shift manager at the 'Moorgate Children's Home' in Bolderdale. Although he was mainly on the night shift, he did occasionally fill in for the other shifts from time to time, covering for staff holidays and staff sickness."

"At last, we seem to have some kind of connection. We've got Preston connected to Social Services, Miss Buxton had just retired from Social Services and, with a bit of luck, Armstrong's employment with the pharmaceutical industry may have linked him with them somewhere along the line. Have we had any luck with the key found in Rothwell's diary?"

"I called at Bentley Sir, but as we thought, it didn't fit Preston's locker. The next stop is the left luggage depot at the bus terminal."

The office, in which Ann Buxton and her friends had had such a wonderful and unforgettable party, was now cloaked in a feeling of sadness and loss, the window blinds closed in respect. After Janet, the young office junior who had been sent on that fateful journey to check up on Ann Buxton, had told her harrowing story to the rest of the staff, even the male members unashamedly shed tears of grief.

The office manager now had a problem on her hands. What to do with all the presents which had been presented to Ann and were now in the office storeroom. After much discussion, it was decided that each person should take back the present which they had bought for Ann since she had lived alone and, as far as anyone knew, had no relatives for the presents to be past on to. Most however decided to donate the gift that they had bought, to charity .It was only after the presents had all been sorted that the office manage noted that there was still one parcel unclaimed. Since no one was able to claim the present, and there was no indication who it was from, it was decided to open the package to see if the contents could give us a clue..

The manager removed the red and white paper outer covering, to reveal a plain brown cardboard box, again there was still no indication who the donor was. She opened the top of the box, "what an unusual present" is all she could think to say, as she removed a ten inch tall cheap egg timer from within the cardboard box. It would have been ten inches tall but for the fact that it was broken in half and most of the sand had run down into the bottom of the box. From under the sand the manager could just see the corner of a piece of paper protruding upwards. She reached into the box and removed the paper, her hands began to shake. There was no name on the paper, but there was writing, writing that made the manager drop the paper onto the desk top as the cold sweat ran down her spine.

'THE SANDS OF TIME HAVE RUN OUT FOR YOU'

"Nobody touch it, don't touch a thing, I'm calling the police."

"Baxter you had better come with me, we've just had a call from a Mrs. Woodside, she's the office manager at the office where Miss Buxton worked. Apparently, something very odd has turned up at the office, something which she thinks we should see right away. Don't ask me what it is, I don't know. From what the duty Sergeant told me, she wouldn't discuss it over the phone and she sounded quite distressed."

Cline parked up in the Social Services car park and placed a Police sign on the windscreen. The car park was covered by a wheel clampers firm and they only need half an excuse to clamp the car, and that's the last thing he wanted right now.

He approached the receptionist and introduced himself.

"Mrs. Woodside is waiting for you Inspector, you'll find her on the tenth floor. I'm afraid you will have to use the stairs, the lifts are out of order again."

Cline took one look at the old man on reception. "I think he's ready for a Zimmer Frame. It's to be hoped that poor sod doesn't have to climb up ten flights of stairs or there'll be   another death at Social Services."

By the time they had reached the tenth floor, they were both sweating like stuffed pigs. It was one of those very hot sultry days when it was an effort just to stay awake. "The first thing we do when we get away from here is to go for a pint. I don't know about you Wendy, but I am absolutely knackered.

At the top of the stairs on the tenth floor, they were confronted with a set of double fire doors guarding the entrance to a long corridor, which serviced a number of different offices along its length. As they passed through the fire doors Cline remarked, "I'll bet you the first pint, that the office we want is right down at the far end of the corridor."

"Looks like I'm buying the first pint Sir."

They entered the door marked, 'Mrs. Woodside Office Manager'

They first entered into a small reception area, lightly furnished with three sit-up-and-beg chairs and a reception desk. Before he could press the bell push at the side of the frosted glass sliding window, a door to the side of the reception desk opened and a young girl's face appeared around the door jamb. You must be Inspector Cline, follow me please, you are expected. The door led into a larger than life open-plan office area.

"You wouldn't like to bet another pint that Mrs. Woodside's office or desk is at the far end of the office?"

"No thank you Sir, something tells me this is not my lucky day."

"Coward."

"Thank you June, you may go home now. On the way out leave a message for the cleaners to leave this floor until they hear from me."

"I've managed to clear the staff out of the way for the rest of the day Inspector, so we can talk in confidence."

"Good, now what is it that you thought so important, that you wanted me to come over here straight away?"

"It's this Inspector." She pointed to the egg timer and wrapping where they still lay on her desk. "After we discovered what was in the box, I decided it would be better if the police were to look at it. We've no idea who sent it, or when it was delivered, it's just a complete mystery to us all."

"So what's so unusual about a broken egg timer Mrs. Woodside?"

"By itself nothing Inspector, but with this note, you tell me." She then removed the note from her desk drawer, where it had been placed for safe keeping; with the hot weather all the office windows had been opened, and the last thing she wanted was for the note to have been blown out of the office window, before the police had looked at it.

"Since I unwrapped it, nobody has touched either the egg timer or the wrappings. I put the note in my drawer, but as you can see I used a pair of tweezers to do so."

"If you know of any of your office staff, or mail room staff that have touched any of this, I would like them to pop into the station to have their fingerprints taken, and that includes yourself of course."

" It's only to eliminate those prints from the ones we find on the package and egg timer etc. I can assure you, once eliminated, they will be destroyed and none of the prints will be kept on file. Are you sure you have no idea how or when the present arrived?"

"No Inspector, we didn't decide to open the presents until after lunch, and by then anyone could have walked in here without us knowing. Just a mo, with all what has happened, I had forgotten all about the phone call."

"What phone call?"

"During the party, reception down stairs rang up and said someone had left a parcel for Ann on the reception desk. I told the man on reception to send them up with the parcel. He said he couldn't do that, since he didn't know who had left it, he had just found the parcel when he returned from paying a visit to the gents."

"So who eventually brought the parcel up here? If the lift was out of order, I can't see the old man bringing it up ten flights of stairs, he would have kicked the bucket by the third floor."

"We don't know, unless the old man got the mail boy to fetch it up."

"Then you had better make sure he comes with you to the station, we will need to check his fingerprints anyway. Have you a spare box to put this lot in?"

"Yes, I should have one under my desk." Baxter carefully packed the present, along with the wrappings into the box ready to take to the forensic lab.

"What type of cases did Ann Buxton work on?"

"As you can imagine Inspector, having worked within the Social Services ever since leaving school and reaching retirement age, she had worked in a great number of different departments. For the first few years she worked in the office for Foster Parents and then in the Child Protection Department. During the past few years she worked in the Department for the sick and disabled."

"Would you say, that the type of jobs that Ann became involved with, would put her in a position, which would make people dislike her sufficient enough to want to kill her?"

"God Inspector, I know our job isn't always very easy or straight forward and, we do quite often get bad press, but whether that would be sufficient enough to incite someone to murder, I very much doubt it."

"Naturally, with it being only a short time since Ann's death, we have no idea why she might have been killed. Not withstanding your belief, that her death is not work related, I cannot dismiss it off hand. Having said that, it would be of great help to us if we could look at Ann's work files, or whatever you like to call them here."

"We call them case files Inspector. There is no way without a court order, that I could let you take the files out of the office, we never know when we need them. However, trusting that whatever you find will be kept to yourselves, other than what is required for your murder inquiry, and since this is to find out who killed one of our own, I have no objections to you looking through the files, here in the office. That way, if we need the files in a hurry they will still be where we can get hold of them at a moment's notice."

"That will do for now, thank you; first things first though, we must get this package to our lab boys. We will be in touch again, right now we have to tackle those stairs, at least we will be going downhill."

"You wouldn't believe it would you Wendy, now we are going down, the blasted lifts are working again, at least we'll get to those pints you're going to buy that much quicker."

Thirsts quenched, spirits raised again, they arrived at the lab in far better condition than they did on the tenth floor at the Social Security Office.

"Glad to have you back Sir."

"Believe me young man, I wouldn't be here if I didn't have to be. Is there any chance you could check this lot while we wait?" Baxter placed the parcel on one of the desks. "Fingerprints would do for a start, it really is very important."

"It always is with you Inspector, I'm pretty well busy at the moment but I'll see what I can do this time, but I don't want you thinking you can make a habit of it."

"That's great thanks."

"You two go and get yourselves a drink in the canteen upstairs and I'll see you back in here, in say, one hour's time."

The hot drinks were in contrast to the cold beers they had just downed thirty minutes previously, but they were still more than welcome.

"At last Sir, it is beginning to look as if we have a link between the victims, something to do with the Social Services."

"Don't forget Wendy, I don't believe Rothwell is connected to the other murder victims, there's certainly no indication that he had any connection with the others, or even with the Social Services. I don't wish to say too much at the moment, but I am sure we will find Rothwell's killer a lot nearer to home than the other killer."

"Why makes you think that Sir?"

"Somebody must have leaked the story to the Press, and I am in no doubt it wasn't anyone from our team. However Wendy, from what we, or should I say, what I found out at Rothwell's old school, I have a jolly good idea who killed Rothwell. At the moment though, I don't have any sound motive or proof to support my beliefs, although I feel that revenge has a large part to play, somewhere in this convoluted plot."

"I wish you would let me in to what you found at Rothwell's old school. I'm sure if the head master had said something significant, I would have picked up on it, unless of course, it was something you saw in the school register, which I didn't get the opportunity to look at."

Again, that little trait of Cline's showed itself, as he winked at Baxter at the same time as he touched the side of his nose with his right index finger.

"Christ Sir, if I understand you correctly, you believe that someone from our station killed Rothwell? I hope we are all safe Sir?"

"You are Wendy, don't worry about it. Just keep you mouth closed until I get the evidence I need, then everybody will know, this is just between you and me. When I'm ready Wendy you will be the first to know who it is."

"At least I think it must be a man Sir, since it was an all boys' school."

"Maybe, maybe not. Right now let's get back to the lab and see if the lads have anything for us."

"We've managed to lift two lots of prints off the wrapping paper, one set off the egg timer and one set off the paper with the writing on it, I would say the writing was done with a word processor, I'm sorry that's all I've got for you."

"From the limited number of prints that we have managed to lift, I would be very surprised if they don't belong to the staff at the Social Services, I'll let you know after we have checked all the office staff. We also did an E.N.S.A. test on the note paper, to check if there were any indentations from material that was written before the note with the egg timer we may just have got lucky, but there was nothing. Apart from the writing on the paper, the rest of it was blank and the paper was just ordinary A4 size plain paper, sold by the thousand every day. If we had a killer, then maybe we would be able to match the paper to any found in their home."

"What did you make of the egg timer?"

"Not much Sir, It's just one of the cheap egg timers found at most seaside resorts such as Blackpool or Scarborough. I doubt if it was ever used as an egg timer, in this case, I think it was sent just to make a point and send a shiver down the spine of the victim."

It was only when they had got back into the car that Cline remembered he was supposed to be back at the station interviewing the Rep from P.F.C. Pharmacy.

"Wendy, when we get back to the station, you chase up the fingerprints from the Social Service people and get them over to the lab boys for comparison as quick as you can. Meanwhile I'll check and see if the Rep has turned up."

"I'd forgotten all about him Sir."

"Sorry I'm late Serg, I believe you might have someone waiting for me?"

"Yes Guv, he was about to give you up for dead. I'll get one of the lads to take him to your office. That will give you a couple of minutes to get yourself sorted out."

"Thanks Sergeant."

"I'm sorry I've kept you waiting, but it's been one of those days again. I'm afraid no one has told me your name. I'm Inspector Cline by the way."

"I'm John Pond, don't worry about the delay Inspector, I'm self employed and, as long as I fill my quota, there's no problem. I hope this may be of help to you Inspector." Pond reached into his brief case, removed a sheet of paper and handed it over to Cline.

"I think that will help, it's a brief outline of Armstrong's short stay at P.F.C."

"I see from this list Armstrong used to call at hospitals, nursing homes, and residential homes etc. Did he ever call on children's homes?"

"Yes, he did Inspector, they are listed on the other side of the sheet."

Cline turned over the sheet of paper and scanned the list, his heart missed a beat, when one particular name stuck out from amongst the rest. 'Moorgate Children's Home."

"Why would he be calling on Children's Homes?"
"Why not Inspector, children get cuts and bruises, they become sick, they use bandages and dressings, just like anyone else. We supply a very comprehensive range of medical appliances and surgical equipment, as well as drugs. The main orders are usually for antiseptic creams, bandages, sterilizers and scissors, all the things that you would expect in a first aid room."

"When did Armstrong work for P.F.C.?"

"About sixteen years ago or thereabouts, give or take a year a two either way." "I take it I can keep this list?"

"By all means Inspector, that's the reason I brought it here."

"Thank you Mr. Pond, you've been a big help, I'll get someone to show you out, I've kept you from work long enough."

At last, Cline had something to be happy about, he now had the first conclusive connection between Armstrong, Preston and Buxton, that is if Buxton had had dealings with the home. Cline felt she must have, since she had been involved with children. First thing tomorrow morning, he would contact Social Services and check.

D.C. Poole was trembling like a frightened child. He had been trying to pluck up the courage to ask Samantha out for a date, ever since the first time he had laid eyes on her in the staff canteen. Now he was face to face with her he was lost for words, he could feel the heat in his cheeks and, he knew by now that his face would be as red as a freshly cut beetroot, it was the fear of being rejected that was the source of his embarrassment.

After all, why would a girl as beautiful Samantha wish to go on a date with him when there were hundreds of other, far better looking chaps around for her to take her pick from. By now, his legs and arms felt just like jelly, as he tried to mouth her name. "S…S…Samantha, w…will you come out with me tonight for a meal, don't worry I'll pay." There I've said it, she's bound to say no. The relief that he felt, having managed to get his question out was so strong he didn't hear Samantha's reply. "Hello! anyone in there……?" She gently tapped him on his temple. The cool touch of her finger brought him quickly back to his senses. "Didn't you hear me? I said yes, I will be pleased to go out with you tonight. What time would you like to pick me up?"

"Say, eight o'clock at your place?"

"Yes, that's fine, I'd better give you my address or I'll be waiting all night for you. I take it you have your own car?"

"Yes, it's only an old 'Uno' but it gets me safely from A to B with the minimum of fuss."

"Don't worry about it, I don't like men with flash cars they can't afford to run. I'll see you at eight o'clock at my place."

Before he could utter another word, she had gone, never in his wildest dreams did he think she would have said yes to his invitation, so sure she would refuse him, he hadn't been to the cash machine for any money. Three pounds fifty pence wouldn't get them very far.

It was exactly eight thirty p.m. when Samantha and Poole walked into the 'Captain's Table Restaurant'. Samantha looked stunning in a short green velvet dress, green high heel shoes and the finishing touch being a matching hand bag. Poole could only pinch himself on his thigh, just to make doubly sure, that he wasn't dreaming.

Samantha looked at her menu, "Have you been here before? Do you know what the food is like?"

"No, this is my first time, so I have no idea what the food is like. I know it always looks busy, so I can only assume it must be fairly good."

"I would have thought you would have been here many times, with your mates or girl friends after a night on the town."

"I've never been one for going out with the lads, and I have always been shy in asking girls out for a date, you've no idea how long it's taken me to pluck up the courage, to ask you out."

"I'll let you into a little secret Micky, by the way, which do you prefer, Micky or Mick?"

"Mick's ok."

"Ever since I first saw you I have been hoping you would ask me out."

"There I was worrying myself sick, I felt sure you would turn me down."

The meal went well, and the time seemed to fly away. The conversation flowed as easily as the wine, it was as if they had known each other for years. It was eleven thirty by the time they arrived at the cheese and biscuits, never had he spent so long having a meal."

"How are you getting along with Mary White? I believe you're helping her out for a while?"

"She's o.k. I believe she's had a rough time of things lately, she's just lost her mother after nursing her for ages. From what she has told me, she has had it rough for most of her life, since her father left home when she was about eight years old, her mother had a break down and Mary had to go into care for a short time. Now that her mother's gone, she said the only company she now has, is the pet parrot, which

I suppose is a bit sick really. I mean, fancy only having a pet parrot to keep you company at nights. It must be a blessing for her to go out to work, at least she gets the opportunity to talk to different people.

The evening had passed far too quickly for Micky's liking, it hardly seemed five minutes since he'd been standing here on the door step, ringing the bell to summons Samantha. Here he was again, this time to take her home. As she placed her door key into the latch, she turned and thanked Mick for a wonderful evening, and then, taking him by complete surprise, she kissed him lightly on the lips. "I won't ask you in, it's getting very late and we've both got to be at work early in the morning, I should say this morning. We must do this again Mick, but don't wait so long next time before you ask me. Good night."

She turned towards her home and then disappeared through the door, leaving Micky standing on the porch, wondering if tonight had ever taken place. He knew he would have to take some stick from the lads at the station, but what the hell, he was the one who was going out with her, not them.

As he walked into the office that morning he was in seventh heaven.

Chapter 15

"Well Jones, how did you and Moore get on yesterday? Did you manage to have any luck with Rothwell's key?"

"Yes Guv, we checked with the left luggage depot at the bus station and struck gold for once. The key fits left luggage locker No. 31, it would be nice if S.O.C.O. find any identifiable prints, especially a set from Rothwell."

"Good, I'll be over at the Social Services again later on, I need to have another word with Mrs. Woodside. Baxter, I'll see you in my office as soon as we have finished here."

"Close the door Wendy and lock it."

"Baxter looked at Cline, this was a first, never before had she been asked to lock the door behind her and for no logical reason that she could think of, she began to feel guilty."

"It's alright Wendy, you can take that worried look off your face, you haven't done anything wrong. It's just that I don't want to be interrupted by someone barging in on us. Whatever I tell you, or show you in the next few minutes, is between you and me only, and I mean you and me, because if I am wrong and it gets out before I can prove anything, my career on the force could well be short lived."

Cline removed a piece of paper out of his desk drawer and wrote something on it before passing it over, face down to Baxter.

"Remember that name you were so intent on knowing about, the one in the school register, well that's it. No! don't look at it yet, wait until I tell you. When you see the name, don't repeat it, remember, walls have ears in this place. When you leave here, I want you to get a court order, to check the bank accounts for the past twelve months of that person whose name I have put on that piece of paper."

"How will I know at which bank the accounts are held at Sir?"

"I'm not one hundred percent sure Wendy, but check with the Post Office Giro Bank, I believe the Head Office is at Bootle on Merseyside, but I could be wrong, I'll leave that with you to sort out. Now you can look at the piece of paper."

Wendy turned the sheet of paper over and silently read the name. Her face went ashen and her limbs began to tremble." You cannot be serious Sir? Can you?"

"I'm afraid I've never been more serious about anything in my whole life. I still don't know why, and that is the reason only you and I must know. We've got to be one hundred

percent sure before we go public with this."

"If what you say is correct Sir, I can understand why you want to keep a tight lid on this, but why tell me now if you still have no proof?"

"Because I need someone that I can trust implicitly to make certain enquiries for me, and not say anything to anyone else."

"You've no fear on that score Sir, but if we are wrong.....?"

"Not we Wendy, ME. You are only following my orders. I just needed to tell someone and you seemed to be the right person, in one way, I just hope I am wrong."

"Haven't they repaired that damn lift yet?" It was one of those rhetorical questions that required no answer, especially since there was a large, 'Lift Out Of Order' sign stuck to the wall next to the lift door.

Mrs. Woodside had already prepared Ann Buxton's case files and had placed them on her office floor. Because of the vast number of files, the floor was the most logical place to arrange them.

"I hope you don't think I am interfering Inspector, but I came into the office very early this morning and sorted out Ann's files. I've made a list of all the places and departments with which Ann had dealings."

"No that's very good of you Mrs. Woodside, anything that saves me time and trouble is much appreciated."

Cline scanned the list until his eyes came to rest on the one name he had been looking for, 'Moorgate Children's Home'.

"The phone on Mrs. Woodside's desk rang out.

"It's for you Inspector."

Cline took the phone from Mrs. Woodside. "Hello Cline here."

"D.C. Jones here Sir. Goodfellows the Accountants have just called, they want to see you urgently. They wouldn't say what it was about, but insisted that you get over to their office at once."

"Couldn't you have seen to it Jones?"

"I said I would Sir but they said they would only talk to you."

"Ok Jones, leave it with me, I'll sort it out."

Cline passed the phone back to Mrs. Woodside. "I'm very sorry but I'm going to have to leave you. With a bit of luck, with what I've seen on your list, I may not have to trouble you any further."

Alex Goodfellow was waiting for Cline when he arrived at the reception desk.

"You look worried Mr. Goodfellow?"

"Not worried Inspector, just concerned."

"I think you had better tell me, what it is that concerns you enough to send out a panic call for me?"

"I'll wait till I get to my office."

It was only after they were both seated in Goodfellow's office, that Alex Goodfellow started to speak.

"Since the death of Rothwell we've had to re-arrange the work load of the rest of the staff and, in order to do that, we had to empty Rothwell's filing cabinet."

"So why should that be any concern to me?"

"Because Inspector, after we had emptied the filing cabinet, we decided to move it to the other side of the office. When we moved it we found this on the floor, it must have been hid under the bottom drawer of the cabinet. I've no idea just how long it could have been there but, from the cleanliness of the envelope, I can't believe that it has been there for very long."

"So what's so special about an envelope?"

"Here take a look for yourself Inspector, it's what is written on the envelope that should really interest you." Cline took the envelope from Goodfellow and then read the address on the outside."

'To the police in case of my sudden death or disappearance.'

Using his handkerchief instead of gloves, Cline placed the envelope into a plastic bag and then into his pocket. "Thank you Mr. Goodfellow, I won't open the letter now, I'll wait until I get it back to the station. If you turn up anything else, you know where I am."

All the way back to the station, Cline could feel the letter burning a hole in his jacket pocket.

At last he was seated at his desk, his office door locked and the letter laying there on his desk in front of him. Now donning a pair of gloves, he carefully opened the envelope using a letter opener, so as to cause as little damage as possible. He must have been sat there for at least five minutes with the letter in his hand, not daring to read it for fear of what it may reveal although in his own mind, he couldn't help but feel that the letter would only confirm his so far, unsubstantiated theory.

He withdrew the letter from within the envelope, opened it out and laid it on the desk in front of him. That was the only way he could stop his hands from shaking the letter, he was so wound up. The first thing that struck him was the neatness of the writing. It was obvious that the letter hadn't been written in haste, and a large amount of forethought had probably gone into it.

'To Whom It May Concern'

With luck, this letter will never see the light of day. If on the other hand, it is now being read, then it means all the years of mental anguish and unrelenting desire to gain my revenge, have been in vain.

The anguish and desire for revenge began many years ago, September 1969 to be precise, when as a young teenager, my family moved to Bolderdale. Right from the very first day that I attended Bolderdale Comprehensive, I was subjected to the most systematic bullying from the older boys and, in particular by the so called leader of the gang, who for no apparent reason, had taken an instant dislike to me.

Whether my accent had anything to do with it, I'll never know, not that I talked posh you understand, I just didn't have that Yorkshire Accent which the other lads seemed to have.

At that time drugs, namely cannabis resin, were starting to appear on the scene with regular frequency. The leader of the gang, a boy nicknamed 'Biff' turned out to be the local drug pusher, for want of a better description.

First of all, he would force the younger lads to hand over their pocket money or dinner money in exchange for drugs, and then, made sure they used the drugs in order to get them addicted. Then they would be only too happy to hand over their pocket money.

I was determined that there was no way I was going to hand my money over to him and his gang of thugs. It was then that, I learnt that if one was to have principles, then it was usually at a cost. In my case the cost was almost daily beatings. Things eventually came to a head, not the head teacher I'm afraid to say, one day in January 1970 when, intending to show all the other lads who had plucked up the courage to defy him, Biff decided to teach me a lesson that I would not forget, and at the same time set an example for the others. That was when I received my free lesson in pain therapy, I also received several days bed and breakfast at the expense of the Health Service in the care of St. Andrew's Hospital.

The final beating, that finally hospitalised me, took place in the play area of Bolderdale Comprehensive School. As I lay on the concrete footpath which surrounded the school pavilion, on that cold, wet wintry day in January 1970, I swore two things to myself. One, I would never forget Biff's face, no matter how much it may alter with age, and two, one day I would seek him out and take my revenge.

After a good number of years in Her Majesty's Armed Forces, the events of that January afternoon began to fade somewhat, they say time heals all wounds. Then there was a bullying incident involving my son at his school, and all the old memories and mental scars returned with a flourish, that's when and why I decided to leave the forces and get myself a job in civvy street.

I spent quite a lot of time in Bolderdale, looking for property and work and, it was during one of those visits that whilst I was walking through the main shopping centre, who should I see walking towards me as bold as brass, but Biff. He had changed somewhat, but it was his cold eyes that gave him away. He didn't recognise me, it was only after I introduced myself and his face lost all it's colour, that he realised his past had come back to haunt him. It wasn't too long before he had arranged a job interview for me, anything to try and keep me quiet, by now, I had started to blackmail him. I had found out that he was a serving member of the police force, and any reference to his activities during his school days would not do his career any favours. I never understood how he got into the police force, I would have thought his teenage history would have been recorded on files somewhere. Now I had found him, it was my turn to make him suffer, and suffer he would.

Tonight I have made arrangements to meet him at the 'Blue Lady Night Club'. I don't believe he has too much money left now, he's been leaving me £400 every month in a locker at the left luggage office at the town's bus station, for the past several months. I'm meeting him tonight on the pretence that this will be the last payment. I want to see the look on his face when I tell him I lied and the payments would have to continue. His last drop at the bus station was £100 short and there was a short note with the money saying he had wanted to make a one-off final payment of £3000, the note also said he had arranged a bank loan in order to raise the £3000.

Just for the record, Biff was the one who suggested that I could make quite a lot of easy money, mugging the Toms in Turpin Road. He said they would never complain and so I would never get caught. He probably thought if I had another sure way to make some easy money I might just leave him alone. No way, to start with it was never about money, it was about making him suffer, but as the money began to pile up I did become greedy.

213

Since you are reading this note I won't be needing the money anymore, will I?

One of these sheets of paper is the note he left me in the left luggage locker, you should be able to get a good set of prints off it.

Please tell my wife and children that I really love them and I'm sorry for any distress that all this might have caused them. Oh! I almost forgot, Biff's real name....you know him as 'SUPERINTENDENT KNOWELS'.

The letter was simply signed Peter James Rothwell

(Jimmy)

Cline sat there in silence, hardly daring to believe what the contents of Jimmy's letter had just revealed. His emotions were a mixture of pleasure because it appeared that, at least one of the murders had been solved, and deep sadness that one of his fellow officers had brought the Police Force into disrepute.

Cline put the letter, along with the note from Knowels to Rothwell back into the envelope and locked it safely away in his desk drawer. It was only now that his emotions were changing to one of anger, not at Knowels or Rothwell, but at himself as he remembered the day at the café in the town centre, when Poole saw Knowels coming out of the Post Office.

Then there was the day Baxter at the Bus Station, had seen Knowels near to the left luggage office.

And to top it off, the sudden few days Knowels had taken off work at the time Rothwell was murdered. Had he slipped up?, or was it only with hindsight, that the facts now started to make sense.

Still thinking aloud. Well, it must be done. He reached for his phone and, using a direct line to the outside, this was one conversation he couldn't afford to be overheard by anyone at the station, he rang the Chief Constable. Five minutes later they had made an appointment to meet.

"Now then John, you were very brief on the phone, but from what I can make out it sounds very serious. In one sense I hope it is, I've had to cancel an important meeting with the Police Liaison Committee to accommodate you. You didn't say too much on the phone, in fact you really didn't say anything, you didn't even say who you were talking about."

"I know Sir, I tried to keep things to a minimum on the phone, you can never tell if you have a crossed line or not. It's not good Sir, in fact, to put it mildly it's bloody bad."

Slowly, and trying not to show any emotion one way or another, Cline reported the events of the past few days, cumulating with the letter from Rothwell. He then sat back and awaited the Chief's reaction.

He could see the droplets of sweat slowly running down both sides of the Chief's ashen face, as he read Rothwell's letter. The Chief jumped up out of his chair, thumping his desk at the same time, "Damn it John, we are going to be the laughing stock of the whole police force. It would appear that, we are not satisfied with the fact that our crime detection and clear up rates are probably the worst in the country, but now our own senior officers are going on the streets committing murder, you couldn't make this up".

"Sir, after I arrest Knowels, he'll be wanting a senior officer to be present at the interview. Who do you suggest?"

"Don't you worry yourself about that John, I will only be too happy to be in on this one.

Between you and me John, I have been waiting for this moment, to get rid of him for years, but God forbid, I never wanted it to be for anything like this."

"It reflects so badly on the rest of us. From what you have said, I still can't believe he was ever admitted to the force in the first place. I will come with you when you make the arrest, I don't want any piffling technicalities being used as an excuse for an improper arrest."

"Who else knows about this John?"

"Only WDS Baxter Sir. I thought it best to keep it between us for now. I didn't want Knowels picking rumours up from the grapevine and do a runner before I got a chance to get my hands on him."

"Good."

"If you don't mind Sir, I'd rather not make the arrest just yet, I'm expecting some further information within the next couple of hours or so. The more ammunition we have at our finger tips when we interview Knowels, the better I'll feel."

"That will suit me fine John, it will give me time to clear my diary and get things sorted out at this end. I'll see you in your office in a couple of hours time and, remember John, not a word to anyone, when the shit hits the fan, I don't want it falling anywhere near us."

Baxter arrived at the station at the same time as Cline. "Wendy, not a word, my office straight away."

"Now then Wendy, remember no names out loud. How did you get on with the Post Office?"

"I spoke to the manager and asked if they held an account for the person in question. At first he was reluctant to help until I explained to him the seriousness of my enquiry and, at this stage, I didn't wish to see any accounts, I thought I would move forward one step at a time. They do hold an account for him, I'm almost sure it's who we are after." Baxter wrote the name down on a piece of paper Victor Knowels. There were other similar sounding names, but none spelt the same. Once I knew there was an account in existence, I arranged a court order, which I faxed over to the Post Office Giro Head Office. I've been on the phone to them to check that the faxed court order will suffice, they said they should really have the original. So I've actually been over to Bootle and back on the back of a Police motorcycle to present the court order and collect the accounts. I've never been so frightened in my life." Wendy passed Cline a brown envelope.

"Anything useful been happening while I've been away?"

"You could say so." Cline briefed Baxter with the details of Rothwell's letter, and his meeting with the Chief Constable. "At least there will be no doubt now Sir, especially if the bank statements back up everything."

"Ok, let's take a look at those accounts and see if they us help in any way." Cline opened the envelope and took out a copy of Knowels's bank statement. He placed the copy on his desk so they could both read it. "There you are Wendy." Cline pointed to a number of entries showing that each month there was a withdrawal of £400.

"According to Rothwell's letter, Knowels was about to hand over £3000 as a last, one off payment, there was no way Knowels could afford that, unless he had other savings tucked away somewhere. As you can see for yourself, the account is almost empty, the balance is only £27.97p. It's easy to see why Knowels would want to get rid of Rothwell.

Before the regular £400 per month withdrawals began, the account looked quite healthy with a £5000 plus balance. Something else crossed my mind earlier on, when Knowels found out that Rothwell had been pulled in over the muggings in Turpin Road, he must have been shitting himself, worrying what he might say during his interview with us. Don't forget it was at Knowels's suggestion, that Rothwell started the muggings, so for one reason or another, he had to get rid of Rothwell. He must have been praying that Rothwell would be released from custody in time to keep the appointment at the Blue Lady Night Club. You know Wendy, it's ironical really, if the Chief Constable hadn't been getting all that stick from his golf buddies about the prostitutes, and then putting Knowels under pressure, to pressurise me to clear it up, Rothwell would never have been caught. Knowels must have thought he could get rid of Rothwell, before we actually caught up with him. I cannot understand though why Knowels just didn't warn Rothwell off."

"That's easy Sir, I take it the only way Knowels could contact Rothwell was through the left luggage locker. The last payment of £400 out of his account, was three days before the surveillance was set up at Turpin Road, Knowels would have to wait until his pre- arranged meeting at the Blue Lady. It does seem however, that he had already decided to get rid of Rothwell, because there is no sign of Knowels having the £3000 for the so called final payment."

"That's a good point Wendy, I suppose we may never know the true, whys and wherefores of this case. For instance, I cannot understand why Knowels couldn't find out where Rothwell lived, unless he didn't want to give anyone cause to be suspicious."

"Don't forget Sir, Knowels probably only knew of his Christian names from their old school days." "Don't forget Wendy, we believe Knowels got Rothwell his job at the accountants, so one way or another he must have known, or could quite easily have got to know, whatever he needed to know about Rothwell. Anyway it is all academic now. The cut throat murders must have been the real spark that gave Knowels what he thought was the perfect way to get rid of Rothwell, and put the blame on someone else. I think he was the one to leak the information to the press, that way, if Rothwell's death couldn't be attributed to the 'Cut Throat killer', at least it could be put down to a copycat killer. It's all starting to make sense now. No doubt he would realise we would know eventually that we had more than one killer, but pinning Rothwell's murder on him, would have been very difficult without any kind of motive, or anything to point us in his direction."

The phone on Cline's desk rang out, bringing their meeting to an abrupt conclusion.

"Yes!"

"The Chief Constable's waiting for you in the canteen Sir. He said you were expecting him, I wish you had told us he was expected Sir, he caught us all having a cuppa on duty."

"Sorry about that Serg, tell the lads not to worry about it, the Chief won't even have noticed, he's got other, much more important things on his mind at the moment. I'll tell you all about it later on."

"Ok Wendy, let's go and get it over with."

Cline made the introductions.

"Baxter, that rings a bell, didn't we meet once before, wasn't it at one of the Police Federation Dinners?"

"About three years since Sir."

"By the way John, I hope your lads don't make too much of a habit of drinking tea and coffee whilst on duty, like the uniform lads. I'll have to have a word with them later."

"Don't worry about that Sir, I'll have a word with the duty Sergeant as soon as I get a minute."

Cline and Baxter had only just sat down at the table when the Chief stood up. "I don't think we should put this off any longer, do you? Let's go and get the son of a bitch."

As they drew up to the front of Knowels's home, they could see his car parked on the drive. Three times they knocked on the front door, to no avail. By now the Chief was visibly angry, he turned to one of the uniformed PCs. "Get that front door opened NOW."

As the door succumbed to the weight of the sledge hammer, it flew open giving a clear unobstructed view through the hallway to the kitchen at the rear of the house. Cline was first into the hallway, he could see Knowels in the kitchen, suitcase in hand and about to leave by the back door, unfortunately there was nowhere for him to go, the back door was locked, with the key nowhere in sight.

He realised there was nothing he could do now, the game was up as far as he was concerned. Then his mind started racing, what the hell am I thinking about, there's no way they can connect me to Rothwell's murder, I didn't even know his name until after he was picked up for the muggings. I'll just bear with it, and bluff it out.

"Going on another holiday Superintendent?"

"No, just getting ready to take some clothes to the dry cleaners. Anyway, what's the big idea of breaking my front door in? Did you think the house was on fire?"

"Nice one Knowels, it's no good trying to act all innocent." Cline read him his rights, at the same time, stepping forward and slapping Knowels's wrists into a pair of handcuffs behind his back.

"What do you think you are doing? Have you forgotten that I'm your senior officer?"

"Not any more you're not, not if I have anything to do with it." The Chief Constable had entered the kitchen to the surprise of Knowels. "And just in case you have forgotten, I am YOUR senior office. Cline show him our warrant."

Thirty minutes later, Knowels was safely locked up in one of the Police Station cells, by now the place was abuzz with rumours and innuendoes, the arrest had been so sudden that the station had been taken by complete surprise. The Chief Constable had taken every precaution in trying to keep the operation as tight as possible. The uniformed officers used at Knowels's home, had been specially seconded in from another station.

In fact, the first that Cline's station knew of Knowels's arrest,was when he was marched through the front door at the station. The arrival and entrance to the station had been arranged to cause Knowels as much embarrassment as possible.

Even before Knowels had left his home, he was shouting and screaming false arrest and was demanding that his solicitor, Reginald Bywater, should be waiting for him when he arrived at the station.

"How do you want to play this now John?"

"Knowels's solicitor hasn't arrived yet, so there isn't a lot I can do with him just at the moment. I suggest I let him stew for a time, while I go back to his home and see if the lads can find the murder weapons. I think he might have been so cock-sure that we would never make any connection between him and Rothwell, that he may have hung on to the murder weapons. Did you want to come with me Sir?"

"Try and keep me away John. I'm afraid you've got my company for the rest of the night."

They arrived moments before Mrs. Knowels. The look of astonishment on her face, as she was confronted with all the police personnel traipsing to and fro through her home, told the whole story as far as she was involved, it was obvious she had no idea what was going on, and had been taken completely by surprise.

The Chief Constable took her to one side, before she had time to enter her home, and explained in the best way that he knew the reason behind all the activity, but without causing her too much distress.

At the end of a five hours search of the house, garage and outbuildings, they had found nothing which could link Knowels to Rothwell's murder.

"Well John, unless he admits to murdering Rothwell, you are going to have to rely on Rothwell's letter and Knowels's bank statements. I'd feel a lot happier if we had the murder weapons, I guess he must have thrown them away after all. A good lawyer could soon discount Rothwell's letter as just sour grapes, don't forget, Rothwell's not here to confirm the contents of the letter John."

"If he was Sir, we wouldn't have had cause, to arrest Knowels in the first place."

"You know what I mean John."

They were in the car on their way back to the station, when Cline was struck by a strange idea. "Sir, if you wanted to hide something that you didn't want the police to find, and you knew they would leave no stone unturned, where is the one place you would think it would be safe to put it?"

The Chief Constable sat in silence for a few moments before answering. "Surely not John, he wouldn't, would he, not the station?"

"Why not?"

"The crafty sod, you seriously think he would hide the murder weapons back at the station, right under our very noses?"

"What better place to hide a tree, than in a wood. I'm only guessing Sir, but surely it's worth a try."

It took precisely thirty two minutes to completely search Knowels's office at the station, and again nothing.

"Well, that's it John, you will have to make do with what little evidence we have, and just pray that Knowels puts his hands up to the murder, not that I think for one minute that he will."

"Just one mo Sir, I don't normally believe in lucky coincidences, but remember where I told you Rothwell's letter was found. Baxter quick, give me a hand over here with this cabinet. Remove the bottom two drawers, and then we'll take a look at the bottom of the unit."

"But Sir, we've already looked in all the drawers of the filing cabinet."

"I know that Baxter, listen to what I said, take the drawers out and look at the bottom of the cabinet. When you checked the cabinet before, you only checked what was in the drawers, not what was underneath, this time, I want the drawers removed completely so that we can see into the bottom of the cabinet."

After the bottom drawers had been removed, Cline leant into the cabinet. The inside of the cabinet was a dirty brown colour, and the first look inside the filing cabinet almost missed the two pieces of brown masking tape one placed each side of the cabinet, between the bottom of the cabinet and the lowest drawer and close up to the front. With the lower drawer in place, and in the fully opened position, it would still have been impossible to see the masking tape.

Cline had almost missed the tape with the drawer removed, so there was no wonder they had missed them during the first search.

Now wearing a pair of gloves, he knelt down on the carpet and reached into the cabinet towards the masking tape, with great care he raised a corner of one of the pieces of masking tape until he could remove it completely from the side of the cabinet. He knew from the weight and shape of the package, that he had found what they had been desperately searching for. "YES,YES,YES, we've got him."

He then removed the second piece of tape from the opposite side of the cabinet, turned and faced the Chief Constable, then walked slowly over to the desk where he laid out the contents of the cabinet with the two pieces of tape still attached. There for all to see were one stiletto knife, one sharp kitchen knife and one key, similar to the one Rothwell had hid in his diary.

"Baxter get these over to the lab, I want them tested for prints straight away and the results back here as soon as they can. Tell them to check that there is only the blood of Rothwell on the knives, and no blood from the other victims. That would certainly complicate things, if we discovered blood from the other victims on the knives."

The Chief Constable turned to Baxter. "Tell the lab that I've sent the knives for testing, that should make them put a bit more effort into getting the results back pretty quick."

"Ok, I'll be back with the results as soon as I can."

"John, do you really want to wait until Baxter returns with the forensic results? Or do you think we should make a start with Knowels? Then, at least we will find out what he's got to say about all this, by then, the results from the lab should hopefully have arrived. Do we know if Knowels's solicitor has arrived yet?"

"He should have by now, we'll know when we get into the interview room."

"I would think they will both be waiting to find out what we've got on Knowels, even more eager than we are, to find out what defence they are going use."

One phone call to the duty Sergeant confirmed, that Knowels and Bywater were both more than ready, to get the interview underway.

Knowels and his solicitor were already seated next to each other, when the Chief and Cline entered the interview room and seated themselves directly opposite them at the table. A uniformed officer remained standing inside the room just near the door. The chief switched on the double tape deck, after which Cline made the introductory statements and reminded Knowels that he had already had his read rights. Since this was Cline's case, the Chief had already agreed that Cline would do the interrogation, and his presence was one of observation and the right of Knowels to have a senior, or equal, ranking officer in attendance during his interview.

As he spoke Cline looked across the table straight into the eyes of Knowels. "For the duration of this and any subsequent interviews, Superintendent Victor Knowels will simply be addressed as Mr. Knowels or by his christian name Victor."

It was Cline's intention to unsettle Knowels from the offset, by removing his rank he hoped to make Knowels feel less superior, which could put Cline at a psychological advantage.

Bywater raised his hand in protest. "Before we commence, on behalf of my client, SUPERINTENDENT KNOWELS, I would like to complain about the length of time he, or should I say we, have had to wait for this interview, it's absolutely disgusting."

Cline ignored the sarcasm in Bywater's voice, "I'm sorry about that, but we had a few enquiries to carry out first." Then turning to Knowels. "Now then Victor", it was Cline's turn to show a bit of sarcasm in his voice, "would you care to tell me where you were on the evening of Thursday the twelfth of July this year and the morning of Friday the Thirteenth of July this year?"

"No comment."

The Chief Constable suddenly and, without warning, thumped his fist on the table, causing everyone in the room to be startled, "If it is your full intention to continue your replies with a no comment response, then I cannot see the point in my presence here at this interview. Now tell me, do you want a senior officer present, namely me, so that you can answer any questions correctly, or are you going to continue to behave like a silly bugger with this no comment nonsense? Because if you are, then I will leave you with Inspector Cline, the choice is yours."

The room remained deathly silent for what seemed like an eternity, but must have only been for about two minutes, whilst Knowels was anguishing over what to do. He turned his head towards his solicitor for some guidance or sign of what to do, but there was none. Then Bywater slowly gave Knowels a gently nod, to which Knowels responded with a quiet "ok."

"Ok what."

"Ok, I'll answer your questions."

"So where were you on those dates in questions?"

"I went out for a drink."

"Did you go alone or did you have company?"

"I went alone."

"So, where did you get to? Surely you must remember which pub you went into, do you have a regular haunting place?"

"I was on a pub crawl all night and I didn't get back home until the early hours of the next morning."

"Bolderdale is not that big a town, surely, if you were out on the town for that number of hours, you must have run into somebody you knew, somebody, who could give you an alibi."

"If I had known at the time I was going to be a suspect in a murder investigation, I would have taken my autograph book with me and got everyone I saw to sign it. I could even have done a strip tease on the pub bars just to make sure that people remembered me."

"Mr. Knowels, it is a well known fact that, amongst the workforce at this police station, there is not much you like better than to go out most nights for a drink, it then follows that there must be countless barmaids and bar managers who know you, and would be able to remember you from that night."

"I'm not saying I didn't see or bump into anyone I knew, I'm just saying, I had that much to drink, I cannot remember who I saw or where I drank."

"How well did you know James Peter Rothwell?"

"Who the hell his he?"

"I'll ask the questions if you don't mind, and for the record he's the guy we think you murdered. So I'll put it to you another way, did you know James Peter Rothwell?"

"No."

"That comes as somewhat of a surprise to me Mr. Knowels, since in your position of Superintendent, were you not presented with a report, dealing with the apprehension of the mugger of the prostitutes in Turpin Road?" "Is that not correct Mr. Knowels?"

"Yes, you know very well it is."

"Then you must also know that the person who was caught red handed effecting those muggings and then subsequently arrested and brought to this station for questioning, was none other that James Peter Rothwell, I s that so?"

"Oh! that Rothwell, naturally I'm aware of his existence and his death, through your investigations."

"Could it be, that the reason you seem so calm about the charges that have been made against you, is because you believe we have no evidence to substantiate our charges? Well you can take it from me, we have all the evidence we need." Cline swore to himself that he saw Knowels squirm on his seat.

"Is it not true that you actually attended the same school, Bolderdale Comprehensive at the same time, back in the early 1970's?"

"I cannot be expected to remember back to those years, that's 20 or 30 years."

"Well Biff, it cannot be too difficult to remember all those years back, apparently Jimmy Rothwell remembered those years very well indeed. Besides, both your names are entered in the school register for the same years. I suppose Jimmy may have had good cause to remember those years. What would you say to that? Do you think it may have something to do with the fact that you were responsible for putting Jimmy into St. Andrews Hospital?"

The look on Knowels's face was now one of despair, how on earth did that clever sod Cline find out about my name, Biff, what else has he dug up from the past? The crafty sod knows a lot more than he is letting on, where is he getting all this information from? It cannot be from Rothwell, at least

I shut him up. Knowels's fidgeting had turned to a shuffle, first his left leg over his right leg, and then vice versa, he had become very agitated.

Suddenly, and to everyone's surprise, Cline brought the interview to an unexpected close and Knowels was escorted quickly back to his police cell.

"What on earth are you playing at John? It was obvious from the way he was squirming on his chair, you had him well and truly rattled. Why didn't you keep the pressure on him? I would have turned the thumb screws even tighter if I had been you. You may even have been able to get a confession out of him, I hope for your sake you know what you are doing."

"Sir, there is no way Knowels will admit to killing Rothwell, at least not yet, I've only let him know a little bit of what we already know. Now he his really confused, he will be in that cell right now worrying about just how much we really know. You saw his facial expression when I reminded him of his old school nick name, Biff. By the time I've finished with him he'll be like a pressure cooker with a faulty safety valve, building up to blow. I may get him even more worried and eager to talk by suggesting we have found a link between him and the other murders."

"We haven't, have we?"

"Of course not Sir, we now know for a fact, the other murders were committed by a female. Knowels was just trying to use the earlier murders as a cover, for Rothwell's death."

There was a sharp knock on the office door and Baxter entered and walked over to Cline's desk.

"Sorry to interrupt you Sir, but I thought you would want to hear the good news. The lab has checked the weapons taken from the Super's office, and they have come up with a set of the Super's finger prints on both the knives and the key. The key as been confirmed as a copy of the key

Rothwell had hid in the back of his diary. They are 99% sure that the knives are the murder weapons, at least that is, for Rothwell's killing. They did find traces of blood on the hilt of one of the knives, blood that matched with Rothwell's blood, that by itself doesn't mean anything, but they will have the proof one way or another when the D.N.A. results come back, they will take a few days Sir. From what I've heard on the grapevine, most of the lads are saying good riddance, so I expect there is not too much love lost with regards to Knowels's demise."

"There's no need for that."

"Sorry Sir, I'm just telling you how it is outside this room."

Cline rose to his feet. "Now let's go and turn the screws and reel him in. I don't know about you two but I'm about ready for bed, so the soon we get this over with the better it will be."

The usual formalities over with, Cline took a long hard look at Knowels's face, the change in his appearance over the past twenty minutes or so was remarkable. All the cockiness which had been present at the start of the previous interview had disappeared, now replaced by a look of guilt and concern for his freedom. His face looked haggard and drawn, whatever it was that had been going through his mind during the break, it certainly had had, a dramatic effect on him.

Cline produced Rothwell's letter, which was secured in a clear plastic cover, and placed it under Knowels's nose, a copy of the letter was also handed over to Bywater, Knowels's solicitor.

"Take a good hard look at the letter in front of you, take your time there's no rush, then tell me what you think about it."

229

It was evident to everyone else in the room that, as soon as Knowels began reading the letter, it started to have a detrimental effect on his mental health. The fear in his eyes was all too evident to see, as the undeniable belief that the game was lost. Self preservation was still strong in his mind and though he was no longer confident and blustering about his innocence, he still had not confessed to any crime. Cline even felt a tinge of pity for the man.

Knowels picked up the letter and threw it across the table at Cline, "That doesn't prove a bloody thing, he's made it all up. In fact, I wouldn't put it passed you to have written it. You've no proof at all that I even knew this so called Rothwell, let alone killed him. You'd do anything to pin this on me. You never did like me, did you?"

Cline ignored the remark and bent down to the floor and picked up the plastic bag with the two knives and the key and placed them on the table.

Knowels turned to Bywater. "This is a set up, I've no idea where they got those from but I'm telling you here and now, I've never seen any of these before in my life. Get me out of here, the next thing, they'll be trying to pin the other murders on me as well."

"Then please explain to me Mr. Knowels, if you can, how come we found all these three items taped to the inside of the bottom of your office filing cabinet?"

"Don't bother asking me your stupid questions, all I know is I didn't put them there."

"Then it's remarkable how your finger prints came to be on all three items, and given a couple of days, no doubt we will also discover your D.N.A."

The quick tan that Knowels had managed to attain during his short holiday, seemed now, to be turning a peculiar shade of yellowy grey, all signs of any healthy colour to his face had now drained away. There was no need to touch his skin to know that it would be cold and clammy, the shock that, no amount of denials or blustering of his innocence, could protect against, had set in. It was the final acceptance and realisation, that this was one situation that he had no way of escaping from and, it was only the quick reaction of Cline in reaching over the table, that protected Knowels's face from hitting the table top.

Cline brought the interview to a halt. "Constable, go and fetch Mr. Knowels a cup of tea please. Knowels very slowly regained his senses. "How do you feel now? Do you wish to see the M.E.?"

"No, I'm ok."

"Inspector Cline, before we continue, I think I should have a few words alone with my client."

"No, No, I've had enough, there's no need, let's just get it over with."

Cline waited until Knowels had drunk his tea, a courtesy no doubt, that would not have been afforded Cline if the boot had been on the other foot, before restarting the interview.

"Do I take it, that you now wish to change your plea?"

"Yes, Yes, just let's get out of here."

"For the tape please Mr. Knowels, you are charged with the murder of James Rothwell, how do you plead?"

"Guilty, for Christ's sake, guilty, now can we get out of here, it's so claustrophobic. It's obvious the bastard was slowly bleeding me dry. Just before I killed him, we decided a one off payment of £3000 would be the last one, but I knew different, so I decided to get rid of him."

"No way was he going to bring up my school boy days to the attention of the Chief Constable, and spoil any chance of promotion I had coming, or even my dismissal from the force."

The Chief with a wry smile looked across at Knowels, "Your days were already numbered in my book, no way were you ever going to be in a position for promotion, I would have seen to that."

"You can tell the Chief and me now, did you intend to kill Rothwell, or was it an accident."

"You must be thicker than me Cline, how can using two blades to kill someone be an accident. It had never been my intention to kill him, but when the other murders began, the thought struck me that, perhaps I could use them to help cover up Rothwell's death, so I thought up the idea of a copy cat murder, that's why I leaked the story to the local press."

"But you killed Rothwell before the story appeared in the papers."

"I didn't know at the time, that I had missed the slot for that evening's papers, just my luck, but he had to go. After his arrest, I couldn't afford for him to be walking about any longer. Can I go now?"

"Back to your cell yes, home no."

The interview was suspended at 01.55.

"Constable, take him back to the cells."

"Well done John, at least that's one out of the way."

"I'll say well done Sir when we have wrapped up the other murders. I'll see you in the morning Baxter, in the incident room. We'll have to let the others know what's been happening. Good morning Sir, I'll keep you directly informed of any further developments now that I haven't the Super to report to, that is unless you are going to send someone else over from area to replace him."

"John I will be sending someone over to replace Knowels as soon as I am able, but he will have clear instructions that he has nothing to do with your murder enquiry, you report directly back to me. Now let's all get off home and get some shuteye."

Chapter 16

It was bright and early when both Cline and Baxter arrived in the incident room, although bright, was not an adjective that you would best describe their appearance, after only the minimum amount of sleep.

By seven thirty all the team was present, all waiting to hear first hand of the events of the previous night.

"Now everybody calm down. No doubt by now, you and everybody else at the station, will have heard one version or another of yesterday's events, with regards to Superintendent Knowels. He has admitted killing Rothwell, so as far as you are all concerned, at least for now, you can concentrate on the other murders."

"This morning I'm in court for Knowels's formal hearing at ten o'clock, so until then I want to go over what we have so far. At least we now know that we are looking for a woman killer, even though we have no idea who she is. Are we looking for a woman who has not entered our enquiries yet? I'm not going to repeat all we've said before about the women we've already interviewed. We know there is a substantial amount of money involved with respect to Armstrong's murder, but personally I don't think these murders are about money. Are we sure, that the reason the Armstrong clan lied to us is, as they say, Kenneth Moss and Ruth Armstrong being a couple or, was this a double bluff to cover up the fact that Ruth Armstrong was having a lesbian relationship with, either Mary Duncan, or even the young receptionist Jenny. Don't forget it was Jenny that Ruth Armstrong rang the day she was first interviewed, she may have been ringing to warn Jenny what to say to us, not Kenneth Moss. If Mary Duncan was having an affair with Ruth Armstrong, it would be to Mary's advantage if Ruth's husband was out of the way. That would also give Mary Duncan access to Armstrong's money, by virtue of her relationship with Ruth Armstrong"

"To be honest Sir, as enlightening as your ideas seem to be, I still believe the killer is someone who, as yet, has not been in the frame as the killer. Besides we still have no connection between any of the women in this case with Preston or Miss Buxton."

"Have you any thoughts Poole?"

"Well, it's more of a query really, than an idea."

"That's ok, let's hear what you have to say, it might help."

"I don't understand why the killer, and I can only assume it was the killer, would send Miss Buxton the egg timer. If it was to cause her distress, then it obviously didn't work since she never saw it, though I suppose the killer would not have expected that. I think that the egg timer was supposed to be representative of the length of life, i.e. three score years and ten, and the glass was broken to let the sand run out, meaning that Miss Buxton's life had run its course. As we have said before, the egg timer was a waste of time because Ann Buxton was drunk as a newt and never got to see it."

"Ok, thanks Poole, for now I think the best lead that we have is with 'Moorgate Children's Home'. We know Preston worked there, Armstrong called there as a rep and Buxton had a connection through her work with the Social Services. One of you check the photos we got out of Preston's locker, check to see if there is any furniture visible besides the picture of the boys, if they do, you never know some one at Social Services may be able to recognise it. I know I'm clutching at straws but we must try and consider anything possible, they must have a central purchasing department.

I have a gut feeling that Preston's photos were taken at the Moorgate. I just hope we aren't going to uncover a child abuse scandal, I'm sure that really would make the Chief Constable happy. The press would really have a field day with that, at least they wouldn't be able to lay it at our door this time, Knowels is already under arrest, besides he's the wrong sex. At some time, somewhere, the killer must have had cause to hate all the victims, but it's hard to believe that someone like Ann Buxton could knowingly harm anyone, according to Social Services she was probably the most liked person on their staff."

"Poole, I want you to go down to the local press office or library and search the records going back, say, 25 years. I have no idea what you are looking for, but I feel something happened many years ago, and I believe 'Moorgate Children's Home' hold's the clue."

"Jones, you and Moore make sure Mary's got all she needs to get her reports up to date, use my report to tie up any loose ends with regards the Rothwell murder, you'll find it in my top left hand drawer."

"Baxter, I'll pick you up after I've been to court with Knowels, it's time we spent some more time with Mrs. Woodside at Social Services. I have this feeling, but don't ask why, that before too long, time is going to be at a premium, so let's not waste it. You all know what to do, so let's get on with it."

Mrs. Woodside was just leaving her home, when Cline and Baxter entered her front garden.

"Good morning Mrs. Woodside, I'm sorry to upset your Saturday morning, but I need to examine Ann Buxton's case files again, I'm sure we missed something the last time we looked."

"I cannot do that today Inspector, I don't work on Saturdays and besides I'm just off to do my weekly shopping, surely it could wait till Monday morning?"

"I suppose that will be alright, as long as you remember, that I'm conducting a murder investigation, and you will be able to shoulder your proportion of the blame if we have another murder before Monday, after which, we discover that information withheld within Ann Buxton's files could have prevented it. Remember Mrs. Woodside, you said yourself, you and your staff have no idea whatsoever why Ann was killed, so it is not beyond the realms of possibilities that you yourself could be next on the killer's list."

Mrs.Woodside needed no further inducement to assist them. "Now you really have got me worried Inspector, don't you think I should have some kind of protection just in case?

"Not at this stage Mrs. Woodside, the best protection that I can give you is to apprehend the murderer and to do that, we need people like yourself to give us your maximum assistance and support."

"Ok, Inspector let's get down to my office. The sooner you get this killer, the sooner I'll be able to sleep better at nights, after you've just put the fear of God into me."

The lifts were still out of order, but at least it now looked as if the maintenance crew were busy trying to detect the fault. Who knows, we may be able to have a ride down later on, was the only comforting thought going through Cline's mind as he started the long and arduous climb up to the tenth floor.

"I had an idea you may be back Inspector, so I left the case files on my desk."

"Look Mrs. Woodside, we are likely to be here for some time, why don't you continue to do your shopping down town, and we will see you back here when you've finished. I promise you, we will take care of your files and we will not be removing any from your office."

"I suppose it can't hurt, if I can't trust a policeman and an Inspector at that, who can I trust, I'll be back as quick as I can."

Cline smiled to himself, she may not have been so trusting, if she had known about Knowels.

"Ok Wendy, you take that half, and I'll take this half."

"What exactly are we looking for Sir?"

"I've no idea, but I'm sure we will know when we find it. Before we start, see if you can find us something to drink, after that climb up the stairs again I'm parched."

I'll go and see what I can scrounge.

Ten minutes later, Baxter returned with a tray of tea and biscuits.

"Sir, I think there's something you ought to go and take a look at in the back room."

Cline followed Baxter into a small back room at the end of the main office. The room was a miniature kitchen with microwave cooker, sink, kettle, small fridge/freezer and a couple of wall cupboards.

"So what am I supposed to be looking at?"

"On the wall behind you Sir."

Cline turned around to face a notice board on the wall, the board being covered with press cuttings, most of them looked recent, but some appeared to be from some time back.

"I was reading through those cuttings whilst I was waiting for the kettle to boil, when I happened to read that old press cutting, the one in the middle of the board. Take a look Sir and see what you make of it."

Cline read the headlines, "Parents Fight With Social Services On Their Front Door Step"

There followed a more detailed account of the incident. The Social Services had removed a young child from her parent's control, after reports of physical and sexual abuse on the child by her step father came to light, when the child's school gym teacher, Mrs. Ivy Johnson, noticed bruises on the child's limbs and body during a P.E class and brought it to the attention of the Social Services.

The child had been removed from her home and placed in temporary care at 'The Moorgate Children's Home'. According to the report, the child had never accused her step father of abusing her, but because of his habitual drunken bouts and his violent behaviour when under the influence of alcohol, it was assumed, rather than proved, that he was guilty and the child was put in protection for her own safety.

"Hello, what are you doing in here?" Mrs. Woodside had returned from her short shopping trip down town.

"We were just having a cuppa, I hope you don't mind. W.D.S. Baxter spotted that cutting in the middle of the notice board." Cline pointed to the cutting in question. "Can you recollect that particular case?"

"Oh! that one. Yes, I remember that very well. A pretty nasty case all round, that one, it caused quite a bit of adverse publicity at the time, as you can well see for yourselves from the press cuttings."

"I noticed that the girl's name is not reported in the press cuttings."

"As you know Inspector, neither we, nor the press, are allowed to give out the names of minors."

"I take it her name must be in your case files?"

"Yes, we will have her name, but I still can't disclose it to you Inspector."

"Since the incident took place many years ago, the child is now no longer a minor, I cannot see there is a problem. Besides, I don't want the name for publication purposes but to help my murder investigation. Don't forget, we still don't know if there will be any more killings, but more to the point, if there are, who will be the next on the list."

"I'm just going to have a look at my files, there is something I need to check."

Mrs. Woodside walked to her desk and delved through the files, finally she took a file from one of the piles, opened the file and laid it open on her desk top." I just have to go to the ladies for a few moments Inspector, I won't be too long."

Cline walked over to the desk and looked at the file, without touching it. There on the very first line was the name "Mary Allbright."

Cline carefully, but quickly, read the report before Mrs. Woodside returned.

"What happened to the step father? Was he ever charged with physically or sexually abusing the girl? I must admit, I cannot remember the incident."

"No Inspector that was the problem, we didn't have sufficient proof against him and, since the girl never accused him of any wrong doing, there was no way we were ever going to obtain a conviction in court. We still felt however, that there were sufficient grounds to have the girl taken away from his jurisdiction for a while, so we placed her into Moorgate Children's Home, just for a few months."

"Were there any further incidents involving the girl and her step father after she was returned home?"

"No Inspector, in fact, a couple of weeks after the girl was returned to her home, her step father committed suicide."

"Where's the gym teacher now? Is she still teaching?"

"Mrs. Johnson, I'm afraid you will have to get in touch with the Education Department to get that information." "Will her address be in your files somewhere?"

"I doubt it, we would have no reason to have it on file, all we required was the name of the school, and if we had needed to contact the teacher we would do it through the school."

Cline was beginning to think that Mrs. Woodside seemed to have forgotten that she had said she couldn't give them any information with regards to the girl, and at this point he certainly was not going to remind her.

"Which school did she attend?"

"'St. Hilda's Infant & Juniors' in Church Street, it's now called, 'St. Hilda's Middle School'."

"I think we have covered about everything we can for now, Mrs. Woodside, you've been a really great help to us. I'll try not to disturb any more of your weekends. Oh! I hope you have no frozen food in your shopping, it will have defrosted by now."

"The only frozen food is for tonight's meal, so it doesn't really matter if it has defrosted. I'll find my own way home Inspector, I should really get all these case files locked away before I go home."

"Sir, look at that, it looks like the lifts have been repaired, the floor indicators are lit up."

"Thank the Lord for that Wendy, I didn't fancy having to walk down ten flights of stairs again. It looks like Lady Luck may have decided to shine on us at last."

On his return to the incident room, Cline found Poole pacing backwards and forwards waiting for him to arrive.

"What's up Poole? You look as if you've got ants in your pants."

"Sir, I think I've found something really interesting which I think you'll like."

"Go on then Poole, let's hear it."

"Not yet Sir, there's something else you should know, I think someone tried to kill me."

"Why would anyone want to kill you?"

"I don't know Sir, but I'm sure it was no accident. I was on the large expanse of footpath outside the newspaper offices, when I heard the sound of a car engine revving up, then I caught sight of the car mounting the footpath with all four wheels, and drive straight for me, that was no accident, I managed to jump to one side, but not before the car caught my legs a glancing blow, as it sped passed me. I didn't see the licence plate, it happened so quickly, all I can remember is that the car was blue."

"Are you all right? Do you want to see the M.E.?"

"I'm ok apart from a few scrapes and bruises to my hands and legs. I've already seen the M.E. Sir, I suppose I was very lucky to escape like I did, do you think someone didn't want me poking my nose into the newspaper archives, for fear of what I might find?"

"I suppose that depends on what there is to find out, and about who, besides, who knew you were going to the archives and when?"

"Well someone evidently did."

"I take it then, that you never got to see the archives?"

"Oh, I got there alright Sir, I was a bit shook up at first but it soon passed. Take a look at this Sir, whether it's anything to do with our murder case or not I don't know. I'll leave it for you to decide."

Poole handed Cline a copy of the same newspaper cutting which he and Baxter had seen at the Social Service Office, earlier that day.

"I'm sorry Poole it looks like I've wasted your time, I've already seen the cutting earlier this morning."

"Right everybody, you've all been updated with the events to date. There is no way that we are going to get any info from the Education Department until Monday morning, so it's back to the 'let the fingers do the walking' technique. I want every Johnson within a twenty five miles radius of Bolderdale town centre contacting today. If you don't get a reply, keep ringing until you do, otherwise get the address out of the phone book, and don't forget the cable phone numbers. One of you get in touch with the phone companies, check for ex-directory numbers for an Ivy Johnson. We need to find her and find her fast,

I have this feeling that she could be the next victim. If the killer knows what we have found, then she will want to silence her before we can get to her. Get Mary and Samantha to help." "Samantha's not in today Sir and Mary went home sick first thing this morning, I think it's the monthly problem Sir."

"I really wanted to know that Jones, you'll just have to manage the best you can."

"Sir."

"Yes Wendy."

"Why don't we just contact the school at which Mrs. Johnson teaches or taught at?"

"We could if it wasn't Saturday, the school will be closed until Monday morning."

"I know Sir, but we could get hold of the caretaker, he'd be able to get hold of the headmaster if he's at home and we could arrange to meet him at the school."

"Now why didn't I think of that? Ok Wendy you get that set up. The rest of you continue with those phones just in case Wendy has no luck with the caretaker."

"Sir, we're in luck. The headmaster will see us at the school in thirty minutes."

"Have you spoken to him on the phone?"

"Yes, Mrs. Johnson doesn't work there any more but he should still have her address on the school records, that's why we are going to meet him."

The school caretaker was already standing at the gates on their arrival. The main gate was still closed and padlocked, but the small footpath gate was opened wide as if it was inviting them into the school premises.

"There's no need to rush Sir, the headmaster hasn't arrived yet, he shouldn't be too long though."

The words had hardly left his mouth, when a blue Ford Scorpio pulled up behind Cline's car and a scruffy looking, middle aged man dressed more like a scarecrow than a head master, emerged from the driver's door.

"I hope you haven't been waiting too long, I came as soon as I got your message. Excuse my appearance, I don't usually leave my home looking like this, but I was doing a spot of gardening when your Sergeant rang me, when she told me it was important, I just dropped everything and jumped in the car. So, how can I be of help?"

"I'm Detective Inspector Cline, and this is Detective Sergeant Baxter, she's the person who spoke to you on the phone earlier. I are trying to contact a Mrs. Ivy Johnson, I believe she used to be a Gym Teacher here?"

"As I told W.D.S. Baxter, Mrs. Johnson retired some time ago. If you follow me I'll go and get you her address. Before she left, she did imply on several occasions, that she and her husband were thinking of moving down south, nearer to Devon after she retired. I've no idea if they ever did move or not."

Ten minutes later Cline was back at the school gate, with hopefully, Ivy Johnson's present address, tucked into his jacket pocket.

"When Mrs. Johnson talked about moving, did she ever give any indication to which part of Devon they preferred?"

"No, not really, I do know they spent a lot of time on holiday in the Dartmouth region of Devon."

"Thank you, I'll let you get back to your gardening, while there's still plenty of light."

As soon as they were back in the car he rang the station. "Get D.S. Jones and D.C. Moore over to Mrs. Ivy Johnson's home at once, and tell them to stay there until they hear from me. The address by the way is Dart House, Water Lane, Bolderdale."

Back in the incident room, Cline instructed Baxter to ring the Johnsons and inform them that two C.I.D. officers were on the way to speak to Mrs. Johnson, so could she please make herself available for them when they arrived. "Try not to worry them too much, just enough to make them aware of the fact Mrs. Johnson may be in some kind of danger."

The Johnsons' phone rang once before Baxter head the voice on the other end. "Hello love, did you have a good journey down? You are late ringing, I thought you would have rung two or three hours ago."

"I'm sorry, is that Mr. Johnson?"

"Yes, who's that? I thought it was my wife ringing."

"I'm W.D.S. Baxter from the Bolderdale Police Station. Is your wife the same Mrs. Ivy Johnson who used to be a Gym teacher at St. Hilda's Infants and Juniors in Church Street?"

"Yes, that's right, Oh! My God, she hasn't been in an accident has she? I thought there was something wrong when she didn't ring up earlier."

"No, calm down, she hasn't had an accident, we just need to speak to her urgently, we think see may be able to help us. As we speak, Two detectives are on their way to speak to you. I take it from what you first said when you picked up the phone, that your wife isn't in at the moment?"

"Yes that's correct. By now she should have arrived in Dartmouth in South Devon, she should have rung back a couple of hours ago, as I said before. She must have been in a traffic hold-up on the way down."

"Has she gone away on holiday?"

"No, she's gone house hunting in Dartmouth, she left this morning at first light. Normally I would have been with her, but I've still got a couple of months left before I retire."

"Did she book a hotel before she set off, or is she waiting till she gets down there?"

"What's with the big rush to get hold of Ivy? You are starting to worry me now, can't you wait until she gets back? She's only down there for three days."

"It's nothing for you to worry about Mr. Johnson," although by now, Baxter herself, was beginning to feel a little unsure about Mrs. Johnson's safety.

"The detectives will explain everything to you when they arrive. In the meantime do you happen to know where your wife is supposed to be staying tonight?"

"Yes, it's the Star Point Hotel at Brixham. That's just a few miles from Dartmouth."

"How did she travel? By car or public transport?"

"By car, she drives a little mini."

"What's the registration number and colour of the car?"

"It's bright red, IVY 60 J. I bought the registration plates for her sixtieth birthday. Hold on a minute, there's someone at the door." There was a brief pause before Johnson returned to the phone. "It's your detectives, do you want a word with them?"

"Please would you ask Sergeant Jones to come to the phone?"

"Peter, stay with Mr. Johnson until you hear from either myself or Inspector Cline, I don't know what has happened to Mrs. Johnson but things are starting to look bad again. She's supposed to be in Devon, but, as yet, has failed to ring in. Try not to worry him too much, as soon as we have something to tell you, we will give you a ring."

Baxter passed on to Cline everything she had just learnt on the phone.

"Ok Wendy, you had better get hold of the Star Point Hotel and see if Mrs. Johnson has turned up or not. I'm beginning not to like the sound of all this, I just hope we are not too late."

The phone rang before Baxter had chance to use it. "Sir, its Jones for you." "Yes Jones."

"Sir, it may be something or nothing but Mr. Johnson has just told us that, just after his wife pulled out of their drive this morning, he had a phone call from a woman wanting to speak to his wife. The woman said she was looking for someone to give private lessons to her children. He told the woman that his wife had just left home and was now on her way to Devon. It wasn't till later, that he thought it was funny that someone should want his wife to give private lessons, she had never given private lessons before, and besides, who needs private lessons in physical education. Since the woman didn't mention his wife by name, he just assumed the caller had the wrong teacher and, after she abruptly hung up, dispelled the incident from his mind. Whilst he was on the phone, he remembers seeing a blue Escort parked across his front drive, which he thought nothing of at the time."

"Did he happen to get a good look at the driver?"

"He said he could see it was a woman, but didn't get a good look at her face because it was shielded by the mobile phone she was using at the time. Reflecting back to the phone call, he now believes it must have been the woman he was talking to. All he can remember about the woman is that she wasn't all that old, she may even have been quite young, he couldn't be sure, he was sure however, that she had short black hair."

"Ok Peter, stay with him, we'll be in touch as soon as we know something."

"Bad news I'm afraid Sir, whilst you were talking to Jones, I rang Star Point Hotel and they have confirmed that Mrs. Johnson hasn't arrived yet. She's now about four hours overdue from the time she was expected."

"This is looking worse by the minute Wendy, I definitely don't like the sound of things now. Get onto Traffic, I want an all police force alert, from here down to Brixham in Devon. We need to find that mini and fast, or I'm afraid it looks like we are going to have another body on our hands. Another thing that sent shivers down my back is the description of the car parked outside Johnson's drive, blue he said, the car that tried to knock Poole down outside the newspaper offices, was also blue."

"I take it you believe the woman in the car is the killer we are after. If that is true Sir, she may even have taken off after Mrs. Johnson down to Devon, Mr. Johnson did say that his wife had only just left. Mrs. Johnson would have had no reason to think she was being pursued, so had no reason to speed, whereas the killer could soon catch her up if she put her foot down a bit. From the Johnson's house, there is really only one way to get onto the road south, so it wouldn't be too much of a problem for the killer to catch up with Johnson."

"I hope you are wrong Wendy, for Mrs. Johnson's sake at least. Just for once Wendy, I thought we may be one step in front of the killer, but it looks like she is still out there, calling the shots. It's as if the killer knows every move we make, almost before we know ourselves."

The incident room door burst open, after Knowels's arrest, Cline had stopped locking the door since the source of the press leaks was now locked up. The Duty Sergeant dashed in to inform Cline that Birmingham Traffic Police had found Mrs. Johnson's car abandoned at the Frankley Service Station on the M5 motorway. "There's no sign of Mrs. Johnson."

"They've checked the immediate area with no luck as yet, they are carrying out routine questioning in the area but they don't hold much hope of getting a lead. The mini's engine was stone cold when the car was found, which means, if someone has taken Mrs. Johnson, they are long gone."

"Thank you Sergeant, let me know at once if you hear of any further developments."

"Christ Sir, it looks like on top of everything else, we could now have a kidnapping on our hands."

"Just when I think that things can't get any worse, looks like I'm wrong again. Poole, you'd better get the Chief Constable's office on the line for me, I hope he's in at a weekend, it's about time I let him know what's happening. Besides, right now, we could do with every bit of help that we can muster, and that means the public and, in order to do that, we need the Chief back on board"

By seven thirty that night, all radio wavelengths and television station networks had transmitted the Police appeal for witnesses to the suspected kidnapping at the Frankley Service Station earlier that day. Now, all Cline could do, was to sit back and wait, and that, was something he was not very good at.

It was half past ten in the evening before the next development took place, again it was the duty Sergeant who brought the news. "Sir, we've just had a call from a Mr. East in Darlington."

"Darlington, you mean Darlington up the A1?"

"I didn't know there were any other Darlingtons Sir. Anyway, that's the one.

Mr. East and his wife have just returned today from a trip to the West Country,

they were nearly at home before he turned his tape cassette off, to listen to the radio. It was then that he heard the appeal. From all accounts, they had pulled into Frankley Services for a short rest and a cuppa. As is usually the case, the café on their side of the motorway was closed, so they had to cross over the motorway foot bridge to the café on the south bound side. It was whilst they were crossing the foot bridge that they could see two women apparently having an argument. One woman looked to be in her late fifties or early sixties and the other woman was about thirty, but she could have been older, it wasn't too easy to judge since they were a good distance away from us."

"Mr. East said it looked as if the younger woman was punching the older woman. He said he ran over the bridge to see what was exactly going on, and to see if the older woman was in need of some assistance. By the time he got to the place where he had seen the two women struggling, he just managed to see the two women driving off in a blue Escort. Mr. East believes the younger woman was driving, the older woman appeared to be sat up in the rear of the car. At that point, if it had not been for the fact that earlier, the younger woman was hitting the older one, he would have thought that they were mother and daughter."

"Did they manage to see the registration number of the Escort?"

"Yes Sir, we are in luck. A 123 LMA Mr. East said it was easy to remember because his wife is called Alma."

"Great, good news at last, have you checked the registration?"

"Yes Sir, but you are not going to like the answer."

"Just tell me Sergeant, who owns the blue Escort? Things can't get any worse than they are now."

"I wouldn't put your shirt on that Sir. The car is registered to a Mary White, a W.D.C. Mary White to be precise Sir."

Cline's jaw dropped a mile, the colour instantly drained from his face, it was a good few seconds before he recovered his composure. "You've just got to be joking. Tell me Sergeant, you are joking and this is a wind up."

"I'm afraid not Sir, besides I wouldn't dare joke about something as serious as this with you."

"Ok Sergeant, thank you."

"Did I hear that correctly Sir? Mary White is our murderer? It just doesn't make any sense Sir."

"Sense or not, you heard the Sergeant. How on earth is Mary involved in all this? I thought the girl involved was Mary Allbright. I know for a fact that Mary has never married. So where's the connection between Mary White and Mary Allbright?"

"Perhaps Mary has sold her car and the re- registration has not gone through the system at Swansea."

"That would be nice if that were so, but I saw Mary in a blue car only this week."

"Have we got an address for Mary?"

"Yes Sir, it's 13 Boston Avenue."

"Ok, I'm on my way out there, meanwhile Wendy, get back onto traffic, I want Mary White's car found and found pretty damned quick. Then get S.O.C.O. down to Mary's home, tell them I'll meet them down there. I'll have to get in contact with the Chief again, and I can tell you, I'm not relishing that for one second. Poole you go and get the car ready for us and I'll see you downstairs in ten minutes. Wendy, you'll need to get the search warrant sorted out as well."

It would have been the understatement of the year, to say that the Chief was not too happy that yet another member of his force was a murderer and was now the subject of a nation wide hunt. Ballistic, was a word that readily came to mind, when trying to describe the reaction of the Chief Constable.

At five minutes before midnight Cline and his party arrived at the home of Mary White. "She may be in bed Sir, she did go home sick."

"Sick my backside, she knew what our plans were for the day, and was determined to stay one jump ahead of us, she won't be in bed, she's out there somewhere with Mrs. Johnson. It looks as if we have forced her hand, she may have made a grab for Mrs. Johnson before she intended to. If she had planned to carry out the snatch at this time, I don't think we would have been in a position to get her car registration number or even a vague description of her."

There was no reply to their banging on the front. "Break it down, we haven't the time to mess about, I want the house searched from top to bottom and pronto, Mrs. Johnson's life could depend on what we find or don't find here. If we need a pantechnicon to haul the stuff away, then get one."

Chapter 17

It was two in the morning, and after several hours, before Cline, Baxter and Poole managed their first cuppa in the canteen. "God, I was ready for that Sir, my throat feels like it's been scrubbed with a ball of wire wool."

"I know what you mean Wendy, it's so humid and sticky tonight, and I must have lost a stone in weight."

"Do you think Mary really is responsible for all these murders Sir? I know she's been through a rough patch of late, what with having to look after her mother for the past couple of years, and then having to watch her die. It must also have been hard on her when her father died. I just cannot believe that someone who can show so much love and caring for her mother, could go out, and kill someone in cold blood, not just once, but at least three times as far as we know."

"What do you mean after her father died? Her father's not dead."

"What do you mean Poole, her father's not dead?"

"The other night I took Samantha out for a meal, now don't look at me like that, it was only a date. Samantha told me that Mary had been telling her about her childhood, including the time when her father had left home, when she only about eight years old."

"Now that's very strange Poole, because now you mention her father, I can distinctly remember her telling me that her father had left home, leaving her to cope with her mother's illness, and later in life, her death. So how did this business about Mary's father dying come about? Who told you Wendy that her father had died?"

"She did Sir, it was quite some time back now though, long before she went off work sick to care for her mother."

"What do you two want to bet that Mary went to Moorgate Children's Home? I think you will find out that Mary Allbright is really Mary White. Why she changed her name, I have no idea, we will have to wait until we catch up with her before we'll be able to answer that question. One thing I am sure of however, when this gets out to the press we are sure going to be the laughing stock of the whole police force."

The canteen doors flung open as a uniformed P.C. dashed in.

"Sir, you are wanted in the radio control room straight away."

As Cline entered the radio control room, he sensed that the atmosphere could be cut with a knife. What's happening Sergeant?"

"Sir, one of the traffic patrol cars has just spotted White's Ford Escort and is now in pursuit, they tried to stop her but she managed to evade them."

"Christ Sergeant, why didn't they just follow at a safe distance? If anything happens to White we may have a tough job locating Mrs. Johnson."

"Don't forget Sir, we only know that the Escort is registered in her name, we didn't know if she was the driver or not."

"So you are saying the Escort was being driven by a woman?"

"Yes Sir." "And do we know if there were any other passengers in the car?"

"Not as far as we can tell at the moment, the pursuit car has now been informed not to push the Escort too much. For all we know Sir, Mrs. Johnson may be trussed up on the rear seat or in the boot, so the last thing we want, is for White to crash the car."

"Where are they now Sergeant?"

"I'll patch the car radio through to the room speakers Sir, then everyone can hear and you will know exactly what's happening."

Cline could now hear the co-driver of the pursuing patrol car.

"She's turning right, right, right off the ring road, into St. Andrews Road. She's accelerating, I think she's trying to lose us, we've just passed St. Andrews Hospital, she's now heading down Jubilee Road, a one way street, the wrong way. Turning left, left, left into Firbeck Avenue. It looks like she's heading back towards the ring road. Can you set up a road block to stop her with the stinger?

Cline grabbed the mike. "Negative, I repeat negative. This is Inspector Cline, just follow her at a safe distance, don't try being heroes, I don't want her being pressurised into having a crash, sooner or later she will have to stop.

"We are back on the ring road travelling west. Speed now 73 mph, now turning left, left. left onto Sheffield Road. Speed now approaching 80mph, perhaps she thinks, if she can get to Sheffield, she'll be able to lose us in all the side streets. Hold on, she's now turning right, right, right into Quarry Road. She'd better slow down, there's a very sharp right hand bend, almost 90 degrees, at the end of the road."

"I'm easing off, I'm falling back, she can't go anywhere, this is the only way back, surely she must know this. I don't think she's slowing down at all, she's not going make it Sir, she's not going to make it. You'd better get the fire and ambulance lads out here, she's gone straight through the wire fencing, it looks like she's rolled over the quarry cliff top. If I didn't know any better, I would say she did that on purpose. We are at the accident site now, just going to have a look. The radio went silent for a few moments, the silence was suddenly broken. "There's no fire, but as far as we can make out with our torches, the Escort is in one hell of a mess. We can't get down to it from the cliff top, the rescue vehicles will have to use the quarry main gate. We'll stay here on the cliff top till they get here, other than that, there's not much else that we can do."

Cline dashed out of the control room, and made to collect Baxter and Poole, after repeating what he had just heard he instructed Poole to contact S.O.C.O. and the traffic accident unit and get a lorry or transporter down to the quarry. "I want that car brought back here and a full examination carried out straight away. Baxter, you come with me."

By the time Cline and Baxter had arrived at the quarry, all the emergency services were in attendance on site, and the paramedics were just loading a stretcher into the rear of the ambulance. Cline dashed over just before the ambulance door closed, "Is it a female?"

Before the paramedic could answer, Cline had jumped into the rear of the ambulance. He could see at once that the blood covered face was that of Mary White.

"How is she, is she alive?"

"Yes, but we need to get her to St. Andrews as soon as we can Sir, if she is going to have any chance of staying alive. Sorry we must get off now."

As Cline jumped out from the rear of the ambulance, he called to Baxter.

"Get in here and stay with her, I want someone with her at all times, if she comes to, I want to know what she's done with Mrs. Johnson. Nothing else matters, understand, nothing."

As the ambulance sped away from the quarry, Cline approached the senior fire officer, "Do you know if there was anyone else in the vehicle?"

"It looks as if the driver was the only occupant of the car Sir."

"We've checked in the car and in the boot, we've also checked a wide area around the car, just in case someone was thrown out whilst the car was rolling over, but nothing Sir.

We'll check again at first light, but I'm 100% sure we won't find anyone else. The driver had been thrown quite a distance from her car, whether she had removed it before the crash, or whether it had ever been fastened I cannot tell, but her safety belt was unbuckled."

"Ok, please keep us informed."

Cline returned to his car, there was only one thing on his mind now and he couldn't help but say it out loud. "We're really in the shit now, if White clogs it, how the hell will we ever find Mrs. Johnson? If there really is Someone up there (he looked out of his car window up to the myriad of stars) help us find her alive."

Cline radioed the station, "Sergeant get hold of S.O.C.O. and tell them to get hold of Mrs .Johnson's hair brush. Ask them to check hair samples from White's car against those obtained from the brush. I want to be 100 % sure that Mrs. Johnson was in White's Escort. If you need me I'll be over at St. Andrews Hospital."

He went straight up to the intensive care unit. He didn't need to be told by a doctor or nurse that the injuries suffered by White, were life threatening. Baxter was seated by the side of White's bed. "How is she? I know, it's a stupid question, I'm just hoping she can come round long enough to tell us what's she done with Mrs. Johnson."

"She's not very good Sir, she still hasn't come to yet. She's sustained serious head and chest injuries. The surgeon said it's too early yet to say whether he's going to operate. Her condition is critical, but stable, and the next couple of hours will tell us which way she's likely to go."

"That's all we bloody need, we don't know if Mrs. Johnson is already dead, or just tied up somewhere, waiting for White to get back to her with food and water. God Wendy, what a bloody mess. She might even be lying in a ditch somewhere, slowly bleeding to death from her knife wounds."

"I'm sure something will turn up Sir, it always does."

"I hope you are right Wendy, I know if it hadn't been for Rothwell's letter, we may never have caught Knowels."

"That's just the type of thing I mean Sir, it's not always down to leg work, sometimes it's simply down to a spell of good fortune."

"I wish I could be as optimistic as you Wendy, we'll just have to wait and see."

"Are we both staying here Sir?"

"No Wendy, you stay here for now, I need to contact S.O.C.O. to see if they have found anything that might help us. I'll get someone to relieve you later on."

"We received your message Sir, with regards Mrs. Johnson's hair brush, and checked as you suggested, I think we can confirm that Mrs. Johnson has been in the back seat of the Escort. Whilst we were at Mrs. Johnson's home collecting the hair brush, your D.S. Jones informed us that Mrs. Johnson was wearing a three quarter sleeved, blue mohair jumper, when she left home for Devon. She was also wearing a tartan skirt. We found strands of blue mohair and hair on the rear seat of the Escort. Naturally, we will need the mohair jumper before we can say the strands, we found in the car, definitely came from Mrs. Johnson's jumper. "

"We also found samples of Indian hemp string on the back seat of the Escort, it could have been used to restrain Mrs. Johnson."

"Were there any signs of a murder weapon like the ones used in the previous murders?"

"None Sir, neither at White's home or in her car. Oh! there was one other thing that may, or may not, be of interest to you, we found a receipt dated yesterday, for a new tyre. The Escort didn't have a spare wheel, so I would guess White had been stuck somewhere with a flat tyre, there is a callout charge on the bill so, the mechanic who went out to her should be able to remember whereabouts she was. Just a thought Sir."

"I hope you don't think I've jumped the gun Sir, I know it's not my place, but I gave the details of the receipt to uniform branch and suggested that you may wish to speak to the mechanic. I thought he may be able to remember if the car had any passengers."

"No, you've done the right thing, any time we can save may be the difference between life and death for poor Mrs. Johnson."

Poole was waiting for Cline in the incident room.

"What's up Poole you look a bit concerned?"

"It's just something that's been niggling me Sir. I've been talking to S.O.C.O. and I asked them who was going to look after the parrot. They said they hadn't seen a parrot."

"What on earth are you talking about Poole? What's with the parrot?"

"Apparently White has told Samantha that the only company she now has since her mother died, is her pet parrot."

"I don't think you need to worry about the welfare of a pet parrot for the time being Poole, I think Mrs. Johnson's safety should be our top priority for now, don't you?"

"But that's the point Sir. If nobody has seen the parrot in White's house, where is it? White didn't know when she set off yesterday morning that she was going to have an accident, besides, if she thought she was going to be away sometime trying to catch up with Mrs. Johnson, don't you think she may have asked one of her neighbours to look after it until she got back? I cannot explain it Sir, it is just a gut feeling that the parrot may just be the help we need."

"Ok Poole. I'll leave that with you. Get the uniform lads to help you if you need to, it may be that the Parrot has just died."

At last, everyone else was out working on the case, this was the first time for what appeared to be ages, that he had been able to sit down alone, and reflect on the events of the past few days. Inevitably though, his mind began to wander, somehow he was on the Yorkshire Moors with his sister and her family. The heathers on the moors would soon be in full colour, the entire area being a mass of purple, a sign that usually heralded the coming of autumn. The trees in the Yorkshire Dales would soon be turning from their summer green, to their reds, browns, russets, oranges and yellows before shedding their leaves, to form a multi coloured carpet, a carpet that no artist with paint brush and paint could ever adequately re-produce.

His thoughts were suddenly interrupted by the ringing of the phone. "Yes, Cline here."

"S.O.C.O. here Sir, We've checked the car tyres of White's Escort, with the tyre cast we took on the lane near the river, where we believe Preston was killed. It is probable that the tyre cast we took down the lane, could be of the tyre, that was changed when she had the puncture. We really need the old tyre Sir."

"Well, if we can get hold of the mechanic who went out to her, I am sure he won't have had time to get rid of the old tyre yet. Have you managed to get anything else?"

"Yes Sir, we have managed to match a pair of White's shoe prints with those at all three murder sites."

"That's brilliant, we are sure they are White's shoes? I don't want any cock ups." "Yes Sir, they are the shoes she was wearing when she crashed the Escort. We still intend to do a D.N.A. test on the sweat, but I'm 100% certain the prints are White's."

"Good, if you need me again I will be over at St. Andrews with White."

He'd just put the phone down when Poole dashed in. "We've found it Sir, we've found it."

"So you've found the parrot, so how does that help us Poole?"

"We found it at one of the neighbours three doors away up the street. White had told them that she may be going away for a two or three days, on a training course to Hendon in London, and would they look after the parrot until she got back."

"Poole I still don't know where all this is leading, what has the parrot got to do with anything?"

"Not the parrot Sir, the parrot's cage."

"For God's sake Poole, don't be so melodramatic, get on with it, I'm busting a gut here."

"As I said Sir, it's the cage, or should I say the sliding tray underneath the cage. That's where the murder weapons had been stored. That's why White moved the parrot, she probably thought we were getting too close for comfort, and just in case, moved the parrot with the cage and the weapons out of our reach. Crafty, hey Sir?"

"Brilliant Poole, just bloody brilliant."

"Forensic are doing checks on the weapons right now, it looks like the case is almost closed now Sir."

"Aren't you forgetting something Poole? We still have to find Mrs. Johnson before it is too late."

"Sir."

Cline turned around to find the duty Sergeant stood in the doorway. "Yes Sergeant, what is it?"

"Baxter has just rung to say that White has regained consciousness but she also said, that the doctors at St.

Andrews don't hold out too much hope that White will recover in the long term."

"Sergeant, do you happen to know who White's solicitor is?"

"I've no idea Sir. It's not something one generally talks about."

"Who's the duty solicitor?"

"Branston Sir. Why?"

"Get hold of him, and get him over to St. Andrews straight away. Tell him I need him now, and don't let him fob you off with some bogus excuse, Mrs. Johnson's life depends on what happens during the next few hours."

"Poole, gather together a tape recorder and plenty of blank tapes. It's about time we heard what Mary White has got to tell us, let's hope she's fit enough to talk to us."

"Thank you for your quick response Mr. Branston, it really is urgent that I get to speak to Mary White, I believe the duty Sergeant has filled you in with all the details?"

"You might be eager to talk to White, and someone else's life may be at stake, but my responsibility lies with Mary White and, if I think she is not fit enough to be interviewed, I won't let it go ahead."

"I'm afraid Mr. Branston, it's not up to you, if the doctors give the go ahead, then the interview will take place. You will be present only to see that the rights of White are not abused."

"As long as the interview takes place in a private room with the doctor's permission, then ok."

"No problem there, we've brought recording equipment along and White is already in a private room."

Chapter 18

It took Cline a further half an hour before he could persuade the doctors to give their permission for White to be interviewed but then granted, only on the strict understanding that a nurse should be present at the bedside, during the whole interview, so that White's medical statistics could be monitored.

The doctors also informed him that White's medical condition was far more serious than her appearance would otherwise indicate, the main damage was internal, to her head and chest. If she appeared over talkative, it would no doubt be due to the effect of the drugs. In reply to Branson's concern over the legality of questioning White, whilst she is under the influence of drugs, Cline explained that he wasn't bothered about gaining evidence for use in the court room, his only concern at this time, was finding the whereabouts of Mrs. Johnson."

The tape recorder was set up on a small table at the side of White's bed. After Branston had spent a few moments alone with White, they were ready to start the interview.

"Mary, can you hear me? It's Inspector Cline."

She slowly turned her head towards Cline, and then turned her head back towards Branston, who in turn gave her a slight nod. She then turned her head back towards Cline.

"Yes Sir" Her voice was very quiet, but still slow and deliberate.

Cline was beginning to feel very uneasy about the whole thing now, and began wondering whether what he was doing was really justified. It must have been the sight of the bandages on White's head and the mass of plastic tubes attached to her body that made him feel that way. Then the thought of Mrs. Johnson lying somewhere, probably with her throat cut, suddenly brought him back to the job in hand. "Mary, what have you done with Mrs. Johnson?"

"I don't know a Mrs. Johnson."

"Who was the school gym teacher when you were about seven or eight years old?"

"I can't remember."

"It was Mrs. Johnson, wasn't it?"

"If you say so."

"I do say so."

"Alright, alright you're right, it was her."

"Did you like her?"

For a few moments there was complete silence. "She's a liar, a liar, a liar, a liar." Now she was visibly agitated.

"It's alright Mary, calm down." Cline waited a few moments for her to settle down again before he started questioning her again. The last thing he wanted was for the nurse to pull the plug on the interview, just because White was getting too upset to continue.

"So you do remember Mrs. Johnson?"

White closed her eyes as she answered, "Yes, I told you."

"What have you done with her?"

"Nothing."

"Why are you lying Mary? We know you met her at one of the motorway service areas, south of Birmingham."

"That's a lie."

"I don't think so Mary, we have eye witnesses who gave us both your description and that of Mrs. Johnson, they also gave us your car registration number, so, what have you done with Mrs. Johnson?"

"I've got a terrible headache, I've gone all dizzy and faint. I can't answer any more of your questions go away and leave me in peace."

"I'm afraid I cannot do that Mary, at least not until you tell me what you have done with Mrs. Johnson."

Branston rose from his chair. "I'm sorry Inspector I really think you should stop now, I think we should let her rest for awhile."

"And I think you should go and have a word with Mr. Johnson, and tell him you are afraid that his wife is more than likely going to die because White has a headache. Nurse can I continue?" The nurse walked over to White and checked all the instrument readouts. "Yes Inspector, for now anyway. If her condition deteriorates, then I will stop the interview."

"Tell me Mary, did your father die or did he walk out on you and your mother?"

White's face was full of hate, her body went tense, her hands clutched at the bed sheets. The mention of her father was like a key that would open the flood gates wide.

"It was her fault, that interfering bitch. She can rot in hell for all I care."

"Who's fault was it Mary? What was her fault?"

"Johnson's, she just had to interfere, she couldn't keep her nose out of things, Miss Bloody Goody Two Shoes."

"She couldn't keep her nose out of what?"

"I told her it was nothing, but she wouldn't believe me, she just wouldn't listen. She had to do things her way, the right and proper way. If she'd kept her nose out all those people would still be alive today."

Branston reached out and touched White on the shoulder, "I think you've said quite enough for now Mary. I think you should wait until you are feeling much better."

"Take your hands off me you pervert, keep him away from me, I know what he wants, he's just like the others."

Everyone in the room was taken aback by the sudden diatribe aimed at Branston. This wasn't the same White everybody knew at the station. The White who could never do enough to help others, the White who had cared for her mother for so long. This White was filled with hatred and a fear of men.

"Are you alright Mr. Branston?"

"Yes thank you Inspector, I put it down to the drugs."

"It's alright Mary, no one is going to harm you in any way. We are all here to help you. Why is it all Mrs. Johnson's fault?"

"Because I told her I'd done it climbing trees in the woods, but she wouldn't believe me."

"Done what climbing trees?"

"I loved to play with the lads in the woods, I was always a bit of a Tom Boy, I hated girlie games such as doctors and nurses. I could climb trees as good as any of the boys, even better than most. I was always covered in cuts and bruises on my arms and legs, but they never bothered me, they were never that bad."

"One day, we dared each other to see who would be the fastest, to climb an old Oak tree which was in the woods close to where I lived. I was almost near the top of the tree when I slipped and fell, I didn't fall all the way to the ground, but landed across one of the large branches lower down the trunk. I didn't break any bones but I was left pretty badly bruised."

"The next day we had a gym lesson with Mrs. Johnson, she saw the bruises when I was in the changing room, changing into my gym kit. She asked how I got the bruises, I told her that I had fallen out of an Oak tree. Little girls don't climb trees she said, and she made it quite clear that she thought that I was lying."

"My real father had left my mother a couple of years before all this happened, if fact my mother had got a quickie divorce and was now remarried. Mrs. Johnson said that the bruising was more in keeping with someone having been physically abused, than someone falling out of a tree. She then reported it to the head teacher (who, by the way would have been my next victim but for the car crash) and who in turn, reported the incident to the Social Services."

"They were just as bad, they wouldn't believe me either, especially that cow Miss. Buxton. I loved my step dad, he was everything my real dad wasn't, the police took him in for questioning, sixteen hours none stop before they let him come home on bail. You see, everybody was so sure that he was the one who had been abusing me and was responsible for all my bruises. That night he went out for a walk and never came home. I went out first thing the next morning to help look for him. We knew, that is, my mother and me, that there was no way he would walk out on us like my real father did. I found him hanging from the very same Oak tree, from which I had fallen, the tree that had been the cause of all this trouble. He must have been so ashamed that anyone could even have thought that he was capable of abusing anyone, least of all his own step daughter, he must have thought suicide was the only way out. God only knows what kind of pressure the interviewing detectives put on him

"So when did you go into the children's home?"

"That was all down to Miss. Buxton's doing."

My father had run away from home a few years ago, my step father had committed suicide, so, as you can see, I was in no danger even if the accusations had been true. But still she insisted I should go in a home."

"Why did she do that?"

267

"She said my mother needed a rest, and to be by herself for a while in order to get over the shock of the past few days. Neither I, nor my mother, wanted me to go into a home, but Miss. Buxton knew best. As far as I am concerned, they all had a part to play in my step father's suicide."

"So where is Mrs. Johnson now Mary?"

She completely ignored the question, she seemed to be in some kind of trance, a type of one-way communication; it was as if she had started to tell her story and she didn't want to stop until it was finished. "They took me to Moorgate Children's Home, that's where I met the so-called nice Mr. Preston."

Mary started to gasp for breath, the mere thought of Preston had induced some slight form of an asthma attack. The nurse dashed to Mary's side and grabbed an oxygen mask from off the wall above the bed and placed it over Mary's face. Within only the space of a few minutes Mary's breathing seemed to have settled back to normal.

Branston stood up and touched Cline on the shoulder, "I'm sorry Inspector, I really must insist that you bring this interview to an end, much more of this and she soon won't be in a position to tell you anything at all about Mrs. Johnson. I know you want to find Mrs. Johnson quickly, but it won't be of any help to you if anything happens to Mary."

"Ok, Branston, we will stop for one hour and no longer and, in the meantime, I want the doctors or nurses to give White something to keep her awake so she is capable of continuing with the interview."

"But Inspector, she's in a very bad way."

"That may be, we either do it my way or we continue with my questioning now, and I will take full responsibility for my actions, irrespective of what happens, at a later date."

"Ok Inspector, one hour."

"Wendy, could you go and bring us all a cuppa each, I need to go outside and make a call. I'll see you back at White's room."

Not being technically minded he could never weigh up why you weren't supposed to use mobile phones in a hospital or on a plane; it must be something to do with the money they can rake off from the pay phones scattered throughout the hospital building.

It never crossed his mind that it could cause some kind of interference with all the electronic equipment, especially the equipment in the intensive and coronary care units.

"Sergeant, have you heard anything from S.O.C.O.?"

"Yes Sir, they rang two minutes ago, just to let you know they haven't anything new to tell you. However, we've managed to get hold of the owner of the tyre repair company who was called out to White's Ford Escort. He's no idea which area the call out was made from, but he gave us the address of the mechanic who answered the call, unfortunately for us, he's gone out on the booze with his mates, and it's unlikely that he will be home before morning. The mechanic's boss has given us a copy of his identity card photo, we have taken copies of it and every copper on the beat has been issued with one. I know it's a long shot, but as we speak, they are going round all the pubs and clubs in the area trying to locate him, while he his still in a fit state of mind to remember anything that will help us find Mrs. Johnson. They are checking all the taxi firms and asking the drivers to keep an eye open for him. That's about all we can do now until morning."

"Right, I've waited long enough, let's get back to White."

"I take it for one reason or another you were not amoured by Mr. Preston?"

Looking directly into the eyes of White, Cline could see that merely the mention of Preston's name filled them with hatred. Whatever foul deeds Preston had committed against her, his death had done nothing to dampen the feelings that still lingered in her now torn body. There was a pause for a few moments before White began answering the question. It seemed she was struggling to either pluck up the courage, or the strength, to recall the nightmarish memory from somewhere within her now aching mind. A memory that had lain dormant, and yet close to the surface of her consciousness for so long, eating away at her sanity.

"For the first three days at the Children's home, I was kept locked up in a darkened room.

I was supposed to be there for my protection but, by the way they treated me, I would not have blamed anyone for thinking that I was there for committing some awful sin."

"I wasn't allowed to leave the room for any reason whatsoever, not even to go to the bathroom. The only time the light was switched on, from a switch outside the room, was when Preston came in with bread and water at meal times, or a bucket if I needed to go to the toilet."

They thought White had slipped back into unconsciousness as she lay there, with her eyes now closed. It soon became evident from her facial expressions that she must have been reliving those dreadful moments that were partly responsible for the slaughter and mayhem and which had caused all the unrest for the residents and visitors to Bolderdale.

Talking must have been like a safety valve to her, relieving the intense pressure that must have been building within her, having harboured all those fears and hatreds for all those years, apparently never telling a soul, not even her mother.

There was still quite a lot Cline didn't know. Where did Armstrong fit into all this? Why wait till now to wreak her revenge? Something must have triggered it all off again.

Soon daylight would be with them, and as yet, they still hadn't a clue to the whereabouts of Mrs. Johnson. With warning or invitation White began talking again.

"On the fourth day, well I think it was the fourth day, Preston entered my room with Miss Buxton. Buxton tied my hands together and feet together and put masking tape over my mouth so I could not scream out. She then threw me on the bed. Preston then tried to rape me but he couldn't because my legs were tied together and I bent my legs up to my chest. From somewhere he produced a knife and cut the rope binding my feet together, I tried to curl up into a ball, no way was I going to let the bastard, get what he wanted, without a fight. Why Buxton had tied my feet together in the first place I didn't know, she must have been aware of Preston's intentions from the start. Then, that cow Buxton left the room to leave him to it, or so I thought, she came back in with a fire bucket full of sand. Then whilst Preston held me down, she poured sand in my ears and in my nostrils until I could hardly breathe and finally gave in to him. They both seemed to know what they where doing, because they never spoke to each other, they must have done it a countless number or times before to other girls and maybe boys as well."

"After Preston had finished with me, I was unceremoniously thrown to the floor, whilst he then had sex with Buxton on my bed. They both then left the room, only for Preston to return and repeat the ordeal with me again, one hour later. He then paid her 30 quid, whether that was for the sex, or because she helped him with me I don't know."

"Tell me Mary, where does Armstrong fit in all of this?"

"Preston came into my room one day, not alone as normally, but with another man who I had never seen before. Preston said he wanted me to do him a favour, or

I knew what to expect. The new man's name was never mentioned, even though he came several times. Every time this man came, they took it in turns to rape me. Once, whilst the other man was putting his clothes back on, I noticed something fall out of his coat pocket: I picked it up after they had left the room, I had to grope about on the floor in the dark to find it, because Preston would still turn the light out when he left the room. I then hid it to look at it at some future date although as a very young girl I didn't know if there would be a later date. In fact it was only after I had left the home and was back with my mother that I had the first chance to read it."

"Surely there would have been someone you could have told about your ordeal at the Children's home?"

"Nobody believed me before, why should they now, besides, remember I was only a little girl and Preston had made it quite clear what the consequences would be if I opened my mouth. I also blamed myself for all that had happened, I rightly, or wrongly, thought that, if I had not fallen from the tree, none of my ordeal would have happened and my step-dad would still have been alive. White was now beginning to become agitated again as the anger and hatred were being replaced by a sense of guilt that it had all been her fault.

"When I left the Children's home I completely shut the whole episode out of my mind, it was only when I had to deal with the Social Services again, when my mum took bad, that all the bad memories started flooding back. It wasn't the fact I was dealing with the Social Services that brought back the bad memories, as much as an incident that took place after they were brought in to help care for my mum. I asked for someone from Social Services to call in to see me because I wanted to try and arrange for extra care. Who turned up? None other than Buxton, she was standing in for someone else."

"My mother had changed beyond all recognition, mainly due to the cancer, since the last time they had met over my alleged abuse case. Because we had both changed our surnames to White, Buxton never made the connection."

"Mary, I really need you to tell me what you have done with Mrs. Johnson? Have you killed her? Where have you left her?"

"I haven't killed her, but I still won't tell you where she is, you are a detective, then get out there and detect. If she dies it will be your fault, they shouldn't have chased me like they did, I was determined they would not catch me alive, I made a mess of that didn't I.? I'm good at killing other people but lousy when I try to kill myself. If I hadn't been in here I would have taken her food and water, just like they did with me, it looks like you might have signed Johnson's death warrant. As I said, it's now down to you to find her in time. I'm very tired now, I want to rest."

"Just one more thing, was it Armstrong's name on the piece of paper you picked up from the floor at the Children's home?"

White's voice was now hardly audible, there was no way he could hear the reply to his question. He feared he may have continued with the questioning for too long, but still believed that, in this case, the end justified the means; only this time there was no end, and the whereabouts of Mrs. Johnson was as big a mystery now, as it had been, when White was first brought into the hospital. At this point, Cline felt there was more to be gained trying to find Mrs. Johnson than questioning White any further, she had made it abundantly clear that she would not be telling them where she had taken her.

They were greeted at the station with the good news that the tyre repair man had been located, and was being pumped full of black coffee in an attempt to bring him down from wherever he was. "At the moment Sir, I'm not sure, if he even knows which planet he is on."

"Just our bleeding luck. The only possible lead we may have Johnson's whereabouts, and it turns out to be a drunken low life."

The long hours without a break, were beginning to take their toll on Cline.

"Sir, don't you think we should be letting Mr. Johnson know what's happening."

"Christ I'd completely forgotten about him. Jones and Moore must be wondering what's happening; Poole, you go and give them a ring, let them know what's been going on at our end. I suppose you had better be frank and tell Jones to get Mr. Johnson prepared for the worse, since we are no closer to finding his wife. I think we had better get the tyre fitter into the interview room, let's see how much he can remember."

Cline and Baxter were already waiting in the interview room, when the duty Sergeant brought the tyre man in, along with a pint pot full to the brim with black coffee.

"Have we got a name for him Sergeant?"

"Yes Sir, Martin Finnegan."

"Christ, I hope he's not Irish. I've nothing against the Irish, in fact I quite like them, but I can never understand a blasted word they say, even when they're sober."

"Wive I've been brung here? Where's mi mates gone?"

"Never mind that, just keep getting that coffee down your throat."

At least Cline could tell from the first mumbled attempt at making conversation, that Finnegan was Irish in name only and not in the way he spoke.

For a full twenty minutes, Finnegan was cajoled, pushed, encouraged and even forced, to drink the pint of black coffee.

"Now then Mr. Finnegan, I believe you may be able to help us."

"I can help you how? Wot do you want?"

He was still having some trouble with some of his words, but the black coffee was beginning to have its desired effect.

"What can you tell me about a blue Ford Escort you were recently called out to? It was a lady who had just had a puncture, but she had no spare wheel to exchange it for the bad tyre. Can you remember her?"

"Can I go home now, I don't really feel too good?"

"Not until you have answered my questions, can you remember the lady with the blue Ford Escort?" Cline produced a copy of his work sheet which had been provided by the fitter's boss, see if this can jog your memory."

Finnegan took hold of the piece of paper and peered at it through almost closed eyes; he was having some difficulty getting his eyes to focus on the writing.

"I remember it now, a cocky cow in a hurry, kept giving me verbal for taking too long to get out to her. Then she started at me again, because she said I was taking too long to change the tyre, it wasn't my fault that the stupid cow didn't have a spare wheel in the boot. "

"Did you notice if there was a passenger in the car?"

"Yes, that wos sumfing else we had a barney about. I said I wanted the passenger out of the car so it wouldn't be so hard jacking up the car. When I went over to the car door to ask the passenger to get out, the driver nearly knocked me over into the road, just as a bloody lorry was passing."

"Did you happen to get a good look at the passenger? Could you make out if it was a man or a woman?

"No, not really, I only got a quick look, besides, it was too dark to see much at all."

"What do you mean, it was dark? Were you out on some country lane?"

"Look, my head is spinning round and round, can't I go home now?"

"You are doing just fine Mr. Finnegan, just try and think back."

"I seem to remember, there was quite a lot of traffic, I told you about the lorry didn't I? That's it, it's coming back to me now. I remember, it was a dual carriageway and the street lights were out; I guess the time clock, or whatever it is they use to switch them on, had failed to operate. You know it's surprising how often the stre…."

"Mr. Finnegan, forget about the street lights for the moment and just tell me what you can remember. Have you any idea at all where you were?"

"I'm sorry, I just can't remember, I've told you all that I can, can I go home now?"

"Ok, Baxter, arrange transport to take Mr. Finnegan home. If you remember anything when you sober up, please ring us straight away, in fact, I would prefer it if you were to call back in here as soon as you get out of bed and we'll have another chat, and thank you for your help Mr. Finnegan."

"Wendy, get in touch with the highways department, get them out of bed if you have to, although I believe they do have skeleton staff working during out-of-office hours for enquiries and emergencies. Find out which dual carriageway has recently had trouble with the street lights not coming on. It could be somewhere on the ring road."

Cline's mobile phone rang out loud, and he thought to himself, why does everything sound three times as loud during the night and early morning hours.

"Sir, it's P.C. Washington here, I've been on duty at St. Andrews watching over W.D.C. White. I'm afraid I have some bad news for you, Mary White had a cerebral embolism ten minutes ago and never recovered, she died without saying another word Sir."

"Died, died. Christ that's all we needed, she was our only direct link to finding Mrs. Johnson, ok Constable."

"Wendy, have you been in touch with the highways department yet? Mary White has just passed away, so they are all we've got left now, unless some old bloke walking his dog should find her under a bush somewhere."

"They are going to ring me straight back, they are just going through their work sheets and records of faults for the last couple of days and nights."

The tiredness that had slowly been taking over Cline's body, as the night got longer, had now been overpowered by the rush of adrenalin at the news of White's sudden death.

Brr, brr, brr, the phone even sounded louder this time, Wendy leaped at the phone and picked it up, "Yes,...Yes... Yes....Ok.... thank you."

"What did they say? Have we got a lead?"

"Well, the only street lights they've had any trouble with recently has been in Universal Road. That's the dual carriageway, leading from the southern ring road into the town centre."

"Great, it's a pity we don't know which way White was travelling when she had the puncture."

"I think we can make a calculated guess on that Sir. We know she picked Johnson up on the M5, south of Birmingham so, if she was coming back to Bolderdale with Mrs. Johnson, looking for somewhere to hide her and since she was on the south side of town I think she would have been travelling towards the town centre."

"That's assuming she travelled on the M5, M6, and the M62. She may have used the side roads."

"No way Sir, besides, it doesn't really make any difference."

"If she was travelling out of town when she had the puncture, bearing in mind that Johnson was in the back of the vehicle, she would have put an extra ten miles on her journey by going all the way round the town to the northern side. No Sir, she would have wanted to get Johnson tucked up safe and sound somewhere away from prying eyes. She must have been aware that someone at the service area would have seen her snatch Johnson, and bundle her into the back of the Escort. She would have taken the fastest route possible to where she has left Johnson."

"Ok Wendy, let's for one minute say you are right, where does that leave us?" They both walked over to the map which White had pinned to the wall at the start of the investigation.

"She can't have been going home that's on the opposite side of town; we never asked where she was, when traffic first picked her up, just before the crash. We know she had dropped off Johnson somewhere between having the puncture, and traffic spotting her. Wendy pop into the radio room and see what they can tell us."

"She was on the ring road Sir, not far from St. Andrews Hospital and travelling from the junction with Universal Road."

"If she had just come from where she was keeping Johnson locked up, then Johnson must be somewhere between the junction of Universal road, the ring road and the town centre. Let's look at the map again."

They both stood there trying hard with tired minds, to see if anything at all stuck out from the rest of the map, anything that merely suggested a location for Johnson, would be a start.

"Oh my God!"

"What is it Wendy? What's wrong?"

"Sir, just suppose you weren't in the police force and someone burnt your car out and you found out who had torched it, but you didn't have sufficient evidence to take to the police, what would you do?"

"I'd probably go out and torch their car. Why?"

"Exactly Sir, an eye for an eye, those that live by the sword, shall die by the sword, all that kind of rubbish."

"It must be lack of sleep Wendy, I haven't a clue what you are going on about. Tell me what am I missing?"

Baxter pointed her finger at the wall map. "There Sir, does that road name ring a bell?"

"Moorgate Avenue, of course, the children's home. Why didn't I think of that before? It's been shut down and boarded up for ages, it would make the perfect hiding place."

By now, Poole was back at the station in time to hear of all the latest developments. "Poole , go and see the Duty Sergeant and tell him I need as many men as he can spare, I'll also need the paramedics, an ambulance and the Fire Brigade in case we have any trouble getting into the building, and I want them all now at the old Moorgate Children's Home on Moorgate Avenue. Wendy grab hold of some torches, then let's get down there on the double."

"Sir, shouldn't we get hold of the council people to let them know what we are going to do?"

"Poole, there are times when I definitely fear for you, forget the council just get on with it."

Cline and Baxter drew up outside the main gate of the children's home, just as two traffic patrol cars screeched to a halt behind them. It took only a matter of seconds, using a pair of bolt cutters to remove the locks and chains securing the heavy wrought iron gates. It was obvious from their shiny appearance, that someone had recently changed the old locks and chains, for new ones.

Two minutes later they were attacking the main door to the home with a sledge hammer. Just as the door gave way to the persistent onslaught, the street behind them came alive with the sound of sirens and the blue light of the Fire Brigade and Medical Services.

Ignoring the commotion behind him, Cline, immediately followed by Baxter, dashed over the toppled door and into the building. The air was acrid and the whole place looked and smelt like a rubbish tip; someone had definitely been in here, since it had been originally locked up and abandoned by the Local Council. By the look of things, it looked as if squatters had, at sometime in the past, sought refuge there.

He could hear Baxter, in his wake, bellowing out instructions to the search teams.

What was once the reception hall, led on to a corridor, Cline turned to the left, whilst Baxter, who by now had caught up to him, turned to the right. Both were now oblivious to the other searchers bringing up the rear. The only thought on their minds now, was, were they in the correct building to find Johnson, and if so, would they be in time to save her?

"Sir, over here."

Cline turned and dashed towards Baxter. "What is it? Have you found her?"

"Over there Sir, in the corner." Baxter had pointed her torch in the direction of what looked like a pile of old newspapers and rubbish in the far corner of the room; he stumbled through the rubbish, until he stood directly over the heap. His whole body was shaking, sweat was pouring down his face and down his back, and it had nothing to do with being hot, it was the pure tension of the situation. Was this the moment he had been dreading for the past few hours, or would he find Johnson alive?

He slowly bent down towards the pile of papers, it was unbelievable the amount of mental energy that he required just to perform this gentle task. He knew it wasn't the physical effort causing the problem, but the thought of what he may uncover.

First he removed one sheet of newspaper, then another, and another until he could see what was underneath.

"Wendy, thank God, it's her, it's Mrs. Johnson."

"Is she alive?"

"I can't tell yet, her mouth is covered in some kind of black masking tape. Hold on a minute, while I remove it."

He was about to stretch out and remove the tape from Mrs. Johnson's mouth, when he heard a movement from the newspapers which still partly covered her body.

"I think she's alive, thank God, I think she is moving."

With the fear of finding a corpse removed from Baxter's mind, she dashed forward in an attempt to help Mrs. Johnson. She started removing the rest of the newspapers and debris as Cline reached out to remove the tape from Mrs. Johnson's mouth.

Baxter gave an almighty scream that nearly perforated Cline's ear drums. He spun around and shone his torch in the direction of the now petrified Baxter, just in time to witness the largest rat that he had ever seen, darting through her legs.

She stood there, her head in her hands, frozen to the spot, as if she had been struck by a bolt of lightning.

The rat scurried away through her open legs, and with a final scream from Baxter, disappeared out through the doorway into what used to be a corridor.

"It's alright Wendy it's gone now, but keep your eyes open, it's more than likely that there will be more of them.

This time he managed to reach down and remove the tape from Mrs. Johnson's mouth. The icy coldness of the flesh on her cheek, that greeted the back of his fingers as he searched for a grip on the tape, sent a cold chill down his spine.

Pulling the tape from her mouth, he could smell the odour of old vomit, he didn't need a doctor to tell him that Mrs. Johnson was dead, asphyxiated by her own vomit.

He rose to his feet, turned to Baxter, placed an arm on her shoulder. "Come on Wendy, I'm afraid we can't do any more here. It's up to the others now."

As they walked out of the Home towards their car in silence, Cline's thoughts were with Mr. Johnson, the only person, for whom he felt any sympathy, in the whole rotten events of the past couple of weeks.

Reaching the car, he looked up to the sky, there wasn't a single star to be seen, only dark ominous clouds. It was then, that he felt the first light drop of rain on his cheek. It had last rained the night of the first murder, namely, when Armstrong had met his fate, perhaps it was only just and proper for it to rain now on the discovery of the last victim.

"Come on Wendy, I think it's about time we all made our way home and got some sleep. I'll let the others know."

"I wonder what tomorrow will bring?"

About the Author

Born into a South Yorkshire mining family, just outside the town of Doncaster, he was brought up with a sense of community spirit and friendliness towards his neighbours.

Although only attending a Secondary Modern school in the early 1950's, he later qualified, first as an electrician and then, as an Electrical Engineer, working in the Coalmining Industry in South Yorkshire. It was during the early 1960's that he was employed as a Laboratory Engineer at the Aircraft Equipment Division of the English Electric Co. at Bradford.

He worked on the equipment of aircraft such as the English Electric Lightening, the Buccaneer and the famous Concorde.

He was married to Dorothy and together they brought up a son and a daughter, the daughter subsequently produced a loving granddaughter and grandson.

Later in life, his work took him to the four corners of England, Scotland and Wales and it was mainly this experience of life's tapestry that he draws upon for his writing.

In addition to being a crossword and puzzle enthusiast, he his an avid reader of crime novels and thrillers. It is this love which inspired him to write his first Inspector Cline novel, adding his own inimitable style to the realms of fictional writing.

He was bereaved just prior to Christmas 2004, when his beloved wife passed away with lung cancer.

Ultimately, he would like, with the help and support of his family, to continue producing 'Inspector Cline' mysteries.

His determined, well motivated and focused writing, could be due to his motto for life which is, "If a job is worth doing, then it's worth doing well"

Lightning Source UK Ltd.
Milton Keynes UK
09 November 2009
146037UK00001B/5/A